OVER ... AND THRO ... TO ENTROPY'S WELL WE GO—

Dore set out on a quest to find Our Father, and, incidentally, the course of The River, while I, Seyt, was left behind, faced with the task of writing about my fabled brother's journey. Without facts, there was nothing for me to do but make it up as we went along. And if Dore encountered symbolism and allegory, he also found love and danger —fighting off armies of overgrown vegetables, theological giants, and treacherous damsels in distress.

But what have I found? Criticism, censorship and a religious war. And if I don't want to become the first martyr to Dore's cause, I'll have to set out right now on my own quest to find—

WHAT ENTROPY MEANS TO ME—

a delightful and intriguing journey on the strange, uncharted planet they call Home.

". . . should shake up the field of sword-and-sorcery fiction."

—*Publishers Weekly*

"The best first novel of this year . . ."

—*Crawdaddy*

Geo. Alec Effinger attended the Clarion Writers' Workshop in 1970. He is the winner of a Clarion prize for best short story, and his stories have been published in science fiction magazines and anthologies, including *Clarion* and *Clarion II*, both available in Signet editions.

SIGNET Science Fiction You Will Enjoy

What Entropy
Means to Me

Geo. Alec Effinger

A SIGNET BOOK from
NEW AMERICAN LIBRARY
TIMES MIRROR

Library of Congress Catalog Card Number 72-182695

This is an authorized reprint of a hardcover edition published
by Doubleday & Company, Inc.

SIGNET TRADEMARK REG. U.S. PAT. OFF. AND FOREIGN COUNTRIES
REGISTERED TRADEMARK—MARCA REGISTRADA
HECHO EN CHICAGO, U.S.A.

SIGNET, SIGNET CLASSICS, SIGNETTE, MENTOR AND PLUME BOOKS
are published by The New American Library, Inc.,
1301 Avenue of the Americas, New York, New York 10019

FIRST PRINTING, JUNE, 1973

2 3 4 5 6 7 8 9

PRINTED IN THE UNITED STATES OF AMERICA

For my parents, for enabling me to write unfettered by the bonds of nonexistence.

For Robin, Harlan, Kate and Damon, for the same.

And always, especially, for Dia.

Contents

. . . Sir, as you and I are in a manner perfect strangers to each other, it would not have been proper to have let you into too many circumstances relating to myself all at once.— You must have a little patience. I have undertaken, you see, to write not only my life, but my opinions also; hoping and expecting that your knowledge of my character, and of what kind of mortal I am, by the one, would give you better relish for the other: As you proceed farther with me, the slight acquaintance, which is now beginning betwixt us, will grow into familiarity; and that, unless one of us is in fault, will terminate in friendship.—*O diem praeclarum!*—then nothing which has touched me will be thought trifling in its nature, or tedious in its telling. Therefore, my dear friend and companion, if you should think me somewhat sparing of my narrative on my first setting out—bear with me,—and let me go on, and tell my story my own way:—Or, if I should sometimes put on a fool's cap with a bell to it, for a moment or two as we pass along,— don't fly off,—but rather courteously give me credit for a little more wisdom than appears upon my outside;—and as we jog on, either laugh with me, or at me, or in short, do any thing,—only keep your temper.

LAURENCE STERNE
Tristram Shandy

WHAT ENTROPY
MEANS TO ME

Part ONE

'Neath His Bronzed Skin His Iron Muscles Played

CHAPTER ONE

Prelude to ... Danger!

She was Our Mother, so she cried. She used to sit out there, under that micha tree, all day as we worked cursing in her fields. She sat there during the freezing nights, and we pretended that we could see her through the windows in the house, by the light of the moons and the hard, fast stars. She sat there before most of us were born; she sat there until she died. And all that time she shed her tears. She was Our Mother, so she cried.

She cried often for our yard, and the chairs that had been put there. We had many chairs on the scrubby lawn between the house and the chata fields. Some of the other estates have iron and stone statues placed around, but none of them have chairs. We have quite a few. Our Mother taught us that she got the idea from reading one of the plays that Our Father brought with him from Earth. We still have many of those books. Sometimes we throw them into the River when it looks like it might flood. But we still have most of them.

I've always liked the plays. I know the one Our Mother meant; I read it years ago. It is by Ionesco. We have the plays of Ionesco, of De Ghelderode, and of Büchner. I enjoy also the plays of Dürrenmatt and Jarry. Of the classics I read Aeschylus and Aristophanes, Shakespeare and Jonson with relish. Our Mother always said that I was presumptuous to display my wide knowledge of the drama, but I do not think so. The Theater is life.

The chairs. Some are wooden, straight-backed chairs. These are gray or olive-green, and their paint is peeling and falling on the grass. There are black enameled iron chairs, and these are subject to rust where the paint covering is damaged. There are a few cold, sweaty stone thrones. Our Mother sat on one of these, with two fluted stone columns rising to her left and right. Behind her a once-beautiful embroidered hanging flapped in the winds, rain-spotted and covered with patches of fungus growth.

There are other sorts of chairs—hammocks hanging and swinging, their canvas bodies bloated with spring rains —but I don't think that it is necessary for me to describe them all. Perhaps you are able already to picture our yard. It is only for background, that's all. If I tell you that there are also skins stuffed with rags set out under the white sky, and that they stay wet longest, and smell worst, how much have I added? You see, I must now continue elsewhere.

Behind the house, on the other side from the chata bean fields, was the River. It was the River of Life, which gave us all our lives and our deaths, too. It sprang, we believe, from the endless tears of Our Mother. Now, impossibly, she is gone, but the River remains. This is our chief defense against those of our family who contend that there is no life after death. Our Mother must still continue to weep in her eternal sorrow, somewhere.

The River was called the Allegheny by Our Father, who took the name from another river on Earth, near his ancestral home. We call it the River of Life, or, simply, the River. Many things could be pulled from the River and dried, but most of us do not consider that to be moral. Wherever the River wishes to carry these things (pieces of wood, broken-down machinery, dead animals and people, boats, our books) is their proper destination, and it would be profane to pull them out prematurely. Some of us do not agree, arguing that it then should be equally impious to enter the River unbidden, as we do for purposes of worship, cleanliness, and sport.

My brother Dore was of the latter group. It is his mission that I am describing, although I haven't really gotten into it yet. He did not go near the River during our monthly devotions, but preferred to pray from the small chapel in the house. He did not swim and dig in the River's bottom as some of the rest of us enjoyed doing. He took nothing from the River, and believed it sacrilegious to add to the burden of the strong current. Nevertheless, it was he whom Our Mother sent. Perhaps if he had allowed himself to sail the River in one of our flat-bottomed boats he would have returned. Then this story would have been told by him, and the details that I am forced to make up out of thin air would have the bite of authenticity.

Our Mother sent Dore, and he never returned. He was the first of our second generation to depart, and Our already-mourning Mother died in her guilt and loss.

Dore was the eldest. He was thoughtful; that is why I argued against his being sent. The mission was meant for one of the more impetuous, less rational young men. Dore would never fight without exploring all the ramifications of everything involved. He might have met his death while temporizing with a grass dragon. If that fits later on, perhaps that will be how I will tell it.

My brother Dore was very young when Our Parents came to Home from *their* home, Earth. He was the first-born, and the only born, at that time. He was still young and alone when Our Father joined the River. (All the rest of us are the offspring of Our Mother and her most sacred tears. This we are taught.) My brother wore the crown that he made for himself when he was first a man, when he coupled with Melithiel, the princess from down the road. He wore a green cloak, fearing in his peculiar devoutness to wear the blue-green of the River. Rather he celebrated the forests, and their masculine and less holy aspects. On special occasions he took for his own a carved wooden throne which was set up on a stone dais (he did *not* take the vacated throne of Our Father); he sat only for short periods of time, a staff cut from the forest in his hand. He did not like to be conspicuous but, in his position, it was difficult for him not to be so.

Dore was the friend of the forest. He was well-liked by lizards. Sometimes in the woods at night, when he built his large fires and slept, he took off his boots; in the morning there would be huge slugs leaving their silvery trails like webwork in them. Better he should have laughed with fish in the River.

The idea of the mission was not originally conceived

by Our Mother, although it is thought by some of us that
she gave the inspiration subliminally to our brother Tere.
She used to do that quite a bit. The mission was closely
related to the reason that Our Parents left their beautiful
red and gray Earth.

Our Parents were nearly superhuman in their powers
and in their inestimable resources. Why then did they
leave their natural home for the unknown territories off-
planet? Was it because their brothers on Earth were jealous
and afraid of their control of supernatural forces beyond
comprehension? Was it because the Earth people hated
Our Parents for their all-encompassing knowledge, their
perfect and blessed relationship to all living things, their
total and consistent morality? No. They hounded Our
Father and Our Mother from their midst because of Our
Parents' overwhelming debts.

One day Tere came in from the fields. He works very
little in the fields, contenting himself instead to measure
the distance between the chata stalks with his eyes and
remark on the good fortune that prevented us from plant-
ing them too closely together. We laughed behind his wide
back, because we knew that he was only shirking. We
have always hated the work in the chata bean fields, but
we did not hate Tere for making our tasks harder. We do
not like him as much as we like others of us, but his lazi-
ness is only part of the reason.

Tere thought of the mission, so I will describe him. He
was second-eldest, and there is a theory current among a
large part of us that the mission was intended as a way to
become eldest. He *is* eldest now, so that theory cannot be
totally discounted; but it *is* uncharitable.

Where Dore was slim and brown, Tere is plump and
dappled pink. He wears silly clothes, trying to appear
regal. He has made for himself a crown; it is much more
ostentatious than Dore's, floppy silk bunches dotted with
colored rock and shell, with trailers of red and blue ribbons. He wears a cloak of heavy blue-green material
caught at the neck with a plastic brooch in the shape of a
fish. Tere is the worrier of fishes, he is not their friend.
As Dore was home in the forest, Tere spends his time in
the pools and watercourses of our land. But he is not welcome there: He just spends a lot of time. He has built a
throne. This in itself is almost inexcusable audacity, for it
is the first chair that has been moved into our yard since

the original lot. It is a strange throne, made of a slick gray substance that we have been unable to identify. He wears slippers of green, shiny with simulated scales so that we will recognize his alliance with the fish. We do not.

Tere came in from the fields on this day. He went past Our Mother, as you must do on the way from the bean fields to the house. He stopped to pray at her feet, and he prayed that her grief might lessen. Her pain was frightening in its intensity. At night we would look out from the windows of the house and watch her. Our Father had built her throne so that she was shaded from the sun by the great tree, and at night the constellation of the Wheel of the Sleeper revolved like a milky halo above her. We could not see her then, but the flashes of light, the shooting stars in the sky fell thickly, like the endless stream of her tears. Though she was obscured by the darkness, her sadness was more palpable. We saw her weeping in the sky and we heard her moans in the groaning of the River. When we slept, we felt her unendurable torment in our dreams, for then our minds were opened completely. We woke several times each night, holding our foreheads and screaming. Now we rest easier, but the moons are still her two red and pleading eyes. It is more than one of us who says that the old days were lighter to bear.

Tere had his inspiration. Someone must make a sacrifice. Would it be Tere? No, we didn't think so. Tere explained his idea to Our Mother: a mission to the end of the River. A mission to the end of existence, to the end of time, to the end of everything that there could be. And, therefore, it could only be entrusted to the leader of us all. Only Dore was capable of making such a sacrifice; perhaps, though, perhaps he might return. Then he would bring back the news that would stop the tears of Our Mother: words from beyond the bar, from Our Father in the belly of the River.

Dore was not a River person, but he accepted the monstrous task without complaint. Our Mother said little, Dore said less. Tere explained it to us all. Meanwhile Dore stood in the house by the great window that overlooked the River. He watched the green water rushing and he smiled. His face was rested and peaceful, his features serene and beautiful. This was to be his sacrifice and he, at least, knew how it was to be made.

Before he left on his journey Dore went down the road

to the house of the Fourth family. He went to visit the
eldest daughter, Melithiel, who was by that family's by-
laws a princess of the blood. She slept with him before
he left, and he touched her small, perfect breasts. He
knew her three times that evening, but he had known
better. In the morning the king of the Fourth family
showed him what Dore would miss by going on the quest
and probably being killed. He showed Dore the joys of
marriage and the joys of family, and he taught him briefly the joys that only the generator of a powerful clan
might know. He took Dore out to a hill a few hundred
yards from the Fourth house. The hill overlooked the
house itself and, beyond, the River. At the bottom of the
hill three children played with a doglike animal. After a
short while the king of the Fourth family's wife came out
from the house. She saw her husband and ran up the hill
to his arms. They embraced, and Dore smiled his small,
knowing smile.

Dore went on his journey. I believe that I was the last
to see him. It was my job, as the tenth-oldest male, to
stand on the hill in our yard that overlooked the River and
hold the standard of our family. I had to stand there one
day out of each eight, and I was there as Dore took his
leave of the house of the Fourth family. I thought I could
make him out, seeing, I think, his familiar green cloak—
the green of the forest, not the flood green of Tere—and
the light glinting from his lovely crown. I liked to sing to
myself, and as I saw Dore start on his way I sang a song
to him, one of his all-time favorites. I dedicated that song
to him, and now I dedicate the memory of that song to
his memory. At that time I wore a simple cloth cap with
a jaunty red feather. My cloak was yellow, the color of
various flowers that I find pleasing. I am a meadowman,
myself.

As Dore passed out of sight on the forest trail, scorning
the broader road that paralleled the River, a chill wind
pushed out of the valley and up my hill. The white sky
darkened, and in a short while rain fell, several full hours
before the regular evening raintime. I did not know then
whether the unusual conditions were an omen or the result of Our Mother's increased anguish. We argue still
about this very thing. It has not been resolved to our
satisfaction.

When I heard that wind, I knew. The pennon snapped

on its staff, and the sound frightened me. The crest of our family, embroidered in white and blue and green on the flag, seemed to be crying out for Dore to return. I knew then that I would never see him again. At sunset I left my post, and I carried the staff back to the outbuilding where it is kept. After I had put it back on its shelf I bowed my head and said the short prayer, adding a few words for Dore's sake. Then I walked around the house to the throne of Our Mother. Nearly all of us were gathered there, sitting on the prickly grass at her feet. I knelt and addressed my prayer of greeting to her. She touched me on the shoulder, one of the few times that she had ever touched me since early childhood. I can remember that I began to cry when I felt her rough fingers.

Our Mother spoke to us. She told us again the story of how she met Our Father in the Earth city of Pittsburgh, and of their flight from the debtors' prison there. She told us of the kindly merchant who sponsored their escape to Home, and how she had taken that merchant to bed, fondling him in gratitude and feeling his throbing manhood within her. She retold the history of the founding of our First family on Home, and the coming of the other and lesser families. Then she addressed herself to the task of Dore, and to his better qualities, so that we should always remember him as a thrifty and worthwhile addition to any family. She told us of his love of the forested lands and his legendary ability to understand the speech of his floral friends, although we knew all this already; she told us of his strong arms. At last she stopped, her holy tears streaming at their constant rate, and we stood before her in silent worship, our arms outstretched. But, of course, she could not leave her throne. Her time had not yet come.

But then we were all made aware that the time was nearer than we had dreamed, and that our lives were to be altered beyond our simple-minded comprehension. It remains to be seen whether or not the changes are of a positive nature. Some of us believe that they are, and some of us disagree.

Dore set out practically unarmed against the dangers of Home's unexplored wildlands. Tere told us about the quasi-religious nature of the quest. He explained that the great and selfless sacrifice of Dore would result in our salvation, at least in the corporal sense; our intentions would be revealed to the River in all their purity, and the innocent body of our brother Dore would serve as substitute for five or six whole shelves of books. Therefore, he must face the Nature of our world (Nature that owes its existence, as do we, to the River) with only the equipment necessary to see him through to the end of his journey. The trip back would be entirely a matter of fortune.

"He will carry, as symbol of our parting with the insane aggressive disposition of the people of Earth, he will carry an empty scabbard. What courage he will require! But our brother Dore is equal to the calling. He is the most qualified among us, and he is, as eldest male, the only one of us whose sacrifice could have any meaning." So Tere put it to us, pausing only now and again to touch his breast and sigh.

I asked Dore about this before he left. He was sitting on his throne, resting his chin on a bridge of his hands. When I spoke he looked up, startled. He seemed embarrassed at being found on his throne again.

"Are you really going out there without even your sword?" I asked.

"No, my brother, I don't think so. If Tere wants someone to go without a sword, let it be he. *I'm* the one who's going, and I'm taking Battlefriend with me. And I'll take everything else that I can sneak out of the house."

He smiled at me, and I saw the pain hidden behind the smile. He took his crown from his head and studied it for a few seconds; he smiled again, perhaps thinking of the days when he first made it, and first made the princess of the Fourth family. He looked up and saw me. For some reason he sighed; he made a gesture which, I am not certain, but it seemed as though he were offering the crown to me. I cannot interpret this; in any event, he shook his head sadly and put the crown back on.

While I sat at his feet our younger sister Lalichë ran to him and jumped into his lap. The scene was so purely touching that I was surprised when Dore failed to laugh in his usual delighted way. Lalichë noticed it too. She looked up at his face, her own nose wrinkled among the freckles.

"Dore," she said, "why don't you put a pine cone on your stick that you walk with?"

Lalichë was five years old and enjoyed Dore's special

favor. But that day his mind was on his journey. He did not answer her.

"Why would he want a pine cone on his staff?" I asked.

"Because Dionysus did," she said. She jumped to the ground again and ran away, laughing and singing and cursing.

"Yes," I said somberly, "you're much more Orphic than anything else."

"It does not matter, Seyt. I have been waiting for a sign. I knew that if I waited here long enough my bird, that tarishawk that rests here each day, I knew that he would come. Our Mother said that if he flew from the right, then I would have good fortune. If he came from the left, my journey would be disastrous for me, and it would bear no positive fruits for you."

"And the hawk? Which way did it come? Did it come from the left?"

Dore smiled once more; his smile was always the most cheerless aspect of him. "The hawk has not come at all," he said. He fell silent, resting his head in his hands. I nodded, though he could not see me; I got to my feet and walked to the house as quietly as I could.

Dore's journey would not become dangerous for two or three days. We all knew that he could stay with the lower families for the first few nights. We had no worries for him until he left the small growth of humanity behind and entered into the healthy, wild skin of the planet that is our Home.

We were wrong. Our Mother told us that he had encountered treachery on his second night away.

Beyond the keep of the Fourth family the estates rapidly fell off in quality. When Dore bid farewell to that king and court he followed the dusty trace leading to his beloved forest. As the sun climbed behind the gritty white clouds he walked to his doom, whistling. In his place I would have sung, and most of the girls would have prayed. But, as Our Mother said on many occasions, it takes all sorts of people to make a world, and that is what made our family great.

The road was unpaved (I have never in my life seen real pavement), rutted deep by the wooden carts of the lower families whose castles and cabins stood to the sides. Roads have played an important role, not only in the entire and majestic history of the human race, but also in the endless procession of literature. Consider the part of the road in *Waiting for Godot* or in the tales of Chaucer. If the road in this history has a lesser importance, it is only because our road is the shorter.

About suppertime Dore stopped his march under a tall, slender pine tree. He opened his wallet and took out the bread and cheese that he had insisted on bringing. Our sister Vaelluin, who had done kitchen duty on the day of Dore's departure, had prepared a compact kit of dried rations in boilable plastic bags, but Dore said that hard bread and stiff cheddar were more in keeping with his quest. It was a poor meal, but Dore had never been used to luxury. He ate quickly, finishing only part of the day's share and saving the remainder for an extra-large breakfast. He packed his wallet and continued his walking, planning to find a place to spend the night in the hour or so before the evening rains.

About two miles farther down the road he arrived at the elaborate mailbox of the Thirtyfourth family. It was a salute to bad taste, combining Doric columns with bastardized Corinthian ornament, a Greco-Roman frieze and imitation Khmer temple statuary, Art Nouveau lettering, and obscenely ornate French Empire neoclassicism on top of Rococo scrollwork. In all, with portico, porch, piazza, and stoa, it stood over eighteen feet tall.

Dore followed the pebble drive up to the front of the building. The path split and went on in opposite directions, making right angles around a rectangular lawn. In the middle of the grass was a statue; Dore knew that it was actually a fountain, but it was turned off during the day. It rather graphically depicted the rape of Proserpina: when it was activated after the raintime, colored lights played on the spray that emanated from an indelicately situated marble orifice.

A heavy iron door was set into the front of the mailbox. The door was decorated with heads of Cerberus and bulls from the Ishtar Gate of Babylon. Across two panels in the middle was a faded reproduction of *The Last Supper* by Dali. A little balcony stood over the doorway, shading it. At the foot of one of its supporting columns was a tall urn filled with white sand and a few crushed cigarette butts. At the base of the other was a cast-iron Negro coachboy, holding a lantern and grinning servilely. On the lantern, as in about a dozen other places, was written

Mr. & Mrs. Walter G. Thirtyfour. Dore lifted the heavy brass doorknocker and pounded it in place.

The knock was answered immediately by a dirty-faced young woman. Her clothes were soiled and threadbare, and her nose was weeping for attention. "Mom says to tell you we don't want any, thank you," she said.

Dore loved her for that. He never needed more of a reason. "No," he said, chuckling, "I'm not selling anything. This is a *real* crown. I am Dore First. I would like to beg your hospitality."

The girl stared in amazement. It is likely that she had never seen any of the First family before. Then she looked at his rich clothing, and at the jeweled scabbard of Battlefriend. "How long," she said, stammering, "how long do you plan to be staying on with us?"

"Just this one night, I think."

"Yes, sir. Fine. Please, sir, if you will sign this book. Do you have any luggage? I can get one of the boys to carry it up to the house. We hope you enjoy your stay with us, and if there's anything you need, *anything*, don't hesitate."

"Thank you," said Dore, "it'll be all right if you just show me the way to the house."

The young woman led Dore back through the trees to the house. The home of the Thirtyfourth family was little, if any, larger than their mailbox. In fact, it later developed that the mailbox, being otherwise without function on our Post Officeless world, served as guest house and part-time brothel. Dore, as an upper-class visitor, would be quartered in the main house itself. But courtesy demanded that he at least visit the mailbox. He hoped that his first fleeting call would suffice.

His arrival put the household in a state of confusion. The head of the Thirtyfourth family (who insisted on being called Walt) ordered a sumptuous feast. This consisted of four courses of hard, dark bread and fine domestic cheese. Dore was unimpressed, of course, but did his best to show his appreciation to his poorer cousins. He explained about his quest, to the amazement of everyone, and begged to be excused so that he might get a good night's sleep. He planned to be on the road again before dawn.

The family sat in stunned silence as he rose from the table. Dore could not understand their reaction until he recalled that a wealthy guest customarily distributed cash gifts after such a dinner. He decided to pretend ignorance, although the conceit was shallow and transparent to everyone. He went up to bed amid the stony silence, embarrassed and unable to bring himself to explain that he carried no money. "Where I go henceforward," he thought, "I shall go incognito." He slipped between the coarse, yellowed sheets and was soon asleep.

In the darkest part of the night, in the most stilly watch, his door opened. The light from the hallway shone in around the silhouette of the formidable and unclad body of Dolksey Thirtyfour, Mr. and Mrs. Walter G's eldest daughter.

Our Mother tutored us carefully in subjects pertaining to morality, both absolute and relative. This is quite obviously a case of the latter. People have intercourse for a variety of reasons, she taught. As a gesture of affection among siblings, as a reward for valiant deeds, as a plighting of troth, for the acquisition of offspring, or to augment the income: These are but a few of the manifold urgings to "make love." Our Mother always took an ambivalent attitude toward sex. We always figured that was because she surely wasn't getting any on that memorial-like throne of hers. Since Our Father joined the spirit of the Home that he built, Our Mother had become a passionate but chaste Penelope-symbol of adequate behavior.

Before coming Home, the story goes, Our Father met Our Mother at a well in Pittsburgh. In that city she was known as a woman of easy virtue, and she had a reputation as an all-around mover. Our Father extended his hand in friendship and invited her to "quit her low-down ways." She was taking various sorts of pills at this time. She recognized in her future husband a person of great personal worth and went with him, abandoning her former loose behavior. *Now* look at her. Dead as Dekker; where does it get you?

None of these thoughts passed through the mind of my older brother Dore as he watched the voluptuous Dolksey undulating toward his bed. He was still half-asleep. He had enough awareness, though, to shove himself over against the wall, giving the girl room to crawl in with him. He was almost asleep again before she did; she spent a good deal of time trying to arouse him by fondling her pendulous, alabaster globes and running her well-formed hands over her flat, sensuous belly. Finally she gave up in favor of closer and more intimate tactics.

Dore realized that he wasn't going to be allowed to go back to sleep. He sighed; then he reached out and grabbed the moaning woman. She responded instantly. She kissed, and scratched, and rubbed, and tickled, and bit. Dore was so distracted by her ministrations that he was unable to gain entrance. Finally, as she trailed her tongue down the tufted hairs of his stomach and massaged his lower back he shoved her away.

"Look," he said, "knock it off. Why don't you just lie there and we'll get this over with."

Still, he found her pleasant company. Sometime later he was able to get back to sleep, but he was glad that he had made the detour.

She was still there in the morning. She woke him with her elbow. "Come with me," she said.

"We already did that. Let me sleep."

"No, we must away. To my room."

"I was just getting very comfortable here."

"You don't understand," she said, her tongue flicking into his ear between words. "My father mustn't find us here. It would be my head."

"How would he find us here? He wouldn't be looking unless you've been dropping hints."

"Never mind. If he finds us in *my* room it will look like simple rape, and that's all right. You're a First."

"I see. Why don't you go back by yourself?"

She demonstrated her reasons, and soon she had shown him enough to warrant his accompanying her to her boudoir. Several minutes later, at one of a series of critical points, Dore heard a chamber door slam shut. Then he heard shouts. Someone pounded on Dolksey's door. "Okay, you imposter in there," a voice bellowed, "that's enough. Get out of there before we come in and slice your real identity to ribbons." Then he heard more doors slamming.

Dolksey looked worried. "You must leave. Father mustn't catch us together."

"Yes, I've heard. Let me get my breeches—"

"Wait. No, go. We have no time. You must fly, my love."

Dore stood beside the bed, naked and confused. Dolksey pushed him to the door. She paused before he departed, looking by turns expectant, disappointed, and angry. Finally she grabbed him and kissed him fiercely. "Flee, my lion," she said, breathing warmly and moistly into his ear. Dore grasped the brass dryad knob and opened the door. Dolksey lunged and caught his hand. She brought it to her lips and kissed the fingers.

"You're really weird," he said, and stepped out into the hallway.

The door slammed shut behind him. He heard the click of the lock.

Dore hurried down the hall to his room. The door was locked and no one answered his frantic knocking. He went back to Dolksey. Of course, her door was locked fast. At last she answered his pounding, whispering to him through the heavy micha planks of her door. "Hurry, my heart. All the rooms are secured. No one may hide you. You must go before my father and brothers come again. They will let you escape if you go now. But if you tarry, for my sake, they will find and kill you. Our love is doomed; I know how your heart is breaking, even as is mine. But go, save yourself."

"Wait a minute!" Dore screamed. "You got my clothes in there! And my room's locked, too. I'm not leaving here without that sword!" He got no further answer. In the stillness he heard the tramping of feet on the front stairs. He hurried, undressed and unarmed, to the back stairway. He checked for guards: There were none. He ran down the stairs and out the back way. He did not stop running until he was across the overgrown yard and safely in the trees behind the house.

CHAPTER TWO

Next: The Radishes of Doom

The reviews are in! What a luxurious feeling it is to get up and know that you've become a celebrity overnight. Outside the door to my tiny chamber was my copy of the Home *Times-Register*, a little local newsletter done on offset by Yord, an older brother of distressing cheerfulness. It is distributed free of charge to members of our family, but it is also available at a nominal cost to foreign households as well. On the third page I was gratified to see a two column-inch critique of my first chapter. The by-line read "The Trunk-maker," but we are all aware that it is our sister Mylvelane who hides behind the allusion. She began by demonstrating her sympathy for my difficult assignment, and says that I have made an auspicious beginning, blending a compassionate portrait of Dore with an incisive view of our family life. The only negative thing she had to say was that I displayed a tendency to exaggerate facts for the sake of interesting reading. That is something that I'll have to watch.

But, nevertheless, I was greeted with a tremendous round of applause when I entered the cafeteria. My chapter was a hit. I am on my way to stardom. Tere himself came over to my table to congratulate me. "It's very much better than ever I might have hoped," he said.

"Thank you," I said, not quite knowing how to take his meaning. I've been writing for years.

"Yes," he said, "and if you ever need any technical assistance, why, feel free to drop by. I was very close to Dore, you know." His smile widened during the invitation, until by Dore's name it was practically a gloat. He may have been close to Dore, but Dore was never anywhere near *him*.

"Thank you," I said flatly, "I appreciate it very much."

"Nothing at all," said Tere, putting his plump pink hand

25

on mine. "Well, I have to get back to work. Uneasy rests the head, you know." I can imagine.

And now I, too, have to get back to work. I have yesterday's chapter before me, and I believe that I will stop admiring it and get on with entangling Dore. Lalichë told me that she's worried about him already. I just smiled and patted her head. "There, there," I said, "he'll be all right. He's a Holy Pilgrim."

"Like Dante?" she asked hopefully.

"Yes, I suppose. He has all the trappings."

"But he's already lost his sword. How could he lose an enchanted sword?"

"It happens," I said.

Perhaps that is where I should begin today. Dore hid in the dense growth that fringed the clearing of the Thirty-fourth family. He was naked, but the warm sun of the late morning kept him from feeling uncomfortable. He did feel mightily insecure, though, for without clothes he was helpless and unfit for whatever social situations he might meet along his journey. He was of course without his Battlefriend, and he knew that facing the unknown terrors of Home unarmed was pure folly. Either he could try recovering his belongings or return, naked, to our house to make another start. He thought for a long time, while the branches scratched his bare skin and the thirsty insects had their way. He considered each possibility, and none seemed to him to have any good points at all. The sun reached and passed its noontime height, and began to slide down the other side of the bowl, arousing the white sky toward the evening rain. Still Dore pondered his dilemma, and could achieve no satisfying solution.

"Are these yours?" asked a voice behind Dore. Our brother was startled, and his nakedness magnified his sense of vulnerability.

"Who are you?" said Dore. It was a strange man, surely not a member of the Thirtyfourth household nor any other with which Dore was familiar. He was holding Dore's captured clothing and, most wonderfully, Battlefriend in its richly wrought scabbard. "Yes, those are my things. How did you get them?"

The stranger smiled and held the clothes and sword out to Dore. "My name is Glorian," he said, "and I have my ways." Once dressed, again Dore examined his benefactor. The man was tall and slender, his skin tanned dark over a well-muscled frame. When he smiled, which he did readily, his teeth were white and strong. His hair was blond and cut very short. Dore was fascinated by the man's eyes, which were the brown of the River after the evening's rain. Glorian's gaze was magnetic, and Dore at last decided that it was because of the clever use of the eyebrows, which were in constant motion. Perhaps the stranger wanted to appear sensitive and aware.

"So tell me about yourself," said Dore. "Where are you from?"

Glorian smiled again. "I have the Knowledge of the working of things. I have come from far away, but I have been with you always. I will be a mystery to you until you discover the simplicity of yourself. I have a strong back, and I love children and parties. Today I wear a ruby on my forehead; this may change as circumstances require. Today I like daffodils, marigolds, and common garden mint. But that will vary, too."

"You said your name was Glorian?" asked Dore.

"Yes. Why do you ask?"

"Nothing," said Dore, shaking his head skeptically.

"I will be of great service to you on your quest," said Glorian.

"What do you know of my journey?" asked Dore, suddenly suspicious.

"Everything."

"Oh," said Dore. There was an uncomfortable silence. "Thank you for finding my clothes."

"Nothing at all. Let's get going."

I have a regular gallery today. Standing behind me are my brothers Jelt, Wole, and Niln, and my sisters Aniatrese, Lalichë, Ateichál, and Dúnilaea. They follow my pen across the page like the spectators at a very slow tennis match. Only Lalichë will disturb me, interrupting at times to clarify some point. A little while ago she asked if Glorian was going to be a symbol. I told her to wait and see.

If only Our Father had had such a friendly, omniscient guide he would never have come to Home, and we would never have been born. If he had had Glorian to help him, he wouldn't have wandered with Our squalling Mother from the prison in Pittsburgh all the miles to Cleveland's teeming decay. Indeed, if Glorian had been there, Our Father would never have met Our Mother, and they would never have been locked up in the first place, and Dore and we would, again, never have been born. It's something to consider.

But, instead, Our Father had only a merchant from Parma. When you say the words "Our Father" around this house, certain key phrases flash immediately through all our minds. This is the result of Our Mother's careful training. She was aware of her power. I'm sure that somewhere behind those incessant tears, she knew that she could mold us through our love, pity, and boredom. *Joy* is the first word that springs to mind when the Our Father reaction is triggered. A wise choice by Our Mother. Joy and happiness tinge all our thoughts of him; we are unsure if that is because Our Father himself was always happy, despite his series of trials, or because whatever reason caused his disappearance is in itself cause for celebration. We are split on this question, but not as split as on others. Most of us believe the former explanation.

The second phrase that roars unstoppably through our minds is *Infidelity doesn't pay, unless in cash.* We always cast our eyes guiltily to the ground. Our Mother was fidel to her dying day, but without a strong father figure around we have grown decadent. Then we think, *Children make up for bad times,* and we wonder if that's all that we are. Lastly we are trained to think, *Love,* and we do, but then add, "Sure, I'll bet," and go to the chapel to pray for forgiveness for these uncharitable thoughts.

Our Father was strong and self-sufficient, but he could not save himself and his charming bride from the invisible nets of the sneep, the Credit Company's ethicless enforcers. It was only through good fortune—or, as we are instructed, the wages of grace—that the merchant had a brother-in-law who ran a book barn in Connecticut. This in-law was shipping a huge load of remainders and used hardcovers to his outlet on a far-flung planet and needed a crew for the transport vessel. Here was a ready-made opportunity for Our Parents to escape the stifling style of life on Earth, and the stifling air, as well. Here was a chance to build a new home on a new, untamed world. Our Father's courage shrank from the idea of leaving the father-world, but grew again at the sound of the sirens. "But I know nothing of piloting a space vessel," he admitted honestly to the merchant from Parma.

"That does not matter," the man said. "My brother-in-law's ship is modern, up-to-date in every way. He has spared no expense in making it the very latest word in comfort and ease of handling. In fact, the entire mechanism is automatic: liftoff, navigation, and orbit when your destination is reached. You, your lovely, wet wife, and your handsome child will be disconnected for the journey, to save the expense of maintaining you during the duration of the flight. Bells will sound once a parking orbit has been achieved and you will awaken, none the worse for your experience, rested and ready to begin your new life."

"But I still know nothing about landing the rocket," said Our Father, liking neither the word "disconnected" nor Our Mother's hand on the merchant's gabardined thigh.

"No matter," said the merchant with a laugh and a wave. "You must satisfy the ground control that the craft contains a live and functional human being, to care for the rocket and its contents on the ground. At that point you can go back to sleep if you wish. Louis' ship will land automatically."

"Well, then, what am I needed for?"

"Someone has to unload the books," said the man.

It is surprising how often a gift of aid in an emergency appears to make the predicament worse. But beggars can't be choosers, I always say. I always say that because Our Mother always mumbled it, trying to make the best of a sorry situation.

"That right there," says Lalichë, pointing over my shoulder, "that's not very true, is it, Seyt?" I admit that Our Mother didn't say it very often. I don't even say it very often. Aren't I permitted *some* license?

In any event, Dore and Glorian cut their way through the underbrush around the estate of the Thirtyfourth family, careful to keep out of sight. Dore was wounded by the pain-filled screams of his precious timber friends, as he hewed a path through a thicket of sapling deys. A few times Glorian saw Dore wince, and asked if something were wrong.

"No," said Dore bravely, "I'll be all right." Soon they had found the slight trail that served these outlying families as highway through the great virgin forest. It was not long before the evening rains began to fall, chilling Dore and making him think for the first time of the comforts he had abandoned for our sake. This was the first night of the journey when he had not found shelter by raintime. He glanced at Glorian, who, because of his elegant white robe and jeweled accessories, Dore believed to be of aristocratic though enigmatic origin. But the new companion showed no signs of discomfort, and Dore was reluctant to suggest a halt. While he had stood alone and undressed behind the house of the Thirtyfours, Dore decided to forego the suspect hospitality of the houses in the neighborhood, at least as far as possible. So the two walked on; eventually the rain stopped, having scrubbed clean the sky, leaving the heavens to the perfect white stars and the two ruddy moons.

After a few hours of silent march Dore stopped by a great pollit, its bark stripping off characteristically in long gray ribbons. "I believe that I'll stop here," he said. "I did not sleep either long or well last night, and this seems to be as good a place as any to take my rest."

"Perhaps," said Glorian, "but if you continue just another few miles there will be a warm supper and a clean bed. And, as neither of us is carrying food, the breakfast in the morning will be a special and heartening blessing."

Dore thought for a few seconds. "What you say is true, but I fear that I have little desire to make the acquaintance of more of my fellow citizens."

"It is true that you may meet unexpected knavery along your way, but surely you expect that. And overcoming it where you find it prepares you to accept your goals at the end of the River." Dore gave Glorian a sharp look. He was concerned that the stranger should be so familiar with what ought to be matters known only to our family. Either Glorian was a force for evil, and then could obstruct Dore if our brother were not worthy of protection, or be powerless if the mission did have validity; or Glorian was a force for good, a guardian spirit from the bosom of Our Father's good will. This reasoning, combined with growing fatigue and hunger, convinced Dore to go along with Glorian's plan.

They saw the lights of the house shining through the darkness before they had covered half the distance. As they came closer the forest thinned, until they stood in a large clearing. In the center of the space was a great stone house, built square and massive and ominous. Dore had pictured a small cottage inhabited by honest rustics. He was unprepared to deal with local baronry.

It is a family characteristic to be unbowed in the face of petty authority. Nothing angers us more than the inflated bureaucrat, the pompous country squire, or the self-important ceremonial functionary. We have several in our own family, and I sincerely feel that they dislike themselves intensely.

I must pause now, because I believe that I'm expected to refresh my guests. They have for the most part sat patiently through the unfolding of this second chapter, with little complaint and admirable courtesy. I will go out and get a few bottles of wine, root beer for the younger children, and set out bowls of potato chips and gebbins.

Now, then. I bid my brothers and sisters to enjoy the spare felicities of my unassuming cell.

"It's coming along well, Seyt," says Dúnilaea. "It's kind of funny to see Dore doing those weird things."

"I'm not sure that you're taking the matter seriously enough," says Ateichál, who currently holds the office of Spiritual Director. Her term expires in two months; I am thinking of running against her in the Benevolent primaries. Perhaps she is already beginning her campaign.

"Oh, I assure you that I am," I say, offering her the bowl of nuts.

"I'm glad he got his sword back," says Jelt. After a while I thank them all for coming, and invite them back anytime. I make it clear that I want to get back to work. Dutifully they rise and go out into the hall, smiling and thanking me for my hospitality. It is the first time I have ever entertained. I feel accepted into responsible maturity.

"Are you going to put me in it any more?" asks Niln.

"We'll see," I say kindly.

At the launching pad in Florida, Our Parents and Dore were tucked into their couches by Louis, the brother-in-law of the merchant from Parma. "Do you still want to go through with it?" he asked.

"You've got your man," said Our Father in his gruff, imagined voice.

"Fine. Now, when the Customs officials on Ferkel's Planet discover you in orbit they'll ask you a few routine questions. You know, registration, cargo, crew descriptions, that sort of thing. By this time the automatic recall system will have restored you to tingling, vibrant life. I almost envy how good you'll feel. After you have clearance to land, you'll have to initiate the automatic entry systems. That's this here. Just flip this single switch from *Off* to *On*. Got that?"

"Roger."

"About the top ten percent of the rocket will be all that will land. This capsule will separate and direct itself toward the middle of a huge ocean on Ferkel's Planet. This has all been prearranged, and flight schedules have been filed, so there will be a carrier waiting for you. Divers from the carrier will meet you and help you and the cargo into a hovercraft, which will take you to the carrier itself. The carrier will make a few other pickups and transport you to Armstrong City, where a chartered plane will fly you to Shepard Beach. When you get there, unload the books, make certain that my agent gets them safely into his truck, and have him sign this receipt. Give him the yellow copy, keep the blue copy, and send the white one to me. After that, you're on your own. Your wife cries a lot, doesn't she?"

"I think she's nervous about the landing," said Our Father discreetly.

"Nothing to worry about, ma'am," said Louis. "It's all automatic. Chutes will open up and everything. Nothing you can do, anyway. Just relax. Everybody all set now?"

"I guess so," said Our Father resolutely.

"All right then. 'Flights of angels sing thee to thy rest,' " said Louis, quoting a truly lovely line from *Hamlet*. Then he disconnected Our Mother and Our Father and Dore.

It went against Our Father's character to relax while there was work to be done. But as Louis pointed out, there wasn't anything he could do, being disconnected in the first place. How remarkable that the merchant's brother-in-law should choose to quote a piece of *Hamlet*, a fictional character more like Dore than is proper to admit. Hesitancy is a key, and nobility, and tenacity. Of course Dore is not mad; but, then, was Hamlet? There is no need to get into that question here.

If Dore was reluctant to encounter any more of Home's settlers, it is because we all feel a great gap between ourselves and the rest of the families. From earliest childhood we are constantly reminded that our family is organized along different lines. We are asked strange questions by other children, and they cannot understand our answers. We tend to draw into ourselves, going outside the limits of our yard but rarely. We certainly have enough company, and enough variety, right here. I do not say that the other families are all opposed to us, for even among themselves they differ. But we have proven that we can get along without them, and they resent this fact.

It was against this disinclination that Glorian argued. "Come on," said Glorian, "remember the food and the bed."

"Oh, all right," said Dore. The two men walked across the short grass of the lawn. The two moons hung in the sky, one on either side of the dark, fortresslike building. They reminded Dore of Odin's ravens, and he knew that it was no good omen. He raised the heavy knocker and brought it down sharply three times. After a short wait the door was opened by a small, bearded old man.

"Who summons Dr. Dread?" said the white-haired gentleman.

"I am called Dore, and my companion is Glorian of the Knowledge."

"I see no companion," said the old man curiously. Dore turned in surprise, and sure enough, Glorian had disappeared. Dore shrugged.

"I am a weary traveler and I beg the hospitality of your hearth," said Dore, letting Glorian play his foolish tricks and take their consequences.

The old man opened his door wider, and stood out of the way to let Dore enter. "Weary, but not wary, eh? Any port in a storm, eh? Better an unknown pallet to a night *al fresco,* eh? Come in. I am Dr. Dread."

Dore went past the Doctor into a large, high-ceilinged hall. Against the far wall was a huge fireplace with the remains of a cooking fire still burning. An arras hung on either side of the fireplace to trap the cool dampness of the stone walls. On a high shelf were arranged heraldic banners, shields, swords, and other pseudo-medieval paraphernalia. At either end of the hall was a great door, made of heavy planks reinforced with iron bands.

"Food is on the table from my late supper," said Dr. Dread, "and you are welcome to eat your fill. As for your bed, you will find a staircase through that door." Here the Doctor indicated the door to the right. "You will ascend

to the second floor, and may take any chamber that meets
your approval. Please excuse my rudeness in not showing
you to your quarters, but your arrival interrupted me at
my work."

"No, thank you very much, Dr. Dread. You've been
most kind."

"Well, then, I will bid you a good night. My work will
not wait. I should warn you not to follow me through the
other door, or try to investigate. What rests in that tower
is my secret."

"Of course. Good night, Doctor."

"Yes, well. Until morning." The Doctor left Dore,
walking across the stone flooring and making very little
sound. He pulled out a large iron key and unlocked the
door, which opened with a fierce creaking. A weird green
light shone into the hall until the Doctor passed through
and shut and locked the door from the other side. Dore
shrugged again and fell to eating his supper.

I receive a note from Tere, no less. "What has happened to Glorian? I do hope you haven't written him out.
I rather enjoyed him. With all good wishes, your brother,
Tere." I remember once when Tere volunteered to teach
a night class in Cake Decorating but no one signed up. He
was angry for weeks. Finally he wrote a letter to the paper, claiming that it was a conspiracy. There may be
cliques among us, and it may be true that Tere belongs
to none of them, but we don't actively plan to ignore him.
It just happens.

Our Mother did her best to avoid the development of
divisive, internal groups. She saw that our family was
growing to immense proportions, and that was bound to
mean a certain alignment along party lines. She worked
very hard to keep us homologous, by making sure that we
all received identical indoctrination, similar environmental
experiences, and equivalent amounts of love, praise, and
frustration. But it didn't work, chiefly because each of us
had more brothers and sisters than our elders, and these
siblings served as a sanctuary from the bleak nonsense of
Our Mother's precepts. She wanted us to be all equal and,
more, identical, so that she could show us off as some sort
of matched collection. I've never really understood her
desire. Was she planning to invite the mistresses of the
other families for tea? What could she gain, besides some
rather nice choral music?

Another note. I have provoked the wrath, social consciousness, or sense of propaganda of Ateichál. She is offended by what I have said about Our Mother. Well, I defy my elder sister to prove me wrong.

Yet one more note. Tere backs her up.

Lalichë comes in unannounced. "They're right, you know," she says, but she's only five years old. She doesn't understand politics.

Our Mother frequently had visions. These always occurred just at dawn, after the morning clouds had formed above her head to obscure for the day the sterile sky. Clouds, of course, hold in themselves the potentiality of rain, a masculine attribute and thus less holy than the receptive earth. But even the clouds are more sanctified than the empty sky. After the heavens were decently covered and the sun had begun its masked journey, illusions on horseback would visit Our Mother on her throne. She never failed to take advantage of the situation, questioning an illusion unmercifully and reporting the incident to us in long dull, hysterical speeches. Most often she was visited by Death, who was brought to Home hidden in one of the thousands of books. We do not know which one, but if ever we find it we'll all live forever. Death spoke in high-sounding riddles, which Our Mother was good at rendering even more obscure, so during the reading of these interviews we sat restlessly at her feet and did other things. Occasionally Our Mother saw a dead king returning from some important war, or a ship with royal purple sails, laden with armed children and searching for the River. In her own way she was a nice old lady. But things change, and they change us. I loved Our Mother but, my brothers and sisters, it is dangerous to romanticize her faults. Surely I am not the only one who will remember them.

It was fortunate that Our Mother met someone as strongly willed and stoical as Our Father. He always knew how to control her. Most of their married life she spent in front of him, with her head bowed. He stood behind her and listened to her weeping. In the spacecraft he rested in the couch below her. Our Father was reconnected first, as the pilot of Louis' vessel. He was astounded to find that, even disconnected, Our Mother put in her quota of tears. He felt wonderful for a few moments. He did not move from his bunk, knowing that there was nothing to do until

he received the call from the ground personnel on
Ferkel's Planet, and he wanted to enjoy the seconds of
peace until Our Mother and Dore were reconnected. Soon
her wailing and gibbering indicated that he might as well
get up.

Our Father sat down at the control panel. He was fascinated that such a complex piece of machinery as the
rocket could be operated so completely automatically. The
controls consisted of the single toggle switch and a fuzzy
section labeled *Radio* set into the gray metal. Our Father
glanced at his right forefinger. "I am gifted with certain
abilities," he thought. "And I am able to use them for my
own advancement and for the betterment of others. What
more could any man desire?" He poised his finger above
the switch and waited. After quite a long time he began
to worry. "Surely Ferkel's Planet cannot have such heavy
traffic," he thought. "How could they have failed to notice
our approach?"

Before him on the viewscreen the planet turned, majestic and egg-shaped. Its poles were capped nicely with
white, but all the rest of the surface was covered with a
dark floral green. Our Father knew fear. He rose from
the control panel and joined his wife.

"I think we're in trouble," he said.

Our Mother sobbed. "Journey to a new home," she said.
"Tomorrow will be brighter. *You* take care of it."

"We were supposed to land in a great ocean. That
planet down there doesn't even have a good-sized lake
that I can see. The only water is one large river. There
seems to have been some sort of inaccuracy."

And so, by a fortuitous mistake, the errant ship brought
Our Parents to our world of Home, instead of the golden
cities of Ferkel's Planet. But trapped in orbit, with the
ship's mechanism programed to land them in the midst of
a nonexistent ocean, they were certainly in desperate circumstances.

"Oh, what will they do?" asks Lalichë fearfully.

"There, there," I say, stroking her fine black hair, "don't
you think I have this all thought out?"

"Oh, what will we do?" asked Our Mother fearfully.

"I don't know," said Our Father. "There must be something. Ah, here!" He had found a small button labeled
Emergency Only. He gave it a sharp push. A low humming caught his attention, and he turned to see a panel

sliding open. He hurried to the secret compartment, which proved to be a sort of broom closet. It was filled with mops and buckets and dustpans. On a shelf in the back were cans of polish and wax, rolls of electrical tape, a small box of tools, and a thick, dusty book entitled *Manual Operation*.

"Well, now," said Our Father jubilantly, "we appear to be saved. It is merely a matter of focusing my faculties and learning to land this craft before we starve, thirst, or strangle."

"I'm behind you all the way," said Our Mother.

"Fine, fine," said Our Father absently, as he began reading the instructions. Several hours later, armed with the knowledge contained in the technical book and a Phillips screwdriver, he had prepared the capsule for separation and a soft landing in the planet's only river. He returned to his bunk, and Our Parents settled back to await developments.

"But landing in the River isn't anything like landing in an ocean," says Lalichë. "They'd be helpless if they survived. There aren't any teams of divers waiting to rescue them."

Lalichë, though bright for her age, has never seen an ocean. A large amount of water is a large amount of water. Beyond a certain point it doesn't make any difference how far apart the shores are; besides, this is historical fact. The screwdriver is still on view in the East Foyer.

It is true that Our Parents, plummeting down from orbit to land in six feet of water, might have been seriously harmed, if not killed, had these been ordinary circumstances. But my dear hebetic sister forgets that the river is *the* River. They landed softly, with barely a jolt. The River welcomed them to Home by running softly and calmly; and when Our Father opened the hatch to push the capsule to land, the River obliged by altering its current. The water flowed transversely, from bank to bank, and soon the capsule was washed ashore. Our Father recognized the miraculous nature of this aid, and wanted to sacrifice something in gratitude. All that he had on hand was his wife and infant son, and a large load of books. He chose one of the latter, of course, a large coffee-table art book; and thus began our tradition of book-tossing. The River seemed pleased.

"Is that really how it happened, Seyt?" asks Lalichë, eating the last of my snacks. "How did Our Father know that he could breathe the air and stuff like that?"

Tere, forgive her. Ateichál, she's still very young. I try to explain to her that either Our Father was omniscient, or he wasn't. And if Lalichë chooses to argue that he wasn't, well, she can expect to lead a very lonely life. That's the point of faith. Isn't she at all interested in the weird green light that so fascinates Dore? Aren't we all supposed to be following with bated breath the hazardous progress of our brother? Perhaps I am being too subtle for her. I will dispense with artifice for the moment, for the benefit of my charming sister.

"That's all right, Seyt," she says. "I was going anyway."

In the morning Dore came downstairs, refreshed and anxious to continue his journey. He met the strange Dr. Dread in the great hall. The Doctor was evidently completing his own breakfast, and gestured to Dore to join him.

"Thank you, Doctor," said our brother. "I slept very well."

"You were not disturbed by any unusual noises?" Dore, his mouth already filled with cold roast, shook his head. "No screams? No pleadings or hideous shrieks?"

"No," said Dore. "Did I miss something?"

The Doctor looked down at his plate. "No, of course not," he said nervously.

"Then I would like to thank you and be on my way. But first, I would be honored if you would let me repay you for your charity. Is there some chore that I might do to relieve you of the labor?"

Dr. Dread appeared to consider Dore's more than generous offer. Then he looked across the table and smiled. "Yes, if you would, I have a small task that needs attention. I myself have been too busy with my researches. If you would, I'd consider it a great favor."

"Not at all," said Dore, and the two men finished their breakfast in silence. Afterward the Doctor led Dore outside to a wooden building behind the house. It was about twelve feet high and twenty feet along each side. There were no windows and but one large door set in the front wall. From within Dore could hear loud scrapings and bangings, and every once in a while there was a thump as something struck the wall.

"Is this a garage?" asked Dore. "What do you keep in there?"

"That's not important," said Dr. Dread. "I want you to reinforce these walls. You cannot fail to be aware that this enclosure houses something monstrous and dreadful. I forbid you to open the door. You would have to destroy my ingenious system of locks to do that, but it has happened before, and the culprits are unanimous in their regret. If you would, I'd appreciate it if you would merely fasten these bars across the timbers. It may be a heavy job, but you will be granting me the most precious gift of all: peace of mind."

"Why, certainly, sir. I'll need a ladder and certain tools. I like to work in an organized and efficient manner."

"A man after my own heart," said the Doctor. "You'll find what you need around the corner of this shed." Dore turned to his labor, and the Doctor left him and returned to the house.

As he worked, Dore did not think of the funny way things turn out. Here he was, the eldest son and leader of the powerful First family, doing carpentry for a neurotically secretive old man. He did not consider himself the least bit dishonored. He did not think that we, his brothers and sisters, would have been disgraced to see him working like a common serf. This is one of the reasons that Dore stands so far apart from us. There are other reasons, and it is my job to make them clear to you, as I've just done.

During a short rest Dore leaned against the tightly sealed cage and looked back toward the house of Dr. Dread. Up in the tower where the Doctor worked, Dore saw the same strange green light flaring from a window. Dore became aware of movement in the distant chamber as huge forms chanced to pass in front of the window and block the emerald rays. Often the shape was recognizably that of Dr. Dread, but sometimes Dore saw hideous sights, as though the Doctor housed towering, monstrous things in his house as well as in the shed. But that, of course, was the man's business, and Dore returned to his job, finishing it shortly before dinnertime.

"Come, my honest fellow," said the Doctor pleasantly, when he saw that Dore had completed his labors. "Let us have a last meal together. You may cover a goodly distance before nightfall, but I'll wager the miles will be shorter on a full stomach."

"Thank you, sir," said Dore. "Indeed, I could use a few moments of rest."

Dr. Dread grasped Dore's arm and directed him toward the house. The old man had a very forceful and direct personality, and Dore realized that under the proper circumstances Dr. Dread could appear to be cold and calculating. What could this man's motives be? What strange goals eluded him?

"I am very interested in you, my son," said the Doctor, seated with Dore once again at the table. "It saddens me that you are leaving, and that we have had such little time to talk, both absorbed in our respective tasks. I am always fascinated by that which makes one individual different from another. This is knowledge that has been hidden by the gods, and it takes a courageous or foolhardy man to tamper with that cosmic casket."

Dore regarded the Doctor over the edge of his wineglass. "Fortunately for myself, I am neither."

"Ah, then why did you find it necessary to disobey my instructions and peer within my coop of wonders? Did you find my collection interesting?"

Dore set his glass down on the table and stared angrily at the Doctor. "You mistake me, sir. I never looked within that fearsome building. I was told not to do so, and I saw no reason to defy you."

"You lie, young man. No one can resist."

Dore was offended. He was angered that the man would judge him to be that weak, and then accuse him of lying. He rose from his chair, his hand straying to the hilt of Battlefriend. "Sir, again I thank you for your food and the lodging, but I—" Dore put his hand to his head. He felt dizzy, as though—

"As though the wine had been drugged," says Lalichë happily. I was so engrossed in Dore's awful difficulty that I didn't hear her enter. Yes, dear little one, the evil Dr. Dread had drugged our brother's wine. Dore felt very sick—

"The room began to spin and then everything turned black, eh?"

Yes, Lalichë, thank you. Dore collapsed in his chair, and the last thing of which he was conscious was the triumphant leering face of Dr. Dread staring down at him.

"Dore wouldn't have been suckered like that, Seyt," says my most tireless commentator. "Our Mother gave us so many good rules to follow. She taught us to judge bad people. Dore wouldn't have been fooled for a minute, once he saw that green light. What's inside that old shed?"

Lalichë forgets that Dore did not think himself to be in any danger. He planned to finish his meal and bid Dr. Dread adieu. Our Mother's set of training principles was neglected for the moment. And, of course, this was the very sort of situation that she was trying to warn us about. She tried to impress us with the frustration of her position: the sole receptacle of wisdom on the planet, confronted with dozens of ignorant children who thought her old and silly. Whenever she said that, we'd all stand and try to convince her that she was wrong, that we didn't think that she was so old. Then she'd ask us to repeat her Precepts of Power. That's what she called them, Precepts of Power. I could never remember them, so I just moved my lips. All the girls had them memorized, though.

Our Mother showed flashes of true concern for our education. She sometimes surprised us all by giving an unannounced quiz. She would go to the trouble of having some of the other neighbors originally from Earth come in to speak to us. She always called them "visiting lecturers," sometimes embarrassing the poor people as they stood before us in their tattered, home-made clothing. We were expected to listen closely, for each guest would recall details and scraps of life on Earth, things we knew nothing about and, perhaps, Our Mother had neglected. I remember once hearing old Charlie Twelve tell us about walnuts, about their sweet, ominous bat-shaped meats, looking sometimes like roast turkeys or warty busts of Zeus. For days afterward we tried to imagine the taste of walnuts, and we've never forgotten our feeling of poverty.

And we tried desperately to include her in the growing relationship and joyful dependence we felt toward our adopted world. Only once did we carry her down to the edge of the River. She was always hearing us speaking of the River in hushed or excited tones, and she demanded to know what was going on. My older brother Sabt built a temporary throne for her in the mud of the

Riverbank, and Nesp and Loml carried her, one holding her ankles, the other supporting her reverently under the arms. She sat with the water washing her feet and gazed wistfully downstream, crying and crying for her lost husband. My younger brother Wole claims that he saw a water sprite bow before the grieving figure of Our Mother. Later in the day we wandered off, one by one, to our chores or to seek other entertainment. So accustomed were we to having Our Mother fixed steadfastly on her throne that we all assumed that she had been returned to her place in the yard. But, sadly, no one had carried her back. She spent the rest of the day and all night by the water's edge, and in the morning when we went out to the fields we were horrified to find her throne empty. We had misplaced Our Mother, and we panicked until a cool head remembered where we had left her. It was a very embarrassing moment when we went to pick her up.

Dore came to his senses strapped to an operating surface tilted almost perpendicularly to the floor. The first thing that he noticed was the ghastly green light in the room, indicating that he had been moved to the Doctor's secret laboratory.

"Ah, welcome back, my young and curious friend. Did I not say that those whose inquiring minds got the better of their caution lived to regret it? Do you not wish that you had followed my advice? It was such a pity to spoil such a rare vintage with the sleeping liquor."

"I insist, my impetuous host, that I never betrayed your trust," said Dore bravely.

"Indeed? But it makes little difference now," said Dr. Dread, turning toward a bank of dials and flashing lights. "You are seeing too much to allow me to permit your escape. What would the innocent townsfolk do, after your tale confirmed their wild rumors and legends? Why, in no time at all I'd have a crowd of angry men out there, screaming for my life. Pitchforks, burning torches, the whole ugly scene. No, I'm afraid you'll have to continue to accept my meager courtesy."

Dore heard a door slam, and though he couldn't see the door behind him, he did witness Dr. Dread's angry reaction.

"Gort!" said the Doctor sharply. "Go back! Go back to your cell!" The Doctor picked out a flaming brand from the fireplace and waved it before him. Dore heard a loud, horrible rustling behind him, and he knew that it belonged to the demonic shape he had seen from the yard. The Doctor screamed, and Dore saw him throw the torch across the room. Dr. Dread hurried to the fireplace, but before he could find a new weapon the monster forced him into a corner. Dore could see it now: It stood easily ten feet tall, massive and globular in shape. It had neither head nor arms, but propelled its huge bulk on several thin, ropy appendages. Dore recalled that it was dark red in color, but looked almost black in the green light.

"Call him!" said Dr. Dread hoarsely. "If you distract him, he'll be easily confused. Save me and I'll let you live."

Dore took a deep breath and called the brute's name. As the Doctor predicted, it hesitated. It seemed to forget its furious attack on Dr. Dread, and stood in the center of the room, paralyzed with indecision.

"My one defense is their stupidity," said the Doctor. "For years I have worked, building them up in size and mobility through selective breeding. Now I have the potential of a truly unstoppable army of vegetables!"

"Vegetables?" asked Dore in astonishment.

"Yes, I see that you're amazed. And well you should be. So should the entire world be, in a short time. Gort is the descendant of generations of genetically manipulated garden radishes. He is my prize, the most locomotive of my plant militia. Also, unfortunately, the most intelligent. That is why I need you, my feckless spy. Tonight I test my new toy. I shall transfer your human essence into Gort's nutritious self. Not your personality, or your memories, or anything like that. Just enough to make Gort a bit more of a man. And," said the untrustworthy scientist, "just enough to make you a bit more of a vegetable. I have dozens of these robots prepared, just waiting for this evening's success. Soon I alone shall rule; with my irresistible army I shall move from conquest to conquest. How can they stop a radish? How do you slay a scallion, a carrot? They have no vital organs at all. They're invincible!"

"He's mad," says Lalichë bitterly. I reassure her.

"I think not, evil one," said a new voice from the

doorway. Our brother still could not see. He chafed against his bonds, but they were too strong.

"Who are you, and how did you get past the guards?" said Dr. Dread.

"My name is Glorian of the Knowledge, and one of the things that I know is that your cause, like all errands of wickedness, is doomed to failure."

"Get me out of here, Glorian," called Dore.

"Yes, my friend." And Glorian came around the platform on which Dore was prisoner. "Here," he said cheerfully, "take this." He put Battlefriend into Dore's hand. Immediately the iron shackles sprang open, and Dore was free.

"How did that happen?" asked Dore in wonder.

"Your enchanted sword conducted my inner wisdom, which, coupled with your own happy innate goodness, overpowered the bonds of corruption. But let us hurry, for our adversary has summoned his planty legions."

"Thanks, Glorian," said Dore, rubbing his sore wrists. "Stand you behind me, for, despite your simple virtue, I see that you are defenseless. I shall try to keep them from you with the strength of my arm, dearest of friends." By now the room was crowded with the insane Doctor's vegetable guards. Great overgrown edible roots they were, milling about on disproportionately cultured secondary roots. The vegetables segregated themselves by variety: All the carrots grouped together, and the onions, scallions, beets, sweet potatoes, radishes, turnips, and garlics. Gort, their nominal leader, was now confused into inertness.

"You may save your arm, my companion," said Glorian, "for you will see that they have none. What the good Doctor has forgotten is that his soldiers cannot grasp weapons, hurl grenades, or storm walls. Let us pass through them and go our way. Do not attempt to wound one, for with your especial sensitivity to green and growing things, you would be yourself disabled."

And so the two men walked unharmed among the giant horrors, while Dr. Dread screeched incoherently behind them. They took their leave of the madman's stronghold and continued their interrupted journey.

"What about Dr. Dread and all his vegetables?" asks Lalichë, with her penchant for tidy endings.

They were all sadly destroyed in a fire. I suppose the

Doctor himself caused it in the extremity of his disappointment.

A victory for Dore! Our brother handled himself admirably in his mystic martial initiation.

CHAPTER THREE

A Woman's Treachery

There is less of a general stir this morning, but I anticipated that. The reaction is essentially that my second chapter was much more fanciful than anyone expected. There is a sharper division among my brothers and sisters, some intrigued by my imagination, others put off by the implausibility and the "misrepresentations." Mylvelane as "The Trunk-maker" in the *Times-Register* is still enthusiastic, applauding my independence and my fearless attitude. I think that I will send her a grateful note.

Now let me begin the day's work. Um. Dore and Glorian have been reunited, once again on their trail to adventure.

The way led deeper into the primeval forest, and the farther they traveled the fresher Dore felt. Soon the horrors of the previous days receded in his memory, and only a few puzzling factors disturbed his tranquil mind.

"Glorian?" he asked quietly, as he walked beside his new comrade. "You knew that maniac, didn't you? Why did you get me into that situation in the first place?"

"Ah, my friend," said the mysterious young man, "I merely provided you with an alternative. It was you alone who chose to enter that domain of evil."

"But I trusted you!" said Dore. "You should have warned me."

"It was something of a test. It had to happen sooner or later, and now at least we are both certain of your valor, if not your prudence. I am very glad that things turned out well."

"So am I," murmured our brother. "And how did you disappear like that? Why did you leave me?" Glorian only smiled. They walked on until late in the day, when Glorian produced apples, dark bread, and ale for their supper.

"These are the last of my supplies," he said. "Even the

46

Knowledge doesn't permit me to conjure rations for your sustenance."

"An excellent meal, my friend. Thank you. Now I suppose we must tighten our belts and learn to make do with what we find." After their short supper they walked some more, and the path grew narrower and narrower. When the rains stopped, the moons illuminated our brother and Glorian standing beside an elder micha, bewildered as the trail dwindled and evaporated among the trees.

"Which way?" asked Glorian. "This is your quest, Dore."

"Let us stop here for the night. Perhaps in the morning something will give us a hint. I'd like not to stray too far from the River, and already I seem to be lost." The two men settled themselves among the huge roots of the micha and wrapped themselves in their insufficient cloaks. Dore addressed a prayer to Our Father, and was soon asleep.

"Seyt?"

What a fortuitous time to be interrupted. I had run out of ideas. It is Relp, this month's Conscience Monitor. I assume that he's come to try my guilt. I welcome him mistrustfully. "Oh, hi, Relp," I say casually.

"Am I bothering you?" he says, sticking to the formula.

"No, not at all. I was taking a break."

"That story of yours keeping you off the streets, eh? Keeps you too busy to sin."

I laugh. Relp takes his position too seriously. "Guess so," I say.

"That's what I wanted to see you about. Now, you understand that this is strictly official business, and personal feelings don't enter into it at all. But whenever the person in my office gets a complaint, it's his duty to check it out. You know that; you've been Monitor."

A horrible experience. I nod. "You've gotten a complaint? Who?"

"I'm not supposed to tell. But just to show you the ridiculousness of the thing, it's Tere. He says you're verging on blasphemy in that history of yours. I wouldn't know. I haven't read it. But be careful, all right? A conviction for blasphemy is a grievous and permanent thing."

I assure Relp that I haven't been doing anything seriously wrong. I'm just telling a story; some of my family want to forget that Our Parents and Dore were *people*, too. They walked around and stubbed their toes and performed bodily functions. Except Our Mother, of course; she just cried. I wish Tere would shut up. I see unhealthy signs of a new regime of religiosity and conservatism.

Relp gives me his official, cheerless smile, tells me to keep up the good work, and leaves. Perhaps I will talk to Mylvelane or Yord, and get them to do an editorial on the freedom of the perceptive artist in our society. Our Parents would have been horrified to see us sliding toward an oppressiveness that didn't include them.

Days passed, and Dore marched further into the heart of our world. He communed with his trees and talked with Glorian, and was actually quite happy. The peace and contentment were something he had never known before, as these are qualities we have sacrificed for our sophistication. He did not suffer from hunger, for his knowledge of the forest and Glorian's kept them well-fed, although Dore observed, curiously, that Glorian ate very little. They refreshed themselves at woodland springs, running toward their junction with the River and not yet holy in themselves.

One afternoon, while Dore was suggesting that they follow one of these streams and thus find the River, the two comrades were startled to hear a loud crashing among the trees before them. Whatever was causing the commotion was still invisible, but Dore drew his sword in preparation. They had met a few small grass dragons and woodcats, but had avoided them without calamity. Now, however, it sounded as though they were about to meet something much larger and wilder. Glorian put his hand on Dore's shoulder. "Don't fear," he said, "we will face this test together." Our brother nodded wordlessly.

As the mystery came closer they heard cursing, in a frustrated female voice. Dore glanced at Glorian, who shrugged. In a few seconds a young lady came into view but did not appear to notice the two men.

"Hello," Dore called, "can we be of service?"

The young woman looked up, startled. "I'm lost in this damn forest," she said, and fell to the ground, crying.

"So are we," said Dore, "but if you like you may travel with us. I believe we will all fare better together than stumbling our separate ways."

"He's right, you know," said Glorian. The young woman looked hesitant, naturally fearing to put her trust in two strange and somewhat disheveled men. Dore had removed his crown and jeweled scabbard after the incident with Dr. Dread, carrying them wrapped in a spare white cloak Glorian had somehow "found." Our brother appeared to be a simple soldier of fortune or other sort of vagrant. Glorian's lithe good looks attracted the young woman, as became evident when she took his arm. Dore was amused by his friend's discomfiture.

"My name is Glorian," said that remarkable man.

"Of the Knowledge," said Dore, still laughing. "My name is Dore."

The young woman stood and curtsied prettily. "I am the Princess Dawn des Malalondes," she said. "I was stolen from the palace of my father by the son of Baron von Glech, our bitterest enemy. I managed to flee before that young rascal Snolli could consummate his rape, but he has been hunting me for days. I'm weak with hunger and hopelessly lost." To demonstrate her point, the Princess Dawn fainted into Glorian's arms. The stranger looked at Dore helplessly, and Dore shook his head in wonder.

"Does not the Knowledge advise you on the ways of women?" asked our brother good-naturedly. "Here, let us permit her to rest beneath this shady tree. We're in no hurry. Be a good man and fetch some water from the spring."

While Glorian was absent, Dore observed their new companion. She was by far the most beautiful girl Dore had ever seen, fairer than even Aniatrese, our own Beauty Queen. The Princess Dawn's loveliness was not diminished by the rigors of her trial, and even the accumulated dirt of her travels could not hide it. Her hair, matted now with twigs and leaves, was of the darkest, purest black Dore had ever seen. Her skin contrasted with it startlingly, so white and unblemished was it. Though she was small and delicate, her form was perfect. Dore wished that she would awaken so that he might see what color were her eyes.

At last Glorian returned with the cold water. Dore did not ask where the man had found the glass. Our brother held the water to her lips, and she began to revive.

"She is very beautiful," said Dore.

"But oftentimes such superficial comeliness masks horrors beneath," said Glorian. "I should have thought you to be the last person to judge such a book by its cover."

The Princess' eyelids began to flutter, and then she sat up suddenly.

"Goodness," she whispered, "have I fainted? Oh, what a girlish, weak thing to do!"

"There, there," said Dore, "you've been through a lot. Just rest, now. Put your head on my shoulder."

The Princess looked around, trying to find Glorian. He was standing a few feet away, looking expectantly at Dore.

"My lord?" he said, trying to catch Dore's attention. "My lord, if all be well with you now, I think that I will take my leave. My wife expects me soon, and a true harridan she is if I'm late. I thank you again, my lord, and trust that all will be to your liking. If I may be of service again, sir, please don't fail to do me the honor. My lady, my lord, I wish you good day." Then Glorian bowed, turned, and walked off through the forest. The Princess was looking into Dore's face with new interest, so that it was only our brother who saw Glorian fade from view after several steps.

"Dore, are you of noble birth?" asked the Princess.

"Yes, truthfully, I am," said Dore, shaking his head with displeasure. "But I desired to travel in disguise, and that poor bungler had to spoil it."

"Oh, he seemed nice enough. And I'm glad that he did," she said softly and moistly.

"Come," said Dore, "let us be off."

"Must we depart so soon?"

"You are being hunted."

"Yes," said the Princess, "yes, of course."

Love is a strange thing. It strikes members of both sexes and all ages. Love doesn't distinguish between rich and poor or good and bad. I recall when I fell in love with Joilliena. It happened after one of Our Mother's lectures on dirt. We were both so bored that we ran back to the house, desperate for diversion. It happened that the rec room was nearly empty, and we played a few games of table tennis. Joilliena was impressed with my top spin, and I gave her a few helpful hints. Afterward we went for a walk outside, unmindful of the evening rain. We held hands, and she picked some flowers for me. We met Dore and his lady, Dyweyne, who were also enjoying the dusky coolness. Dore smiled at me, and I suppose that I was embarrassed. Dyweyne kissed Joilliena's cheek and warned her against vice. But the whiteness of our flowers convinced our eldest sister that our new love was pure. The four of us went down to the River and thought about skipping stones.

If Dyweyne is upset by my introduction of the Princess Dawn, she should recall that Dore never expected to return, and felt that he might as well accept the bounties of fate. I do not intend the Princess to be any actual rival for Dyweyne and I truly hope my lovely sister doesn't take offense. But Dore was in a lonely and somber state, and we have all had experience with the magic of contiguity. And, incidentally, if Joilliena happens to be out there listening, I'd like to take this opportunity to thank her for those golden moments, and promise her many more over the years to come.

Was it love that Dore felt, or merely a sexual infatuation? Of course, he is not available for comment, and this is the sort of matter that belongs to the realm of individual assessment. I could enter into a great dissertation on romance, virtue, and the egotism of love, but I won't. I will merely go on without prejudicial sentiment and allow the reader to close his eyes, recall the last few times that he has felt as Dore does, and decide for himself.

Toward evening the Princess Dawn began to complain of hunger. Dore cursed himself for forgetting his companion's limitations. "I have only some fruit and nuts left from yesterday's meal, my lady," he said. "Here, let us stop and share them. It will be time for the rain soon, and perhaps it will be better to rest."

"My lord Dore," said the Princess softly, "do you suppose that I might have all the fruit? I am famished and palsied with hunger."

Dore was bewildered and disappointed, but he couldn't deny the Princess' wish. Human relationships are not as fragile as swooning poets would have us believe. Indeed, rather than the gentle wildflower, love is most like the sturdy, tough vine. It grows and turns and twists, sometimes strangling its support in its blind upward surge. People just don't understand the human mind. Even after these thousands of years of practice, we still haven't learned the basic facts. The true place of humanity in the scheme of things can be approximated by the appalling frequency with which one hears the words "contrary to popular belief."

After the meal and the rest period, Dore gathered his kit together in preparation for the evening march. The Princess, however, begged him to halt for the night. "You know that today when we met I was nearly exhausted," she said. "I thank you for the relief of your food and this short repose. But I fear that I am sorely in need of one good night's sleep." Again Dore could not refuse her pleasure. He prepared a hard bed for her beneath a large tree, covering her with his cloak.

"Are you not going to share my resting place, my lord?" she said. "You have done so much for me today; surely you are as fatigued as I."

"Ah, but then would I not be as foul as that Snolli von Glech whom you avoid so desperately?"

The Princess Dawn looked up sleepily from her leafy couch. "What I withhold so vigorously from some, I may dispense with joy to others." Dore did not answer, but sat thinking beneath the black, cold sky.

In the morning Dore was awakened by the sound of the Princess moving about. He said nothing, but watched for several minutes as she opened his bundle and removed his crown and jeweled scabbard. She seemed awestruck by their beauty and opulence. After a time she replaced them and tied up the cloth again. She returned to her bed and feigned sleep. Shortly thereafter Dore stood and went deeper into the woods to attend to his morning's business, and to permit the Princess Dawn to arrange herself in privacy. When he returned he found her still reclining upon the ground, but watching him with mirthful eyes.

"Good morning, my lord protector. Will you not greet me as expects a woman lost alone with her truly beloved?" She stretched out her arms and Dore, taken with her drowsy charms, sat beside her. The Princess Dawn laughed to herself, for well she understood the powers of love, those that steal gradually upon a person until he is overwhelmed by desire. From Aristophanes we hear the story of the creation of Men, who originally were made with four arms and four legs, but were divided in half for their sins. All love's goal is now to reunite those sundered parts, if but for a moment. Very crude, but charming. Dore could read from the Princess' sighs that she was becoming anxious for such an atavistic conjunction. In those lonesome woods he knew that he could do no better, and, in love's sweet disorder, could see no reason to begin opposing her designs.

"Ah, Dore, come to me," she whispered. "Nature herself approves: here we will lie in a bed of wild thyme." The Princess lay back expectantly while Dore removed his belt and put Battlefriend carefully with his other treasures. He joined the beautiful Princess and they began their mutual explorations. The bout proceeded without incident until the Princess kissed Dore's ear and said, "Soft, my lord, do not haste. We shall have the day to ourselves." Accordingly, Dore retarded the tempo of his assault, and the two entwined devoted themselves to such intimate games as may be improvised between the roots of a great tree.

Lalichë storms into my room, a rather small thunderclap in respect of her size. She tugs my arm, forbidding me from continuing the passionate adventure. "I don't like her, and I don't trust her," she says. I inquire of whom she disapproves, and of course she means my lusty Princess. I tell her that she is probably merely jealous, an emotion that has caused more grief in this world than any other, in its various guises. What else toppled those topless towers?

"It wasn't me," says my nonagic sister.

"Do you mind if I start this thing toward its conclusion?" asked Dore, for his elbows and knees were scraped raw.

"Let me see," said the Princess, who herself was in a most uncomfortable position with her spine upon a half-buried root. She seemed to think for a few seconds. "Yes, my lord, take me now." And the two, as one, united themselves in moist completion. Almost immediately Dore heard the sound of running feet, and looked up in dismay to see an armored youth absconding with Dore's belongings.

"It's that wretch, Snolli von Glech!" cried the Princess Dawn.

"Caught with your pants down again, eh, my friend?" said Glorian from behind the great tree.

"How long have you been there?" asked Dore angrily. "And why didn't you do anything to stop that thief?"

"Perhaps it would be more profitable to question your

putative Princess," said Glorian, still declining to come into view. "I don't mean to hurry you, but if you would care to recompose yourself, I believe that we can learn some interesting things."

Dore did as he was bidden, staring impotently after the young thief.

"Now," said Glorian, "tell my friend who you are."

The Princess looked at Glorian, and gasped. She cringed against Dore in dismay. "You!" she whispered, her eyes still on Glorian. "Do you guide this man on his quest?"

Dore was confused, for the man who had stepped from behind the tree in no way resembled the Glorian he had known, except in the tone and firmness of his voice. The new Glorian was short and thickly built, with curly brown hair and a dark complexion. He wore a heavy violet tunic and black breeches, and had a silver band about his brow set with a large sapphire.

"Are you Glorian?" asked Dore doubtfully.

"Yes. I have changed because the environment of our relationship has changed. Your studies are near an end, and soon you must take up your burden of responsibility. But first I must make clear to you what has happened, for you have not acted wisely and cannot afford to continue thus in the future."

"And you are familiar to the Princess in your current guise?"

"Very much to her chagrin," said Glorian. "Her family refuses my Knowledge."

"Not I," said the Princess in a quavering voice. "My brother and my father force their will upon me."

"Tell Dore your name," said Glorian sternly. When she did not reply, he answered for her.

"The Princess Dawn des Malalondes is a fiction. This young woman is Narlinia von Glech, the daughter of the impoverished Baron Glaub von Glech. Her brother often teams with her to waylay unsuspecting swains such as yourself. Your crown and your jeweled scabbard will stock next month's sculleries, but your sword Battlefriend will be put to other uses. Your reputation is wider than your modesty admits, and your ensorcelled blade is desired by many. It remains to be seen what results your ardor may have in the wide world, but you have not by any means met the last of the Von Glechs. I begin to think that perhaps this encounter was ordained, and that my decision to leave you to your honor was more momentous than I dreamed. In any event, you are without the protection of your sword, and are in no manner prepared to gain it back."

Dore was ashamed. "It is only now that my judgment begins to uncloud," he said. "What do you suggest I do?"

"Bid this trollop of a princess farewell, and come along," said Glorian.

"I'm sorry, Dore, really I am," she said, with genuine tears in her eyes. "I want to see you again. Can you believe me? I . . . I think I love you." Dore said nothing, but walked away and left her beneath the giant tree. He did not turn around again, and followed with Glorian the forest stream as it led back toward the River.

"You sure make Dore look like a fool," says Lalichë, failing to understand the allegorical device of moral education. I do not intend this history to be merely a collection of simulated exploits. There is in it the potential for a truly useful homiletic tool.

Tere comes into the room, filling it with his officious humor. He always appears to be occupied, but he seems busier than he is. "Women!" he says with a deprecatory laugh and a snort. "Excuse me, Lalichë, but it's true. You can't trust women as far as you can throw 'em."

"Have you ever thrown one, Tere?" asks my sister from within the refuge of youth. Tere doesn't answer. He smiles at me, only apparently amused by her remark.

"Lalichë," he says pointedly, "it was you for whom I was looking. I'd like to speak with you for a few minutes, if you don't mind. Perhaps it isn't a good idea to interrupt our brother at his Gongorism."

"It doesn't make any difference," she says, and both Tere and I wonder at her meaning. Tere takes her skinny arm and the two of them leave my room without a word.

CHAPTER FOUR

The Song of the Sword

I do not here attempt to derogate my brother's reading habits, but merely to indicate the disparity in our interests. Had Dore been as educated in the drama as I, he could easily have found solace. Such topics as love, betrayal, and revenge have fascinated playwrights continuously, for these themes lend themselves excellently to the generation of motion, passion, and dead bodies. Molière, that surpassing non-English Thalian, says that if everyone were clothed in integrity, and every heart were just, sincere, and kindly, the other virtues would be practically useless, since their part is to enable us to stand the prejudices of our fellows. Elsewhere another person, George Chapman, in his *All Fools* of 1605, tells us that "Love is Nature's second sun, causing a spring of virtues where he shines." Thus we have on one hand the recommendation that those noble qualities are necessary to abide the pettiness of the world, and on the other hand a prescription for the cultivation of those virtues: Love. I hope I am not acting presumptuously to add that Love, meaning here either the spiritual or the sensual sort, might best in most practical circumstances be employed when it is an amalgam of the two.

Although the lady was not, after all, the Princess Dawn des Malalondes, Dore recognized in her a certain quality, as though the crimes of her greedy father and brother had failed to win over her soul. Along the way after their meeting our brother found himself giving much thought to her, and to Glorian's veiled promise that Dore would have the opportunity to meet her again. Dore began to hold to that assurance with great hope, perhaps to the detriment of his journey's more worthy goals.

This ability to consider one problem even when most engrossed with another is a typical distortion of one of Our Father's impressive traits. There was nothing Our

Father was if not resourceful; he had an answer for everything, and if sometimes that answer was unrealistic, he was rarely at a loss for another. He could juggle a plurality of weighty matters with little effort. Now, of course Dore tries, and he certainly *considers* a lot, but he somehow lacks the same capacity to distinguish priorities. Our Father always knew the relative importance of his problems, and treated them accordingly.

When the great space-traveling capsule landed in the waters of Life here on Home, rather than the salty ocean toward which it had been aimed, Our Father was little dismayed. Plans began forming before he ever soaked his foot in the River. If he could manage to haul that capsule onto the shore, it would make an ideal cabin and base of explorations. Home was an uncharted world and, even if Our Father had known where he was, he would have known nothing of the dangers of his new environment. A secure shelter was needed before nightfall.

I have already shown how the River itself aided Our Parents by sweeping the capsule up on the muddy banks. Once it rested precariously on the land, Our Father began to give thought to how it might be moved to a safer location. He thought of inclined planes, screws, rollers, blocks and tackles, pendulums, and other simple engines. So lost was he in thought that he did not notice the eyes that stared at him from the leafy verges of the forest. Soon the animals grew bolder, and Our Mother's frantic scratching at the capsule's window attracted his attention. Our Father was surrounded by scores of animals, ranging in size from tiny shrews and dobs to huge, slavering doglike beasts and venomous grass dragons.

Our Father smiled slowly, careful not to make any sudden or threatening motions. He looked at the animals, and they looked at him. He pointed first at the capsule, then up the small slope of the bank. Our Father was amazed when the animals nodded, but said nothing when, one by one, they slid down the declivity and began rocking and dragging the capsule until it rested on the lip of the escarpment.

"I want to get it a little more inland, if you'd give me a hand," said Our Father, and he laughed with the animals at his *faux pas*. Together they wrestled it all the way across the strip of land that separates our house from the

River. They stopped when Our Father judged it to be in a satisfactory place; indeed, it was never moved again, and our house was built up around it. Unfortunately, the construction was done so that the foundation was completed and the upper stories finished before Our Father discovered no doors or windows had been provided for access to the capsule. It was a lucky thing that by this time the books and Our Mother and Dore had been offloaded. We would have a fine museum piece in that space capsule now if we could get to it, but there is an unwritten prohibition against destroying any part of the house.

Later that evening some of the animals returned with a vast assortment of fruits and edible tubers, and placed them before the capsule's hatch as a sort of offering; Our Father wrote in the ship's log—his first and last entry—"We seem to have found our milieu."

The stream that Dore and Glorian were following grew larger as it joined with others along its route toward the River. Soon the two travelers were walking within the confines of a small valley; beyond the rims of the depression grew the towering trees of the forest, obliterating the traces of the sun's light but for the part of the sky immediately above the water. The hollow was carpeted with soft grass and the way was easier, unobstructed by the boles of huge trees. But at night the men climbed the ridge to sleep among the michas and oaks, because the low, wet valley was home for a great variety of predatory insects.

One morning Dore was awakened by the noise of many persons shouting in the valley below. He thought for a moment that he had dreamed the racket, but when it began again, louder still, he knew that another strange encounter was about to begin. He looked around for Glorian but, not much to his surprise, he discovered that the puzzling man was nowhere to be seen. Dore decided to peer quietly over the lip of the low cliff.

As soon as his face looked over the edge the shouting grew louder. Dore could not help but think that the party of men below knew of his presence and had come to speak with him. He stood up and sighed; among these eccentric peoples he never knew what to expect. He would not run from them, and the only way to maintain his unarmed peace was to go down to them.

"Oh, puissant Ugid," shouted one of the feather-robed men when Dore appeared, "we pray that you aid us in our coming battle. Know, oh mighty god of military robustness, that we your servants have followed your laws and made our sacrifices, every one. The Seduevii are your priests and your disciples, no matter what the lying Nomitians have said. Come to us in your guise of loving uncle. Don your lightning helm and thunder sword and whatever else you need. Help us to drive the thieves and rapists from our land."

Dore was quick to realize that these chanting men thought that he was an avatar of some heathen god. It would be a difficult role, but perhaps it would bring him closer to the Princess Dawn. He wished that he could remember her real name.

Love's melancholy is a crippling disorder. In extremities of passion a heroine may do herself or others grievous bodily harm, and the steadiest of military heroes may go sullen to his tent. The symptoms of love's distress are too familiar and unpleasant to be listed again, but the proper treatment, which is simple and effective, is virtually unknown. The secret is diet and exercise. Diet and exercise. A handy formula, recommended by the best classical authorities, easy to remember and easy on your pocketbook, too.

If I may be permitted to light my way with Robert Burton's candle, I will describe the methods given to us by Our Mother. One time my younger brother Auel asked her why one of our sisters recently rejected by the young man of her choice was behaving so strangely. We all laughed with delight at his innocence, but Our Mother, always quick to spot an opening for a lesson, said that his question was not as stupid as it sounded. From behind her veil of tears she began a lengthy and somewhat pointless discourse on the rebuffed suitor and the abandoned mistress. This developed into a practical demonstration, and for weeks thereafter we improved our skills upon a lifelike dummy, "treating" it for shock, water and smoke inhalation, and unrequited affection.

Ovid instructs us that poverty has not the means to fatten love. From this oversimplified maxim Our Mother developed what she called her Sorrow Drill. Whenever we felt the poison of heartache, we were to foreswear our lovely clothes and put on rough, unpleasant garments. We were to go barefoot at all times. Most of all we were to fast, for saith St. Ambrose, hunger is a friend of virginity and an enemy to lasciviousness. Further, Ovid relates that Love yields to business. *Diet and exercise*.

None of us were too excited by Our Mother's ideas, and some of the classicists among us searched for equally authoritarian refutations. One was found in Horace, where he counsels the lovelorn to take refuge in a nearby servingmaid or whatever. Soon, few of us paid any more attention to either side of the dispute and continued at our pleasure, leading to the usual number of broken hearts and blackened eyes. How often must the trite old romantic dramas be played? Is it that we enjoy the distressing scenes and encourage the midnight aches? It is not for me to supply an arbitrary answer.

It is only indirectly that we have learned of love for other than a desirable sexual object. Our Mother never told us of love of beauty, love of one's home, or love of nature; these things we have inferred from her wide-though damp-eyed recitations of Our Father's excellences. Such papers as Sabt's perceptive "Man of the Hour: Our Father's Eternal Integrity" and Talavesía's "The Failure of Mediocrity" have expanded our understanding of the finer things in life.

Our Father lived simply, holding few things dear beyond his home and family. But these beloved ideas he defended with all the occult weapons at his command. Our Mother could never quite grasp the abstract forces that drove her husband to provide and protect. Only when she slept did her misty conscious mind cease to interfere. When she was unconscious her tears were clearer, her dreams gentler, her sentiments more humane. It is a great pity that when awake she was never able to share them with us, for she became unable to express or remember them.

It was not long before other men tried to take for themselves some of the bounties of Home. One day, while making a cool potato salad in the reconverted space capsule, Our Mother heard strange voices. She ran crying outside, where Our Father and his four-footed forest friends were hard at work building our house. She told him wonderingly of the voices from the ether. He knew

WHAT ENTROPY MEANS TO ME   61

at once what they meant; he brushed past her and hurried to the capsule. Sure enough, Our Mother had heard radio transmissions through the capsule's receiver.

"Hello, uncharted world. This is Sagittarius. One Five Four Three Three Seven, do you read me? Over," said a small, distant voice.

Our Father leaned over the panel and spoke into the radio. "This is the Master of Home. What do you want? Over."

"Hello, Home. We are lost and are low on supplies. We request permission to land. Over."

"Roger, Sagittarius," said Our Father confidently, "you may manent thralldom. Do you wish to discuss terms? Over."

"Negative, Home. Feudal circumstances entirely unacceptable. Your world is certainly large enough for all of us. We have your transmission monitored and your position plotted. We shall land far enough away so you needn't worry. Over."

"Roger, Sagittarius," said Our Father confidently, "you may try. Will speak with you later. Over and out." It did not take long. After Our Father put the matter out of his head and returned to his construction work, the intruders tried to put their plan into action. They programed their landing module for a soft touchdown exactly halfway around the planet from Our Parents' settlement. But at an altitude of 60,000 feet the module, floating gently down on several large parachutes, struck something "solid" in the atmosphere. In some magic way Our Father had caused a barrier to exist around our entire world. Perhaps the River aided him. Our Mother didn't know; she was making potato salad at the time. But soon there was another frantic message.

"Hello, Home Master. Do you copy? Come in, Home!" Our Father listened patiently. "Hello, Home. We're stuck up here. Let us down! You can't let us die up here. Any terms you like, but get us down! Over."

Our Father smiled grimly to himself, and assured the immigrants that they would land safely. They came down not far from our clearing and, after swearing fealty and eternal loyalty, Our Father allowed them to begin building their new home. These folk became the Second family. More and more spacecraft attempted to violate Our Father's territorial franchise, and each time they were compelled to bow to Our Father's demands. Through Our Father's farsightedness, we enjoy eminence over all others on Home, from the Lawrence P. Seconds (who have become close friends, coming over often for canasta and coffee cake, and who maintain a certain distinction among the other tenants) down to the poorest of the Sixties and Seventies.

Of course, once the families were safely established in their hierarchic lives, they felt that nothing could stand in the way of their forceful usurpation of power. Several times an armed revolt was put down by Our Father and his animal allies. Since Our Father's disappearance we have feared to mention the possibility of a new rebellion, for Our wise Father often remarked to Our Mother that thoughts of hostility attract an enemy. We have been trained to think only happy thoughts.

Of what did Dore think as he climbed carefully down the steep bank to the group of men below? We cannot say with any assurance. When he reached the floor of the valley he thought it best to let the others initiate the meeting. He stood quietly, observing the two leaders disdainfully as befitted the human aspect of a mighty god. One of the men was tall and gaunt, with a large head shaved bald. He wore a long robe of orange feathers, and Dore was curious about their origin; there are no orange birds on Home with which we are familiar. The other man was shorter and quite heavy. He looked very unhappy, and his plump face and neck were dripping with sweat. He wore a feathered robe also, but his was a dazzling collection of rainbow colors. His shoulder-length black hair was crowned with a heavy golden helmet. The bald man stepped forward, offering Dore his hand. Dore grasped it, and the bald man smiled.

"My name is Palaschine," he said. "I am the leader and chief priest of your cult. This is the king of the Seduevii, King Lebrodias." The king smiled, and Dore shook hands with him, to the dismay of Palaschine. "The king is the head of our secular arm," said the priest, emphasizing the word *secular* for Dore's benefit, and, no doubt, also for Lebrodias'.

"And I?" said Dore pleasantly.

"You, of course, are the great god Ugid," said Palaschine. "No doubt your memory is cloudy after your journey from Heaven."

"Possibly," said Dore. "Do you know of a family called Von Glech?"

The priest looked at the king, who shook his head slowly. "That's all right," said Dore, "I was just checking. I don't have a great deal of time, so why don't you outline the situation for me."

King Lebrodias smiled broadly. "Certainly, sir, if you will follow me. Our encampment is not far away, and we have tables and maps and miniature troop markers just waiting for you. Come, and I will briefly sketch in the history of our troubles."

Well, of course, the background was in no way unusual. The Seduevii were simple agricultural people who were often raided by the hostile, nomadic Nomitians. Dore, or Ugid, was a mythical deity who appeared only once every five hundred years. A prophecy foretold his rebirth and settling for once and all the territorial dispute through force of arms. As far as Dore could fathom, both the Seduevii and the Nomitians were tribes indigenous to Home.

Even here in the deepest cellar, where I have taken to writing, even down in the slimy, dark catacombs beneath our house I am found by the wrathful and contentious interest of Ateichál. She would not deign to come down here herself, of course, but instead sends one of her underlings, young Blin, with a note.

"That thought will mark you, Seyt," says the note. "A belief in human inhabitants previous to Our Parents is dangerous, odious, and a total and indefensible profanity. You have gone too far. Very truly yours, your sister, Ateichál."

I tip Blin generously and he leaves, stopping by the stairs and saying, "I am *not* an underling. I'm a henchman." Ambition and decadence are running unfettered these days.

Dore could not understand how so many people could have banded together and degenerated to tribal barbarities in the few years since Our Parents' arrival on Home. (Is that better?)

In the camp of the Seduevii, our brother was stopped before the pavilion of the king by a minor functionary. He was told to raise his right hand and take an oath that he would serve the just cause of the Seduevii to the best of his ability, so help him Ugid. The functionary was taken aside by Palaschine and reprimanded, but Dore and the priest had a good laugh over the humorous affair inside the tent. A runner broke in to announce that the battle had been scheduled for noon, less than two hours hence. Dore looked thoughtful. A great deal of work had to be done before then.

Dore was enthusiastic about his assignments, taking pleasure in the preparatory stages and following through with perseverance. But often he spent a disproportionate amount of energy on the planning; he tended to draw up lists of materials and alternate schemes, so that the task might have been completed in much less time by someone else, if that person had merely begun immediately upon the business in the simplest way. Of course when Dore completed something it was done prettily, with extra scuff-guards of spare metal, or thoughtful plastic bumpers, or the drainage system designed in a meaningful pattern. In our frequent, tedious board games Dore was the inevitable victor, because he played to a totally alien strategy; and when he won, he did so grandly. He never just wiped out his opponents, he defeated them each in some aesthetic and significant way.

It may be indicative of our shared outlook to mention that Dore was the only one of us who never attended Our Father's school. Our attendance was kept to a minimum, because Our Mother disapproved of our associating with the common children; but every one of us managed to spend a goodly amount of our formative years hiding in the cloakroom. Only Dore, the eldest and, for a time, the only child, was not able to escape Our Mother's weeping and watchful eyes. The school had been founded as a public service by Our Father, in an offhand attempt to prepare the new immigrants for their life on Home. Courses were taught in flora and fauna of Home, the proper duties to the River and Our Parents, hygiene, practical arts and crafts, remedial reading, history of Earth, local government, and French I and II. Our Father himself taught the first semester, and it is a matter of pride among his former students. Following Our Father's hejira, the school was run by the Seconds' lovely twin daughters, Judith and Diane.

The battle presented Dore with the sort of intellectual and artistic puzzle he enjoyed the most. But he was concerned that the schedule would not give him time to prepare as he would like.

Another messenger came into the tent. "Heavenly leader, the armorer must know what periaptic device you desire emblazoned on your shield," he said.

Dore thought for a moment, wishing that he had the time to make some preliminary sketches. "I'd like the River in the foreground," he said at last, "and two towers in the middle distance, with a range of mountains visible between them, and a sun rising between two ice-crowned peaks."

"I'll try," said the messenger doubtfully, "but I think they were planning on something simple, like a seven- or eight-pointed star." He saluted in the manly way of the Seduevii, faced about smartly, and left. Dore sighed.

King Lebrodias came in, sitting at the table with Dore. "This thing is ridiculous," he said, taking off his golden helmet. "It's too soft to even deflect a sword cut. I think Palaschine just makes me wear it to make me look silly. How are the plans?"

"Still incomplete, I'm afraid," said Dore. "I wish we had a better estimate of their strength. I wish we had a better count of *our* troops, for that matter. Look at this report from Captain Tradius: 'We looked upon the camp of the Nomitians, and, lo!, the moons shone upon their burnished breastplates to blind our eyes as the noontime god of fire. And when the wounded Dawn had bled and fallen lifeless, corpse-white, into the sky, the enemy stood marshaled as the leaves upon the trees.' "

"Perhaps we could capture their baggage train," said the king hopefully.

"I think not."

"Attack their flank? That's always popular."

"Where is it?" asked Dore. There was no answer. "I think we'll just find the narrowest part of the valley and block it with our ranks," said Dore without enthusiasm.

"Excellent!" cried King Lebrodias, pleased that the responsibility was at last removed from his shoulders. "Only you, mighty God of Fury, could lead us to victory!" Dore chewed his lip and said nothing.

There is no retreat. I suppose I may as well go back to my room, for I am found out. Lalichë skips down the stairs, evidently happy to see me. I, of course, am always glad to see one of my cherished brothers or sisters. She brings me the morning paper, which I have neglected in favor of an early start. I open it to Mylvelane's column and I see that, while she is still enthusiastic, my work merits only about a single column-inch. It is hinted that Mylvelane has received threatening notes, and I suppose I can guess who sent them.

"Look at the headlines, Seyt," says Lalichë eagerly. That goes to show how my interest in things has changed. I used to read the *Times-Register* from cover to cover, every article: women's and society, recipes, pets, comics. Now I see if I'm mentioned by Mylvelane, and then I read the sports, and, if I have the time, I read the news.

The headlines say, TERE BOLTS BENEVS; *Denies Rift with Ateichál;* To Form Third Party Says Spokesman. I guess that's news, but for all my careless interest I don't really believe in politics. My critical opposition appears to be divided, but I don't have the skill to play one against the other. And we will have to wait to see if the division is anything more than an unprincipled bid for power. Perhaps it is a good thing, as it will split the conservative vote. I used to be an active Benevolent myself, but my tepid politics are being dragged further and further left.

Dore was educated almost entirely by Our Father, who kindly stayed around long enough to set firmly Dore's personality in the ways of courtesy. After Our Father departed, Our Mother took Dore aside and tried to continue his education along her own unsettling lines. Fortunately, even at his tender age Dore knew enough to stare blankly while she sniveled and nod his head often, but ignore the fallacies that tumbled from her mouth as readily as the tears from her eyes.

A tale, uncollected before now in the annals of our brother, assumes that Our Father left to Dore a large body of secret wisdom, hidden in some form within the scores of exotic chairs on the lawn. The originator of this baseless rumor asks what other explanation there may be for the chairs; that is a very good question. It is true that many of them have parts that easily could have been places of concealment, but to some of us this is hardly conclusive evidence. To others it is all that is necessary. There are those of us who are needlessly foolish.

But the fact remains that Dore alone received special knowledge, and we can neither prove nor deny that this learning is what called him to the ghosty council of Our

Parents. We search for clues in what we know of his youth: He worked hard, he played hard. He delighted in making presents for his family; he would take a high wooden stool deep within his sheltering forest and put together leather wallets. Each of us received one on his birthday; then Dore began to make belts for us. We accepted the gifts gratefully, searching them for bits of arcane lore. But such knowledge is not for us, or else we have failed to read the patterns of the leather's hand tooling.

It is sad to think of Dore, alone and the product of such random influences, putting his life on the line for us. Certainly Our Father trained him well and hard, and Our Mother labored for years thereafter, sometimes at cross-purposes to her husband's beginning, but ultimately to Dore's moral benefit. But at last there was Dore, his head filled with teeming strangeness, far from his house and beset by strangers. With enough allegoric responsibility to fill ten books, he is given more by the Seduevii, thoughtless barbarians who want him to fight their battles. And it is we who have cast him out. Tere and Ateichál don't like to face that fact, but it is something that we must live with.

Blin is back with another note. Lalichë takes it from him, as I am much too emotional to deal with it. "If you weren't official historian," it says, "what you have said about Our Mother would lose you your name. You are going to be extremely vulnerable when your period of grace expires, Seyt. To tell the truth, I'm looking forward to it. Regards to Lalichë. Your sister, Ateichál."

I will not be intimidated. I owe it to future generations to give them a rousing good tale as well as unadorned and unpalatable facts. It is a wonder that books get written at all, with such a multitude of petty critics ready with discouragement. Lalichë applauds my fortitude, and I continue.

Dore couldn't think of anything else worthwhile to do, so he went outside and reviewed his troops. They stood in ranks uncomfortably, obviously poorly disciplined. They were farmers and townsmen, not soldiers, and they were armed with whatever each individual thought might be a weapon: pruning hooks, pitchforks, long knives. There were few swords and little armor. Dore was discouraged, for he knew that the Nomitians were accustomed to battle.

"I'll need a weapon for myself," he told an orderly. In a few minutes the man brought Dore an old and battered sword.

"Gulla is mighty angry," said the orderly, "but I promised him that you'd see that he wasn't hurt during the battle."

"Thanks," said Dore, beginning to realize his danger. The more he saw of the men the more he knew that they were in no way fit for making war. He suggested a parlay with the Nomitians, but King Lebrodias was shocked. Such a meeting would cast a shadow on his masculinity. Dore felt trapped.

Our brother stood before his army. "I'm going to ask for volunteers," he said. "I want a corps of strong men, men who will not run from danger. I will fight for you at the front, but I am only one blade. Who will guard my shield arm?" He waited for the flash of dozens of swords in answer to his challenge, but only three men spoke up: a tall, brawny man named Corag, himself a Nomitian outlawed for his wanton killing; a small, dark man called Shendai the Deft, who wielded a single gold-handled dagger; and a youth named Porcellus Tarvin. "All right," said Dore, "these three and myself will be your vanguard. Remember what you fight for, remember your homes and wives. If we fall, do not lose heart, but fight on for our sakes. I bless you all and welcome you who die valiantly to call on me in Heaven. *Valete.*"

The soldiers grumbled and dispersed. King Lebrodias took Dore aside and whispered in his ear. "My good Ugid, surely you're not going to take an active part in this nonsense? What did you mean, 'fight at the front'? A man could be killed, and you're wearing a man's body, you know." Dore made no reply, but stared around him at the quiet, anxious men in the camp. "If you do intend to be up there," said the king nervously, "I hope you realize that my place is here. We can't afford to lose both of us." Dore nodded, and walked away.

He stopped a lieutenant and asked what time it was. "Shortly after eleven, I suspect," said the man. Dore thanked him, and told him to arrange for the mustering of the men at a narrow part of the valley a half mile from the camp. Dore had studied the maps and decided on this part of the valley for several strategic reasons. He knew he could position the men in one of two ways:

either strung out across the valley so that a good number of them would be fighting in the stream itself, a difficult position to defend; or split detachments on the two banks. He chose the former, because this particular part of the stream was pinched and shallow, and flowed into a deep pool. Dore decided to deploy his men unevenly, with concentrations of them on the banks where the fighting would be fiercest, and fewer guarding the stream's passage. If the Nomitians chose to try the center, the men would give way and drive the attackers into the deep water.

"You're not a very good militarist, Seyt," says Lalichë. I wave at her impatiently and continue to set up the pieces.

The Seduevii defenses were dejected as they stood waiting for the battle. The men stationed in the water seemed even glummer, knowing that a slip on the smooth stones of the bottom meant death. Everyone stared ahead and waited for the signal of the sunlight flashing on the polished weapons of the enemy. Dore walked among the ranks and told them to hold their shields steady, those that had them, and to use them as an impenetrable wall. If any man broke contact, the whole line of men was doomed. Cooperation was necessary, and Dore appealed to the courage of the Seduevii, to their pride and honor. At last Dore knew he had done all that he could, and took his place with his three comrades in the center of the front rank.

After a time the enemy was seen, marching along the right-hand bank. Soon their drums and songs could be heard. The Seduevii moved restlessly, and Dore felt his throat go dry. A strange electric tingle found a home in his lower abdomen. He was aware of a constant hum of prayers directed toward his ears.

The Nomitians halted. A man, evidently a leader, walked forward and shouted: "Give us access to your women, grain eaters, and we will kill you tomorrow!" The Nomitians laughed and yelled their own insults when they heard their general's challenge. The Seduevii did nothing. Dore made a quick calculation and he was heartened to see that the Nomitians appeared to have about half the force of the Seduevii, although much better equipment.

The Nomitian leader directed his troops, and they arranged themselves to attack the right bank and the right half of the line in the water. Dore suffered through a moment of indecision when he saw the plan. Should he recall the left part of his line? The Nomitians were holding a part of their men in reserve and concentrating on a single area. Dore's left would not be used at all, but if they were removed the Nomitians would be free to pass. And, suddenly, Dore realized that he had not provided any reserves.

Jelt interrupts me to say that I'm doing good stuff. He really likes the battle so far, he says, and he sits on the basement steps to await developments. Lalichë joins him, and they hold hands and stare at me. I feel unaccountably nervous.

"Steady now, men," shouted Dore. "The wall of shields, the forest of blades!"

"For mighty Ugid!" rose the cry from several throats, but most of the Seduevii were less eager. Dore knew that scores of men were destined to die in the battle, and he hardened his poetic soul to stand the slaughter. He never gave thought that he, himself, might be one of the many to foul the stream with his life's blood; and, at the appointed time, the water began to turn red at his feet. Around him the Nomitians were taking a horrible toll of his comrades. He looked ahead and saw a huge, shaggy barbarian coming toward him with a two-handed ax covered with blood. Dore's tingle grew to a palpitation, but he planted his feet firmly and met the man's charge with an upward thrust of his sword. The villain fell to his knees, his chest slit to cool his steaming blood. Dore realized that the man had been expecting an overhand cut. Perhaps these savages knew nothing of the finer points of swordplay ("Neither did Dore," say Jelt and Lalichë in unison. They have been joined by Auel, Shesarine, and Niln); Dore felt a strange, grim smile play upon his features, and a red mist seemed to float before his eyes. Dore's sword stuck in the man's vitals, and only a desperate parry by Corag, the erstwhile Nomitian, saved our brother from a steely death. Sadly, in rescuing Dore the great bearded Corag was struck from two sides at once and collapsed at his chieftain's feet, where the gurgling scarlet water rushed his soul to join the River.

"Mighty Ugid! Mighty Ugid!" sang many voices behind Dore. The Nomitian leader, fighting several yards to Dore's right, grinned and yelled to his men: "We are

saved, my Nomitian laddies! They have Ugid among
them! He has come, even as our priests foretold! Forward,
the day is won!" Dore did not understand.

"We are lost, mighty Ugid," said Tarvin, the boy. He
pointed to the left bank of the stream. A second force of
Nomitians stood watching above the valley on the high
ridge. If they continued downstream the battle would be
in vain, and if they joined the attack the battle would
soon be over. Dore saw with horrified clarity why the
barbarian forces seemed so small at first. Then Tarvin
pointed past Dore's shoulder, to the right bank. On the
near margin a third party of Nomitians stood ready. "Oh,
mighty Ugid," muttered Dore. While our brother stood
lost in contemplation, Porcellus Tarvin was cut down by a
Nomitian pike.

"Do not slay that one," cried the Nomitian general,
pointing to Dore. "As long as he breathes, the field is
ours!"

"What does he mean, murderer of children?" asked
Dore of the brute who had killed Tarvin.

"Are you not Ugid, god of failure? Have you not come
as appointed to lead the pagan Seduevii to defeat? Once
in five hundred years you come to settle the world's disputes, and now you end for once and all the matter of our
strife. We thank you, Ugid, whose power is irresistible
and false." Dore was humiliated and filled with anger, and
his arm rose and fell before he thought to stay it. The
Nomitian warrior sank in the water, covering the slender
body of the youth he had slain.

A low, sibilant voice spoke in Dore's ear. "Mighty
Ugid, aid them now, for I must take my leave." Dore
turned, and Shendai the Deft smiled and bowed. As Dore
watched, the short, mysterious man cut a path through
the Nomitian hordes, neatly severing carotid arteries and
sword hands with his razor-sharp knife. The knots of
fighting men blocked our brother's view, and he could not
see if Shendai escaped.

Dore did not know what to do. The remaining Seduevii
had grouped themselves around him, chanting his name
mournfully. Those who had not fled continued to fight,
wanting to win a place in their vapid paradise.

"Remember how we promised our women," said one
man boldly, "how we laughed at our dinner tables and
vowed to whip these mongrel savages. Now is the time to

make good that oath. Even while we die our daughters and mothers are suffering. Now, only now those black pigs are doing our lambs. And unless we make some sort of fight, who is to say that they are not doing better for our wives?"

Others voiced their proud thoughts, and were unmercifully slain. "Now," said Dore, trying to make their final minutes seem meaningful, "while your weary arms fall to leave you without defense, as your sturdy hearts prepare to shelter cold steel and quit forever their vibrant task, listen to me. Death is for you a kind of glory, though your eyes burn and your heads buzz too much for credulity. I want to thank you, and I want you to know it's been a privilege being here with you today." Soon the last of the Seduevii had been dispatched, and Dore stood alone on the right bank. The Nomitians waved to him as they passed on their way to their spoils.

Dore sat down on a large rock by the side of the water. He looked at the sword in his hand, covered with gore. He spat in disgust and threw the weapon into the stream. Then he rose and turned his back on the mounds of corpses, and headed back upstream. He saw two legs hanging down from the ridge some yards ahead of him, and he wondered if it were a survivor of the Seduevii or a Nomitian deserter. It was neither. It was Glorian.

"An admirable job, Dore. Fine, fine. You acted with honor." Dore just stared angrily.

"Another test? Did you learn something more about me?" he asked at last.

"Why, yes, my friend. You are a bundle of wonders."

"How are you going to thank Porcellus Tarvin for his help?" asked Dore bitterly.

"Don't overreact, Dore. Life and death. Good and bad. Come on, we have to get going. The rain is starting."

There are about fifteen people sitting on the stairs, looking like fans at a ball game. There has not been a sound for several minutes. They realize I have ended the battle, and now they break into applause. I feel triumphant. I have turned a real success, and the Benevolent Party will just have to do without me.

"That was really neat, Seyt," says Jelt, and I smile and thank him. I am tired, and Dore has much thinking to do. He is sick of his journey already, and wondering about the true meaning of his self-investment. What sanctified reasons could Our Mother have had for asking his death? Why did we listen to her then, when we spent so much effort to overlook her inventions before? How could we have accepted Tere's plan so quickly? Dore will leave that hateful little brook and cleanse his thoughts among his beloved trees. He and I will go upstairs to rest and discuss these questions.

Part TWO

His Mind, Ever Quick To Perceive

CHAPTER FIVE

In the Hall of the Mountain Thing

He was only a filthy peasant. His rags were crusted with the corruption of years of use, and his hair matted with the foulness of his existence. He lived to be avoided, to be struck down into the mud, to be cursed and vilified. He labored, fevered and flecked with pain, in his tiny field of violet bushes.

His name was Vasmahli Odrucajnek. Through the grace and favor of the Baron Riy he was allowed to pass fifty years of life in perpetual toil. The stony ground allowed him a meager portion of its fruits, and the worthy Baron permitted him to keep a quarter of these. Without resentment, without love, without hope, the skeleton of Odrucajnek pricked the soil.

He had a wife and six children. He despised each of them with the only passion that he knew. The noxious dark-green sky was too low, the arrogant land too hard for him to love; the spiteful members of his family were too demanding for him to do anything other than hate. Three of his children had taken their own wives and husbands, silently snapping the worn, uncherished family ties. The others could starve in their lazy apathy if they so desired.

His back would not bend and his arms shook as he filled the baskets with the bright blue beans. His wife would soak them for days to make the bitter tea that sustained them. Most of the beans, however, would be traded for other foods: the tough brown roots that were gnawed like bones; the hard, pealike vegetables that were boiled; and dark, gritty flour to make bread.

Odrucajnek thought of his family. His baby would be on the floor, crying. The other two brats were probably sitting in a corner, their dull faces holding back their tears of frustration and hunger. And his wife would be entertaining a neighbor, wealthier and still appreciative of her clumsy favors. There was nothing, nothing at all to return to, but Odrucajnek was too tired to die.

At sunset, with the wind riding down on him from the distant northern mountains, he walked back to his hovel with his load of beans. The last pink and gray flickers of the feeble sun had barely vanished when a rain began to fall. It rained methodically, the wind dying completely rather than disturb the strictly vertical drop of the water. The rain was cold, and he was thoroughly drenched by the time he reached his hut. No one acknowledged his return, and he ate his poor meal in solitude by the smoking fire.

The task of eating proved too much for his weary body. Odrucajnek threw the wooden plate to the ground and limped to the low bed. The mattress was a torn bag stuffed with straw and crawling with a variety of parasitic vermin. He lay down, not bothering to remove his damp rags, and he began to cough. The fit kept him in agony for a while, as it did every night, but soon he propped up his head and spat. He sighed deeply and fell back down, and was soon asleep.

The nights usually passed quickly, dreamlessly. This night, however, Odrucajnek dreamed uneasily of vague landscapes, and of falling and loud noises. With a start he opened his eyes. The dim light from the fire's expiring flame showed him in shadowed outlines the room he knew and loathed so well. His family was gathered together in the darkness about ten feet from the bed. Soresklya, his wife, crouched in the dirt, her hands covering her mouth as she whimpered in terror. The baby was screaming but neglected. The two older children had gathered stones and were beginning to throw them.

As the clinging webs of sleep blew from his mind he learned why. He was growing. He was twenty, twenty-five, thirty feet tall! With one huge fist he smashed the cabin's wall into splinters. His wondering was broken by a stone hitting his chest. He squinted down into the half-light at his feet. He kicked out, and his already forgotten family was crushed lifeless against the ground, their limbs twisted and their bones powdered. He blasted the remnants of his miserable home with his fingers, grinding all that remained of his past into the derisive earth.

He was fifty feet tall, he was a hundred feet tall! With a scuff of his toe he removed the bluebean fields. He popped the homes of the neighboring serfs apart like so much wet cardboard. In the cloudy blackness he strode toward the mountains. He recognized the fortified palace of his Baron. He got down on his knees and learned that his body didn't pain him any longer. He laughed and laughed and with one grimy thumb ruined Lodejpo Riy's hopes for the ermine and crown of King.

He was a quarter, a half mile high! He thundered the ground as he waded among the hills. He was two, five, eight miles high! The mountains disappeared beneath the waves of gray-green thunderheads. Lightnings hissed out at him, rolling booms of sound followed and he laughed.

He grew. His ponderous weight collapsed the straining layers of rock on which he walked. Once he fell, laughing and shouting, screaming through the wind to the ground out of sight miles below his eyes. Lying there with one arm in the sea, he roared even louder. He grabbed up handfuls of rock and forest and city and flung them about. After a while he quieted, and at last resumed his interrupted night's sleep.

The sun woke him. His eyes opened and were startled by the huge ball of flame hanging in space, seemingly within arm's reach. He himself floated about, swimming in the void. His notion of the universe, his flat world surrounded by tiny and useless stars, was forgotten with ease lent of madness. He did not doubt that the yellow-green ball turning before his face was his own former home. He flicked the small, hurtling moons away and held his planet in the palm of one dirty hand. A forefinger probed, vainly seeking the fields, the huts, the scenes of his lifelong torment. With a snarl that was more than half sob he clapped the injured world to dust. He continued growing.

He was unaware of time, and space was beginning to mean as little. The great, heaving sun was as big as a basket when he reached for it. He pulled it apart, separat-

ing it into tiny pieces as he would a used cooking fire. The
fusing gases failed to harm his scabrous hands. He threw
the parts of the star away and killed it.

He turned his attention to the farther stars, unwinking,
staring in fright, like pinpoints of light slipping through a
satin cape of perfect blackness. He reached, but they were
yet too distant. He raged and screamed and stretched his
naked arms, and in a while he was among them. The
wheeling stars, once so proud in their random formations,
sailing like some mighty fleet on boundless seas, trembled
as he came among them. They were fireflies; they were
gnats and mosquitoes, and he swatted them from his neck
and wrists, brushing them away and slapping them dead.

His musty beard floated light-years from his cankered
nose. Dusty callused feet trailed behind him at an un-
imaginable distance. He smiled when he saw the double
spiral of a galaxy. His lined and leathery cheeks puffed
out, and he blew, wanting to make the pinwheel spin.
Instead, the millions of burning suns whished away, soundlessly, like smoke. He was sorry he had ruined the pinwheel and he put out his hands and grabbed the galaxy,
squeezing the worlds and suns together like a lump of
clay. Hundreds of exploding stars spilled from his hands:
sand running through the fingers of a playful child.

The slowly turning galaxies were all about him now.
They moved proudly, slowly, hanging in the dark and
huddling into themselves against the cold of space. He
came among them. He laughed at them, but they paid no
heed. He questioned them, he threatened them. He
plucked them from their places and dashed them together,
or put them on himself, decorating his hair and beard.

He came to the wall. It was huge, extending up and
down and away in all directions further than he could see.
He stared at it quietly for a short time, feeling again his
relative smallness. The wall was made of dark-stained
planks of wood, laid in rows with gray, flathead nails;
he hit the boards with his fists until his hands were
scraped and bloody. He cried. He had stopped growing.

A monster of night descended, eclipsing great swaths of
stars and space as it drew nearer. The gigantic black arm
reached down and scooped him up. A gleaming copper
band was on its wrist, brighter than all the swirling,
faltering stars. Odrucajnek kicked at the ebony pillar
fingers and he tore at the glistening black palm.

Another immense arm appeared, as terribly white as the other was perfect black. The white fingers bore heavy silver rings; they probed at Odrucajnek's cringing form. The two hands held him trapped, and they closed about him so that he was left in absolute darkness.

He was lifted out of space and deposited on a sheet, blindingly white and clean, which seemed to extend beyond the limits of his vision. Once more, sobbing and cursing, he fell asleep.

When he awoke it was as if he had been reborn. He could remember neither his name nor his pathetic former life. He could not recall the world upon which he passed so many fruitless years or his starlit cosmic adventure. He made no attempt to remember these things.

At the foot of the bed had been placed a suit of clothes. He put on the deep-blue silk shirt and knee-breeches, and they touched his new body with all the gentleness of womankind. On his feet he wound the clean linen cross-gartered stockings, and laced the sandals to his knees. Finally, he slipped on a sleeveless robe of white and gold.

A mirror was set into one of the walls of the chamber, and he studied his unfamiliar reflection closely. His neatly cut black hair, handsome features, and smartly trimmed beard gave him an image of dignified authority. His clothing and his young, powerful body magnified the impression of quiet strength. He gave a brief nod of satisfaction and went out in search of breakfast.

Or so he said. To tell the truth, the story seems a little unlikely. I wouldn't be inclined to believe it without proof.

He stood at the mouth of the cave, yawning into the morning mists. From halfway up his hill he could look out over the green ocean of the forest. The sun had climbed over all but the tallest trees, and burned a pale disc behind the clouds.

The goats stirred uncomfortably in the damp air, anxious to be led out to the sweet grass of the hillside. A few came to stand beside him, nudging him familiarly; these were the first of the herd to shake off the night's drowsiness. They were also the first to hear Dore, as he crashed through the underbrush at the very foot of the hill.

Dore's face was ripped by the low branches, and his arms stung from forcing a path through the climbing briars. The forest had grown wilder as it grew denser,

until now it bore little resemblance to the brighter woods
that he had known nearer our house. He lost his sense of
responsibility to the younger trees and delicate growths
of the forest floor. "Well, enough of *this!*" he said in a
surge of frustration, kicking a clear way through a stand
of sapling losperns.

It's certainly easy to sympathize. After traveling as
long as he had, and going through what he had experienced, I surely wouldn't be too concerned about the bad
karma from trampling a few lousy little plants. It has
always seemed to us that Dore could hear the minute cries
of even the smallest damaged branches and wounded
stems; but after a while your empathic powers must get
overloaded. No one of us would have met such exquisite
tortures as our sacred brother.

"Our *sacred* brother?" I hear you ask. Yes, let me
speak to that for a moment. It was about this time, by my
own made-up chronology, that our sister Ateichál began a
series of sermons on our obligation to Dore, and the
impossibility of ever fulfilling it. At first they were only
the postscript to the monthly devotional services; we had
always made our obeisance to the River on the Eve of No
Moons, and ritually included a prayer for the well-being
of Our Father. Lately, of course, we also prayed for and
to the spirit of Our Mother. But it was Ateichál's bright
idea to include a few short words for Dore's sake. Now
we have the prospect of a religious war on our hands, with
the attendant proliferation of "heresies" and two separate
but equal inquisitions.

We tread on unsure ground, theologically. The doctrines
are still in the malleable state; what eventually evolves
from them will owe its existence not to pre-eminent merit,
but to the shrewdness of the compromises made by the
factions. But at least we have an idea of who's on which
side; a certain spryness is required in answering all but the
most innocent questions, but we know in which direction
to exercise that agility. Pity poor Dore, if you haven't before now. (Could I have failed to arouse *that* much sympathy? Have I failed my assignment already? Then what is
keeping your interest? If you want a better picture of
Melithiel, you lose, I'm afraid.) He is totally at sea; he is
wandering in a wilderness of ethical entanglements, and
he has only his irony-tinged faith to guide him past the
fanatics intent only on his destruction.

He did not see the giant until the latter looed to him. Dore was battling his way through the thinning trees at the edge of the giant's clearing when a thunderous deep voice splintered the early peacefulness.

"Loo," it went.

"All right," said Dore, gazing up startled at the giant on the mountain. "Okay, I'm coming."

"Looool!" roared the giant.

Dore stood on the verge of a forest, staring at the man with the goats at the mouth of a cave. The man was dressed in rags; his hair and bushy beard indicated that he had been living close to the earth for a very long time. He was a giant in stature, and a giant in aroma, even upwind. He stood about fifteen feet tall, and his mighty frame was awesome to behold. He wore tarnished metal bands around his biceps, and a huge club hung from his girdle.

Lalichë is reading this as I write; she suggests that I am subconsciously introducing an overtly phallic symbol here. I don't think so. For me to have Dore meet and overcome a symbol of his masculinity would be to metaphorically castrate our sacred brother. We wouldn't want Ateichál to read that; she always dug Dore's body. (Now Lalichë implies that the symbol is of *my* putative virility, not Dore's. A lot she knows, five years old.)

Our Father was a giant in his day as well, so it may be that I am drawing on *his* description here. Of course, that may be a worse departure from orthodox thought. But who is to say? ("Tere, for one," says my little sister, giggling.) What sort of quest would it be if Dore were to meet only puny threats that stood in his way armed with beanbags? To be of any worth Dore must contend with honest dangers. A giant's as good as any. At least *I* think so. Giants have lots of historic precedent in quest tales.

Our Father was a giant in his day as a result of his wide assortment of menial jobs. Because of Our Parents' financial naïveté, Our Father was forced to take on any number of laborious tasks, none as heroic as those of Hercules but every bit as tiresome. We are told of his employment as a loader of trucks, piling by hand huge cartons of Eaton's Corrasable Bond into vans for delivery. Various sorts of mechanical devices could have done the job in shorter time, but the courts of law that sentenced

Our Father and found him this employment felt that the physical labor might be of rehabilitative effect.

Rehabilitated from and for what? Our Father was unfairly judged, of course, but never did he complain. The august body that decreed his guilt commanded his allegiance, and in his innocent patriotism he could not see the logical fallacy upon which the system was based. He did his work efficiently, and his overseers were envious. The stripes he earned from his boss's cat were more to slow him down than anything else. Our Father still worked, however; see him: sweating through the long, hot days, singing his mournful work chants as he loaded the typing paper onto the trucks. *That* is my image of manhood; not, as Lalichë would have me admit, some mythical grotesquerie or the gross symbol hanging from the monster's belt. (Now she tells me not to be ashamed of my inner urgings. Get out of here; you must flee, my sister, before another of those urgings forces from you the last gasp of mortal life.)

We all know that Dore is lithe, fleet of foot, and of the shrewdest natural bent. It would be reasonable, then, to expect him to be wary of the dangers presented by a scruffy and altogether plebeian giant. If Dore were to turn and run through the forest, the giant would be hard-pressed to follow. This seems, at first glance, to be the course I should have my brother adopt.

No, no, no. If you don't have the idea by now, give up. *Primo,* Dore is bone-weary, nearly starving, bleeding from half- or unhealed wounds, and longing for hominid companionship. *Secundo,* he needs to learn all he can about the nearby countryside, so that he may face the dangers thereof with at least a minimum of preparation. And *tertio,* if he were going to avoid all the rough spots, I would have had him take a boat in the beginning.

So Dore looked up at the monster on the hill. The giant was, in traditional terms, as tall as a mountain. His cave yawned behind him like the greedy mouth of a grave, as the poet has it, hungry for yet more rotting bodies. A metaphoric owl dwelt on a craggy overhang, and his ceaseless, awful calls kept away all but the least sensitive birds and animals.

All these things Dore began to see as he climbed the large boulders on the side of the hill. He became less and less sure that the giant would greet him hospitably, not knowing for certain what was meant by the periodic *Loooo*. The giant was escorting his goats to pasture, down the hill on the other side. Dore continued climbing, and in several minutes he stood gasping for breath at the entrance to the cave.

The opening into the cave was wondrous dark; the morning sun was still too weak to push back the gathered forces of agèd night. Dore stood outside, whistling and rocking on his heels like a bored magazine salesman. Around the cave huge rocks had been sunk between sprawling micha trees and tall, slender losperns to form a sort of pen or yard.

Presently Dore heard a vague looing. The sound grew louder, and in a short while the fearsome giant appeared. He towered over Dore's appalled form, grinning a yellow-toothed and joyless grin. He wore animal skins pinned together with thorns, in the traditional comic-strip cave-man style. He held up one hand, palm facing Dore, and said, "Loo." Dore did the same and said, "Dore." Loo grinned, and bent to the remains of his cooking fire just outside the mouth of the cave. He blew on the coals and soon had the fire going once more. From the blaze he lit two torches, handing one to Dore and indicating that they should enter the cave.

Dore followed him into the cavern, regretting it immediately. Besides the damp, unpleasantly ancient smell of livestock, the equally venerable stink of giant made the air virtually toxic. They proceeded into the heart of the mountain, and soon they were entirely divorced from the light of the sun. Loo halted, putting his burning branch into a niche carved from the rock wall. Dore did the same, and sat upon a flat stone that evidently served as a seat. The giant nodded solemnly and offered Dore some goat cheese and warm goat milk. Dore accepted gratefully; the cheese was old and rancid, but the milk was sweet and frothy.

"Loo," said the giant, refilling Dore's stone cup with milk, "I been expecting you, don't you see. I been sitting in this cave ever since the world began, don't you see, waiting just for you. Now you're here, the prophecies have been fulfilled, and we can get on with it. It's all very interesting."

"What prophecies? How did you know that I was coming?"

"I know, loo, I know it all. You're one of those *humans*, aren't you? I've met a few of you before." Here the giant pointed into the gloom, indicating some grisly bones lying in twisted disarray further into the cave. "Loo, and I'm glad to see you. It makes me feel better, don't you see, sitting here talking to you, drinking a cup of milk. Tell me, what is the news?"

Dore was still looking at the disarticulated skeletons. He was seeking a viable pretext for escape, trying to think of something that wouldn't upset the giant's evidently murderous ire. "Look, Loo, thanks for the milk and all," he said, "but I have to be going. I really shouldn't have killed this much time. My wife's waiting for me down in the forest, and we're supposed to be on a vacation. But why don't you drop by when you're passing through? Stop in; we'd love to have you. There's always room for a friend." Dore stocd, starting to make his way out of the cave.

The giant scowled evilly. "My name's not Loo. I say it a lot; it's a verbal habit like 'well,' don't you see. And you can't leave until I at least test you." He stood, too, and with his longer strides arrived at the cave entrance well before Dore, who stumbled in the darkness. The giant hefted his gateway—an incredibly heavy boulder fully ten feet tall—and blocked the opening.

"You needn't explain your coming, loo," said the giant. "The fact that you came at all, don't you see, is proof enow of your desire for expiation."

You would think, from the pained expression on Dore's handsome face, that just being in the same county as that pungent lair would be the redemptive equivalent of several thousand of the finest candles going. But no, the giant did not agree. He apparently felt a sense of pride in the resourceful and, to his mind, not entirely inelegant uses to which he had put the materials that he found to hand.

At one time, long ago, there was another such temporary "home," which Dore recalled with something approaching the same repugnance. Our Parents and Dore were fleeing the sneep of Cleveland. They had barely escaped, driving their rattling groundcar through the rain-slicked streets of the near West Side. Across the city they drove, prepared at any moment to hear the sirens of the Northeastern Ohio Credit Association's sneepcars.

They abandoned the car on a dark side street, running through the drizzle for the protection of the park. They huddled together under a shale ledge in the remnant of Cleveland's once-famous Emerald Necklace. All night they imagined they could hear the shouts of the hunting sneep, and expected to see at any moment the beams from their pocket searchlights. Dore was still a baby and unaware of their danger; he slept through most of the night, but Our Mother and Father held each other in silence. Our blessed Mother's tears flowed in their holy profusion.

For several weeks the family lived in a corner of the Metropolitan Park, hiding during the day in a wet, filthy culvert. At night they sat out under the silver maples, afraid to speak for fear of revealing their presence to the electronic ears of the sneep that might have been planted nearby.

At last, of course, they were discovered. Our Father was spotted on one of his nocturnal forages by the wealthy jeweler from Parma. The merchant called to Our Father, who, in his blind panic, caught the man and began to strangle him. Our Mother heard the noise of the battle and, fortunately for all of us, was so impressed with the merchant's accoutrements that she decided it would be worthwhile to spare him and rely on his gratitude.

And what gratitude it was! The largest that Our Mother had ever seen, and the only one since Our Father's was shot off in the war.

"Then where did Dore come from, Seyt? That is, without resorting to out-and-out blasphemy?" asks my little brother, Auel, who has just come in.

"Why, hello there, Auel. You know the story, don't you? Surely you've been taught that Our Father appeared to Our Mother in the debtors' prison of Pittsburgh in the form of a shower of gold. Our Mother was impregnated by this shower of gold, and thus Dore was conceived."

I'll wait a minute until he leaves.

Alors. What I was going to say was that copulating with a shower of gold is not the most stimulating thing in the world. It's all right for *him,* I suppose, and it enabled Our Parents to effect their escape ("Hey, Lenny, there's a naked broad and the damnedest shower of gold you *ever* saw!" "We'd better get the doc!") ("Quick now, my love. They have left the doors wide open in their unthinking haste . . ."); but, still, Our Mother was partial to the regular way.

Na'theless, the memory of those sodden, muddy days in the abandoned sewer was forever imprinted engrammatically on Dore's infant mind. It is altogether reasonable to assume that his deep and abiding love for greenlands sprang from this early situation. And after that he avoided all the darker, moister places of his surroundings. But he was trapped in the giant's cave, and these unconscious and nonverbal feelings flooded back and forth through his unprotected psyche. He was afraid, and nauseous.

"Loo, you might as leffer make yourself to home," said the giant, grinning, "because, loo, I get to tell my tale here, and you will be amazed."

The two had returned to the giant's parlor, although in the dim light of the torches Dore could see little. He found his former seat by tripping over it. He sat and listened, all the time trying feverishly to find some way to get out.

The giant told him how he had originally been a slimy peasant named Odrucajnek. Dore nodded absently; he could believe that. The growing part got a bit much, though. Actually, Dore couldn't care less. But the conversation was the only thing he had to stall the giant. Dore sat on his rock, frantically studying the cave and finding nothing at all encouraging.

"Are things realer now?" asked Dore.

"Loo, yes, of course. Before, don't you see, it was all someone else's idea. Now all this is *my* illusion."

"Yes, but how do you know it's not my illusion, as it seems to me?"

"You probably do have your own, don't you see, but, loo, it works within my system. I created this universe. Back at the beginning of time. *Your* time, loo, not mine."

"I don't understand." Dore realized that if he said "I don't understand" often enough, he might die of old age right there in the cave.

"I'm not boring you, am I?" asked the giant.

"No, not at all. I've never seen God before."

"Yes. God. I've never thought of myself as God, but, loo, I suppose I am! It's not so difficult being God, don't you see. You open your eyes in the morning and, loo, there you are. Easier than pulling limbs."

"Tell me," said Dore, his voice croaking with frustration, "how did you come to create the world as we know it?"

"An interesting question, that. I was about to tell you; a revelation, don't you see. Loo, if I'd let you go, you could be my prophet. These others were here first, loo, but they missed their chance. They wouldn't believe me, and I'm a jealous god, don't you see. We'll know, loo, we'll know about you in a while."

The giant stood up again, taking in one hand the torch that he had put in the wall and, with the other, reaching down around the level of his knees to clutch Dore's arm. "Come with me," he said, "and I will show you your test."

"Fine," said Dore helplessly.

Now, Tere and Ateichál are getting just the least bit impatient with this account. I believe from their hints that they were looking forward to something on the order of the Book of Job, that great mock-Euripidean drama. But certainly it is clear that, for me, at least, it is impossible to sing my song as briefly or as beautifully as those nameless authors of Job.

But where I detect irritation in the spiritual cadre (in the final analysis my only true sponsor), I find however only mounting joy in the mundane concerns that surface, ephemerally, to float like bubbles for a time in the imagination of the acquisitive members of our happy band. With me now are Loml and Peytheida, Male and Female Vice-presidents in Charge of Proliferation for the current incarnation of the Ploutos Corporation.

"Good evening, my brother and sister. It is nice of you to drop by to see me."

"It's nice to be here," says Peytheida.

"It's nice of you to have us," says Loml.

I offer them some candied flowers. My tiny cell has become increasingly popular as word of my project, sanctioned as it is by all factions, spreads among our sorrowing tribe. My present visitors are here to investigate the merchandising possibilities that may arise as a direct result of my history. Surely there can't be very many.

I receive for this ingenuous sentiment two indulgent smiles.

"You underestimate your power," says Loml.

"Mightier than the sword, after all," says Peytheida.

Now that I am once again alone, I must consider their excited dreams. Can it be that I am shaping the destiny of not only our own way of life here in the house, but also the course of whatever culture may develop across the length and breadth of Home, our dear adopted world? Reasoned discourse permits no positive reply, and yet . . .

Tourism. For the least instance, how about that monster's torch of a dozen paragraphs past? They would make little plastic images of it, molded so that if they were painted at one end to simulate flame, we would have the allegorical false light, the will-o'-the-wisp of heresy, which is coming to play such a large part in our day-to-day life. The plastic remaining one color, brown, throughout—*voila!* the famous club. I am told that our house and grounds will become a fashionable and lucrative tourist attraction. Why not take the opportunity to supply each pilgrim with a material and permanent keepsake? Sell to them little clubs like atrophied pickle pins mentioned so often in American journals. If they could sell souvenir ladders at the Lindbergh kidnap trial, why can't we have countrified inns, *Antiques* signs in front of every home on the road, with weathered boards and pre-faded letters. Corps of engineers dig lagoons in the yard among the chairs: a boat ride under the summer sky, to view with open mouths animated figures bending at the waist in artificial greeting. Wax dummies of Our Parents and Dore in their favorite chairs. I cannot await this with any eagerness.

Dore and the giant walked deeper into the cave, and Dore caught indistinct glimpses of many sorts of evil things. The corridor went along in a straight line for quite some distance, with no side branches or inlets of light that might promise a possible emergency exit. Then he noticed by the sudden steepness of the path that they were going down into the heart of the mountain. The light of the burning brand in the giant's fist broke on the cave walls against scores of tiny, colored surfaces. It seemed to Dore that the rocky passage was set with a staggering variety and richness of rough gems, and the refracted beams split the darkness with weak flares of red, blue, and green.

As they walked, the giant continued his story. Dore had to restrain himself from pointing out various inconsistencies that occurred to him; he knew the danger of appearing a disbeliever. He was careful to say "Wow!" and "Uh huh" at the appropriate places.

"What happened when you woke up? Where were you?"

"Now, loo, that's also very interesting. I couldn't remember then who I was, don't you see, or even what had just happened to me. I've had to reconstruct all that since."

"And a marvelous fine job of reconstructing it is, too," said Dore. He was sorry it had slipped out before he could censor the sarcastic tone, but the giant never noticed.

Lalichë, my critic, my thesis consultant, has graced me with another visit. And this time I listen to her. She claims that this chapter is growing unwieldly, with a disproportionate amount of description and dialogue. Now, of course, she is ready with a reason for *why* this is happening: it seems to her prepubic mind that I am trying to avoid dealing squarely wit' the problems inherent in my task. I am refusing to "come to grips with (my) material." I am not coping with the actual assignment. I am not relating.

Well, of course. How astute of you to notice. This is the most difficult thing I've ever had to do. I *loved* Dore.

I had planned for the end of this section a longish essay on the problems of writing, much like that of Henry James's Preface to *The Portrait of a Lady*. After all, I am in a peculiar position; I must detail a quest about which I know nothing, and therefore I fashion fiction. (What a play of words there. Mylvelane, Tere, do you notice?) But insofar as I deal with real people and places, I am constrained to limit my imagination. And this paragraph now is a further delay, more procrastination. "What happened to Dore?" they cried, expecting a five-page answer. And so, like Fielding, I will strive and aim to bring this section to a close. It has gone on its appointed length, is quickly reaching that limit of attention span that I can reasonably require of an audience. A few more bits of information to impart in preparation for the action of the following pages, and then I will end. Lalichë is satisfied; and you, my inquisitory readers, you must be patient while I learn to juggle plot and charm.

What the giant told Dore: He told him how he (the giant) had awakened in a room at the end of a long hallway. Along the hall were two other sleeping rooms. At the far end was a large room, decorated with crystal and gold and soft, colored silks. There were no other rooms, and no doors or windows anywhere.

As he entered the room he saw the misty forms of three people disappearing. They were vanishing, evaporating, like smoke from a fire. He saw what appeared to be two giant men, one with the most totally black skin, the other snowy white. With them was a golden creature, smaller and rounder, with long, golden hair. This one raised a hand and waved, just before they all blinked out completely. ("A princess," said Dore. "Some beautiful goddess, no doubt."

"Eh?" said the giant, puzzled.)

The giant sat in their parlor for hours. He put his feet up on a large coffee table, the top of which was dull black and perfectly clean. It was decorated with galaxies and nebulas in infinite detail. When he tapped his finger on the sheet of glass covering the table the stars moved. He lifted the glass and put his hand down onto the blackness; it kept going. They had the whole physical universe there in that coffee table. They were gods, and they had gotten tired of it. The giant had been picked as their successor. The first thing he did was to wipe out the old universe, like washing a blackboard.

"One clean, empty coffee table. Loo, then I got rid of that idiotic palace."

"Why? It sounded great to me." Dore was beginning to lose hope. They were still walking down into the mountain, but their path curved around on itself many times, and every now and then side paths cut into theirs. Dore was pretty well lost. He began to smell the concentrated aroma of cattle from up ahead.

"Maybe. But it was theirs, don't you see. I wanted my own place. So first I created this universe. It's modeled after the old in a lot of ways, don't you see. Then, loo, I created this world to be my home, which is what I named it. Then I made myself into a regular person, don't you see, keeping of course my superior appearance and mentality, loo, so I could watch you and decide if you're worth saving. I have to be thinking of someone to take my place someday, don't you see, and I haven't found him yet."

The broad hint wasn't lost on Dore, but he didn't really put much faith in the story. There were several implausible points.

"Why didn't you make a more luxurious capital some-where?" asked Dore. "I mean, as the Supreme Being of all the universe, this cave can't be the best you could do."

"Well, loo," said the giant, yawning, his baroquely rotting teeth shining in the firelight like ancient, yellowed scrimshaw, "when I allowed myself to incorporate on the human level, don't you see, here on the mundane plane, loo, I forgot to maintain those supernatural powers that went with my former self. This avatar is, you might say, voluntarily without my godlike attributes, don't you see. So I'm more or less here for the duration, if you take my meaning. But," he said, his tone becoming slightly more threatening, "that doesn't mean that I am without my own senses-shattering personal strength, don't you see, and my all-encompassing power."

"I see. But tell me more."

Ah, this giant, this hider-under-bushels. How like the Type of impotent magnitude he is. He is the American Dream, as amusingly portrayed in Albee's *The American Dream*, the ball-less, witless whore who has nothing but his smile and beauty; he is the essence of Genet's *The Balcony*, where people pretend to be and, thus, become the symbol and actuality of authority. This silly giant. And who is to say that his story is all delusion? It is Dore who must refute him. And as long as that great crab-tree cudgel swings at the monster's side, well, *kyrie eleison*.

And so they came, man and myth, to the subterranean enclosures that the giant had built for his animals. There was one large pen in an immense natural cavern, and beyond that another and smaller fold fenced with rough, unstripped hardwood boughs. Both pens were empty now, during the day when the animals were pasturing on the hill. Dore thought of the clean air without and the fresh-ness of the forest, and wished for the same simple luck of the animals.

"Well, loo, the big one keeps the cows, don't you see, and the other is for the goats. Now, tonight they will have a guest, loo, and I hope you don't mind their rough manners. Country hospitality, don't you see. You have come here to your fashioner under the usual burden of guilt and sin, but how am I to know if your repenting is sincere? Loo, yes, a problem: Do I take your word? Ah, the weak point of the theology. So. Tonight you sleep with the cows. Tomorrow night you sleep with the goats.

The evening after, loo, you pass with the pigs further on. And if your desire is such that you do not give up, don't you see, if you swallow your profane pride and weather this ordeal, loo, you win. I suggest you pass the time praying. Takes your mind off the troubles, don't you see."

The giant scooped Dore up in one huge hand, hoisting him up above his head. Dore balanced there for only a moment, until the giant lobbed him in a gentle arc into the largest corral. The thought of the eloquent skeletons of his infidel predecessors was little consolation for the filth in which he landed, heavily, on his back. The giant laughed some yards away, and as Dore turned to say something the monster lifted his torch and headed back toward the daylight, leaving Dore in total darkness, pain, and corruption.

CHAPTER SIX

A Perilous Scheme

Our Mother would have been scandalized. She had a very negative attitude toward filth, an outlook that she was careful to impress on those of us who would listen. We could always tell when it was going to be one of the "dirt days," as we laughingly called them. The sky remained dark, even as the sun rose higher and higher into the heavens' spacy vault. The normally white roof of clouds hung dark and low, unmoving in the morning's windless quiet. Grudgingly we'd rise and dress, knowing that the day would be spent listening to the cleanliness lecture again. Our Mother was waiting, and someone kept attendance reports. (All right, it was Tere. Not to put Tere in a worse light, you understand, but Tere always seemed to have more sharp pencils than anyone else.)

The air would always be chilly when we left the house. We'd walk in groups of three or four as slowly as we could among the chairs on the lawn, clucking our tongues, staring sullenly at the clumps of needle grass. At last we'd get to Our Mother's throne, despite all our efforts to get lost on the way. The usual early devotions were said, though with less enthusiasm than on ordinary days. Our Mother noted no difference, however, as beaded with dew on her stone seat as the throne itself. She stared out over our heads, blinking rapidly and nodding as regularly as a metronome. Only Tere noticed that our prayers were rushed with impatience; Our Mother just gurgled her holiness, but Tere came around afterward to our rooms. "Let's try to understand her," he'd say. "She's having a hard time now that Dad" (Dad?) "went off. The least we can do is be tolerant, okay?" Then he'd punch each of us on the shoulder, smile winningly, and mince away.

On dirt days he'd help her out. He'd stand next to her in front of one of the pillars, where he could watch each of us. Our Mother would do nothing for a long time, letting us soak up the unpleasantness for as long as an hour. A great idea for a play, eh, Lalichë? The audience is seated all at once, and while they are coming in the curtain is slowly falling, hiding some imaginative and interesting scene. After two and a half hours they are permitted to go home. *Naja*, then Tere would hand Our Mother her sword. She looked very silly with it. The broadsword would get heavy as the afternoon went on, and, instead of holding it before her symbolically, she took to resting it on the arm of the throne, or letting it waver dangerously close to Tere's inadequate breast. It did not take long for the sword to lose whatever metaphorical significance it might have had.

We were watching other things, anyway. How fascinating became the embroidered hanging behind the throne! It filled with the first afternoon breezes, bellied out and emptied, and slapped back against the pillars. Our Mother's voice droned on, accompanied by Tere's distracted "to be sure"s. After several more hours Our Mother wept to her conclusion. The sun would be too low for us to work in the fields; someone would shout, "Let us then cleanse ourselves in the healing holy waters of the River," which was just an excuse to go swimming. Those of us who believed in that sort of thing left in a group, and the rest of us headed back to the house for some table tennis or shuffleboard in the rec room before supper.

Once, though, after Dore left, we had a special dirt day. In the first place, it was the only one since our eldest brother's departure. This was the longest respite we had ever enjoyed. "Perhaps," we had thought timidly, "perhaps she'll never do it again. Because of Dore." But it was not to be. We sat about her, arms folded around our knees, boys and girls tickling each other with blades of grass. The morning passed as usual, and we started to get caught up in the rhythmic *fwap! thub* of the tapestry after the noontime winds began. But we slowly noticed that the sky was doing odd things. The heavy, threatening clouds lightened to their accustomed grayish-white, then began to thin in the middle so that they collected in bunches at the horizon. The sky above was bright blue, the only time it had been clear within my memory. Everyone fell silent except Our Mother, who spoke on from behind her tears. Tere slipped away, not unnoticed by anyone. We watched him loose a bird from a cage behind the micha tree. At first sight I believed it to be Dore's tarishawk, but as it circled closer I saw that it was a redskip, a small swiftlike bird officially known as Dodham's racer. No one is sure who or where Dodham is.

Tere tried to return to his position next to Our Mother without attracting attention, but we all made a great show of smiling to him and waving. He stood in front of the pillar and stared at the ground. We refused to acknowledge either the clear sky or the bird. We were unsure how Tere had managed the cloud thing, but we were united in wanting to deprive him of his silly triumph. The dirt day went on from there as usual, but it had given us material for speculation.

As Dore lay imprisoned in that filth, he must have given thought to Our Mother's teachings. She had never made a distinction between involuntary dirt and dirt of one's own free will. Surely Dore could not be held responsible for whatever uncleanness he suffered in the giant's lair. But he must have felt a few moments' guilt nevertheless. Could we dare to interpret the physical soiling of Dore's person as a symbol for the disorder of his intellectual self? Tere the messianist would be happy with this slightest of slaps at Dore's new stature. Ateichál the fundamentalist, now, might with reason be upset. I must therefore decline to voice an editorial preference.

That intellectual disorder might best be described in Dore's own terms, in the words of his motto: *Creative equilibrium*. This is the principle of having one's cake and eating it, too. Or closing one's eyes and letting it all go away. It happened generally that by the time Dore had thought things out, events had progressed to the point that his choice had been narrowed to one mandatory response. We can all appreciate how that has its good and bad points.

Dore thought in the muck. He traced plans in the slime on the floor, invisible in the absolute darkness.

"We don't have time for that," whispered someone behind him.

Dore was startled. "Who is it?" he said.

"It is I," said the voice. "Glorian."

"Ah, fine. What do you look like now?"

"What does it matter?" said the mysterious stranger. "I

have fair hair and a ruddy complexion. My back and spine are my best parts."

"Then you wear a ruby?"

Glorian laughed. "You are learning quickly," he said. "Yes, I have a yellow ruby on my forehead. It leaves me vulnerable to ailments in my joints, so let us get out of here soonest."

"How? The situation looks hopeless to me."

"They all do," said Glorian. "But faith works wonders."

"It is well that faith does, because I can't," said Dore.

"Right this very minute there is an angelic Person waiting outside the mouth of the cave for you. If we can manage your escape within the hour, that Person will be in a position to cut a great deal of time from your trial."

Sabt, the fourth-eldest male, has cleverly caught my *lapsus linguae* there. No doubt Glorian himself would never slip so, to reveal to Dore that the journey was indeed some sort of initiation. I can remedy the error easily enough, by simply making our brother ignore its significance. But do I now have to explicate the whole myth structure to you? No, I believe it best to go on, to let you piece the picture together on your own.

This doesn't satisfy my brother Sabt. The trouble with writing this in plain view is that everyone feels qualified to criticize each development. I suppose I am the only one of us who knows what I plan to do, but all the brothers and sisters in the house have suddenly become experts. It's *my* project, and my symbols are my own.

"Since when?" asks Sabt. "Dore was much more my brother than yours. You have a responsibility to us as well as to him. You seem to think you're writing this for your own self-aggrandizement. I'm sure Ateichál would find that an unwholesome attitude."

"What sort of . . . Person?" asked Dore, *ignoring Glorian's slip.*

"Oh, a sexless ethereal sort. Girded round with flowered garlands. Visible yellow aura. Smells of anise."

"Do you have a plan?"

"Yes," said Glorian. "Here's my plan. . . ."

Well, that got rid of Sabt. No one seems to be at all interested in the ingenious ways I find to extricate Dore from the diabolical situations in which I place him. All attention is focused on the merest modifiers, on the minutest descriptions that I drop more as filler than anything else. If I say that Dore finds a chain of red roses in the pen, and binds it about his waist to symbolize the union of carnal and spiritual desires, I do not intend my dear brothers and sisters to interpret this in a negative light. Compromise is a fine, true thing, although the word appears to have adopted a pejorative sense lately. Dore *hesitates,* which in itself implies action at *some* time. This is well-known; I am shocked that some of us are becoming outraged at my innocent observations. Dore may be holy nowadays, but when I knew him as the Will Incarnate he messed around a lot.

I was embarrassed by Sabt's return. He read what I had written after his departure, growing redder and redder through the last paragraph. He made a few notes, saying nothing, and left once more. The days of the liberal atmosphere seem to be numbered. With Sabt was my younger sister Shesarine, who is still with me. She would like to know what the Person mentioned by Glorian represents. I thought originally that the Person was to combine masculine and feminine elements, as the River combines the strength and fructification of the male and the fluidity and receptivity of the female. This hybrid Person would then be an external projection of the forces currently at work within Dore himself. The Person would remind Dore that all work and no play, etc.; part of compromise in this situation would be, necessarily, to allow a certain standard of pleasure. But this pleasure must be tempered and accepted in the proper spirit; the Person would explain to Dore that the red roses were essentially the same as the red robe so often seen adorning the Virgin Mary: the red of Eros, transformed from base animal drives into a pure and holy Love. Shesarine thought that this was dumb. All right. Never mind, then. It'll take longer than an hour for Dore to escape and the Person will be gone. Okay?

"We must wait for nightfall," said Glorian.

"Fine," said Dore. "How will we be able to tell when it gets dark?"

"Easy. We'll just wait until the giant returns with the cattle. You can sit here where he can see you, putting on a grand show of enjoying the whole thing. Then we'll just stealthily follow him back through the tunnels to the front entrance and slip away."

"What about the huge rock he uses as a gate?"

Glorian winked at me. I nodded gravely. "Don't worry," he said to our brother, "I have a feeling everything will be ready for us."

Very soon the two men saw the flickering of the giant's torch. It shone redly, a tiny point of light in the universe of darkness. It seemed to hover motionlessly for hours, as the giant drew nearer down the long tunnel. In a while they could hear the lowing of the cattle. Dore looked around for Glorian, but of course he could not see him. "Glorian?" he whispered. There was no answer. "Glorian, where are you?" he said, louder. The man had disappeared again.

There were a few thumps and bangings, evidently the giant opening the gate to the pen. Dore stood and pressed himself against the wooden timbers so that he might not be crushed or trampled by the herd of cows. The animals filled up the pen, milling about noisily. The torch, which had been placed in a holder, began to float again as the giant prepared to leave.

"Well, loo," said the giant, "how's it going so far?"

"All right, I guess," said Dore.

"Good." They were both silent for a moment. The torch waved as the giant gestured broadly. "All this, this is real life, eh?"

"Yeah. Strange."

"Real life, don't you know." The giant laughed sadly. "We do such silly things. Loo, but it's still great. Being an individual, don't you know."

"I suppose so. I've never been one."

Our Father was *the* individual, and so it is difficult to accept Dore's statement without looking deeper into our brother's often torpid thought processes. From early childhood, word reaches me, Dore knew that eventually he would be the one to have to go out in search of Our Father. He lived for years with the responsibility constantly coloring his relationships in the house. He could not avoid distancing himself from us, although he was by nature the warmest of friends; he was aware that we could not fail to demand that he do this thing. He was sorry for our guilt long before we ever felt its subtle pains.

I have to come up with some answer to Shesarine's charge that I am cheapening Dore's sacrifice by turning him into "just another Christ-figure." What can I say? By sitting outside the framework of the story, much like the levels of audiences in Kyd's admirable *Spanish Tragedy* (a play I have often suggested to Vaelluin's Lawn Theatre summer stock group. They insist that Neil Simon draws better), I can obtain a degree of, well, not *objectivity*, I suppose, but at least a studied carelessness that enables me to present Dore in all of his two or three aspects. Christ? Well, there are parallels, but aren't there always? You can hardly fault me for showing touches of the greatest of all influences. I am very fond of Christ; but Dore's character is more complex than that, and his story is much more resonant with allusion than simply a Christ/Prometheus thing.

Dore's journey was an historically imperative event. But even so we all feel responsible for whatever fate befell him. We regret our ever listening to Tere, although none of us would go so far as to wish to change places with Dore. But where Our Father was the very essence of leadership (the story goes), Dore gave himself over to vacillation. In him indecision masqueraded as "reason," and our leaderless family suffered unknowingly. Our Father's crown, which is still on display from nine in the morning until five-thirty in the evening in the West Foyer, is a massive gold affair. Dore made himself a simple circlet of metal, but Our Father wore a heavy helmet, ribbed and studded with bloodstones and Spanish topazes. We *need* someone to assume that emblem of strength and sureness, but no one quite that capable seems to be coming up through the ranks.

Dore felt a moment of panic as he noticed the bobbing of the torch. The giant was preparing to abandon him once more in the strange and foul cell.

"Glorian," whispered our brother, never taking his eyes from the slowly diminishing light. "You there? What are we going to do?" There was no answer but the soft murmurings of the cows and the squishings of their hooves in the mud. Dore was confused and frightened. He was usually pretty good when he had a choice of actions; somehow or other he always came through, late or not. But the situation was so unpromising that he couldn't see anything else for it but to do as the giant wished.

He was not able to say how much time passed, but in a while he saw the giant's torch approaching again. This time he was able to guess that the monster was escorting the goats. He said nothing as the giant led the animals past the cowpen. When the light of the torch had faded somewhat, Dore felt a reassuring tug at his sleeve.

"Be ready," said Glorian.

"Ready for what?"

"To escape, of course. We'll follow noiselessly behind the giant, ever keeping the light of his burning brand as our guide to liberty and reminder of the constant shining flame of hope."

"Have you taken care of the giant's boulder yet?"

"No," said Glorian, "but be still. He returns."

"Loo," came the call. "That's it for tonight, don't you see. Have a good rest, now. Don't sit up all night reading. Those cows will wake you early."

"Thank you," said Dore as the giant was swallowed up by the darkness of the tunnel.

"By the way," shouted Glorian, "where are the guest towels?"

"Quiet," said Dore, thrashing about in the dark for his mysterious ally.

"No worry," said Glorian, "he's quite out of earshot by now. Come; let's follow before we lose his light altogether."

"He's not out of earshot," said Dore anxiously.

"Sure he is."

"We'll see," said Dore, vaulting the fence and landing lightly on the stone floor. He trusted that Glorian had followed; again there was no reply. Dore shrugged and set off in pursuit of his captor.

If you're reading the original manuscript (which in a few hundred years will no doubt be precious and a thing of wonder), you will see that I have crossed out a large section of dialogue. Dore and Glorian continued their discussion at some length, giving, as I intended, further insight into their deepening friendship. Shesarine grew impatient, and Lalichë (who joned me at "Where are the guest towels?") agreed that I should just get on with it. No one seems to appreciate what I am doing. This is a major task, this document that I have been *urged* to write. There is much more to it than just the hacking and hewing of the hero. Am I the only one who sees the

significance of Glorian? Shesarine says he's effeminate, "if
you know what I mean." Sure, I know what she means.
But it's obvious that she doesn't know what *I* mean. "Why
bother?" I ask myself. Lalichë has the answer to that:
Tere, Ateichál, and their holy sideshow. Glorian's a symbol,
all right? A symbol. For the R - - - r. I must admit that I
just realized that last night. It came to me in a vision.
After Joilliena came to me in a sour mood. The other
girls won't talk to her at lunch.

All right. Shesarine's gone back to her desk in the
office of the Ploutos Corporation. I'll get back to the
adventure. Maybe I'll condense it a bit, now; I think I
have the next one all worked out, and I'm anxious to get
to it. Lalichë doesn't like the giant, anyway. She's nice, but
she's only five. She'll really be something in another seven
years or so.

Good. We have Dore and possibly Glorian following the
weakening glow of the giant's torch. The tunnels seemed
strange and threatening in the gloom, more so because
Dore was trying desperately and unsuccessfully to recognize a feature or landmark. His current fear was that the
giant was not, in fact, returning to the surface and the
exit, but rather taking some side tunnel to whatever goal
excited his gianty mind. Dore pictured himself trapped
deep within the bowels of the mountain, lost forever and
at the unsavory and unimaginative mercy of Loo. He felt
an urge to stop and go over the situation with Glorian, to
point out this and other possibilities which should not go
unconsidered; fortunately or unfortunately (it is for you
to decide), Glorian was unavailable for comment. A tingly,
lightheaded feeling in his abdomen reminded Dore that in
the childhood-monster darkness he would not be able to
find his way back to the cattle pen. He wished that he
could calmly shrug his shoulders.

Ahead, the seductive light of the torch shone steadily, as
though the giant and Dore had entered a long and un-
curving corridor. Dore took a deep breath and increased
his pace, thinking that for a time he was safe from dashing
out his life against the walls of a sudden turn. He thought
of Our Mother, whom he believed to be still doing her
usual things, safely and grotesquely seated on her backyard throne. He thought of Our Father, Dore's own founding Father, whose strange and unanswerable desertion
had made our brother's journey necessary. What motives

had sent (or driven?) Our Father from his wife and son, from the grand new home he had carved from the alien wilderness of an unknown world? Speculation was error (and is now heresy, from which you just don't recover), and only facts could satisfy our questing young minds. Dore thought of us, his brothers and beloved sisters; he thought of our stations and persuasions and occupations, of all the discriminating and otherwise useless distinctions we had invented to tell each other apart. He considered our feelings, how we must blame ourselves for his sacrifice, how we must lose sleep at night worrying about his well-being, how the days and months go by without even a card from him. He chuckled to himself there in the sunless pit, filled with nostalgia and homesickness and other pointless emotions. He entertained himself with thoughts of home and remembrances of us until the giant grabbed Dore's shoulder from behind.

"Loo, you laugh," said the giant. "What amuses you?"

Well now, of course Dore recalled that being caught like this had turned each of his predecessors from a novice to a corpse. Dore had to think quickly. He couldn't.

"You haven't seen Glorian, have you?" he asked.

"Eh?"

"It's not that I was trying to escape, you know. I just thought that a short walk might do me good. I couldn't get to sleep. The cows."

The giant had Dore once again tightly within his grasp, but even in our brother's state of extreme panic Dore realized that the giant was leading him toward the mouth of the cave, rather than back to the cattle pens. A simple error on the part of the giant? Dore thought it best to keep the monster occupied until Dore might make a break for freedom. But through the giant's boulder of a gateway? Dore wasn't thinking that far in advance.

"I understand," said the giant. "And well that you couldn't, don't you see. The others, loo, those deaders up ahead, now, they *did*. They spent the whole three nights, loo," here the giant spat in disgust, "their whole sentence they spent with those filthy beasts. But not you, don't you see. How holy could they be sleeping with animals? Loo, but you couldn't bear it. I'd have eaten you if you could." The giant sounded proud, and congratulated Dore with a bruising tap on the back.

Dore was silent for a long moment. "You mean I'm free?" he said at last.

"Well, loo, you've passed your first test, don't you see."

Dore wasn't as alarmed as he should have been, because he heard "first" as "First."

When at last they returned to the giant's parlor, Dore was worried to see that Glorian had failed to remove the great stone from the cave's mouth. The giant lifted Dore and placed him on a smooth flat slab of stone, cold and damp and ten feet above the floor.

"Hard comfort, eh loo, but better than you found with the kine," said the giant. "Now sleep you well, for we have much to talk about in the morning."

"Don't you see," added Dore in a whisper. He watched the giant prepare his own simple bed, and waited soundlessly while the torch was put out. Dore was again left frightened in total darkness, but this time he was soon asleep.

A knock! a knock upon my humble chamber's portal. A pleasant change, I will grant, from the unadorned bargings of my casual siblings. I will leave my desk for the unusual pleasure of welcoming a visitor rather than tolerating an intruder. Excuse me.

It is Dyweyne. Or rather, it *was* her, and I reproduce for you now our puzzling conversation. I welcome her in, my eldest sister, with great pleasure, for it is rare that she leaves her barren cell to visit with the other members of our family. She is tall and slender, with dark-brown hair piled on her head in intricate mounds and knots. Light strikes red sparks from the countless fascinating planes. She wears an unofficial crown, a barely visible golden band about her brow. The crown, not one quarter of an inch wide, signifies more that she was Dore's consort than her rank as eldest female. She dresses simply in a yellow robe, the color of the garden flowers with which she passed her days until Dore's departure. Since that day she has worn a white cloak of celebration and mourning over the robe, gathered on her breast with a golden pin in the form of a small doglike animal. She carries with her tonight the yellow flower she picked to give to Dore on his return. The flower is, of course, dead and dried.

"Welcome to my poor apartment," I say to her.

"Thank you, Seyt," says Dyweyne. Her voice is very low, and she drops her eyes shyly often as she speaks.

"Is there something I can do for you?"

Dyweyne stands from the chair she accepted upon her arrival. Before she turns away I see that there are tears upon her pale, friendly cheeks. I am shocked and afraid. What have I done?

For a few seconds there is a nervous silence. I smell the rich, earthy smell of Dyweyne, as though she had been once again working in her abandoned gardens. Dyweyne can control her flowers, but, too, she can control the basic animal urges of all of us. Our emotions are never hidden from her, one reason that she has chosen to secrete herself far from our riotous nonsense. And, deftly, lovingly, graciously, she can mold our emotions and change them: change envy to love, change pity to love, change anger to love. But she doesn't. She is humiliated by her ability.

"Why are you doing it?" she asks, her voice cloudy with feeling. "Why are you picturing Dore so unfairly? Why do you show him acting so stupidly, so grossly? Don't you remember?"

I can say nothing. This is the first sign of dissension that I have had to recognize. Dyweyne *cares* about Dore and, I know, she cares about me. What a discovery, that I may be negligent. I thought that I was above that.

"I'm sorry, my sister," I say to her, embarrassed. "I thought that for my purposes I was treating him fairly."

She nods sadly. *"For your purposes.* I, too, am doing the history of his travels, although you probably do not know of that. It is not as publicized as your official account and, truthfully, it is not as nicely wrought. But it *is* sincere." Dyweyne begins to weep copiously. I am helpless.

"I'd . . . I'd be honored to see it sometime. I could help you with it," I say lamely. My sister, chaste, loving, sorrowing, does not answer and departs. I am profoundly affected.

In the morning Dore was awakened by the noises of the cattle which the giant was leading out to pasture. He could not see them because his neck was fastened to the slab by a large iron staple. His hands and feet were bound to the damp stone with heavy chains.

"You should not have trusted the giant's strange hospitality," said Glorian.

"What else could I do?" said Dore, staring at the sedimentary ceiling. "You proved of remarkably little help."

"My ways are my own. Everything in its season. In the fullness of time. There is yet more to this episode."

"Free me, or there won't be much."

"No chance now," said Glorian, hiding deeper within the cave, "the giant returns!"

"Loo, there. You are awake. Good," said the giant.

"Why have you done this to me?" asked Dore.

"Ah, don't you see, you brought it on yourself by not fitting the bed," said the giant.

"But it's made for someone of gigantic proportions," said Dore in frustration. "I didn't have a chance."

"For you are not virtuous," said the giant. "If you were good, don't you see, you'd fit my bed. There is little enough good in the world."

"Not so!" cried Glorian, springing from his place of concealment.

"Who is this?" asked the giant. "Are you here for pain, or to effect an escape?"

"I am Glorian."

"What?" said the giant.

"Glorian," said Dore helpfully.

"And I am Despair," said the giant.

"Is that your name?" asked Dore.

"Bunyan or Spenser?" asked Glorian.

"Neither," said the giant impatiently, "loo, I'm a different one entirely."

"What's happening?" asked Dore.

"You were beginning your argument?" said Despair, the giant.

"Yes, thank you," said Glorian. "Why do you hold Dore, my companion, captive upon this noisome rock?"

"Well, loo, so he won't wriggle in the Scotch Boot."

"No," said my symbol, "why hold him at all?"

"He's evil, don't you see," said the giant, playing nervously with the cord of the great cudgel that hung by his side. Evidently, Despair was not used to such close questioning.

"And if I could prove the nonexistence of evil?"

"Eh?" said Despair.

"If I could show that your fears are groundless?"

"What fears?" asked Despair.

"If I demonstrate the universality of goodness?"

"I would set him and you free," said Despair with his disconcerting grin.

"Then, do you believe in the goodness of God?" asked Glorian.

"He *is* God," said Dore.

"Well," said Glorian, "that will simplify things, You *are* good, eh?"

"Loo, certainly."

"And by 'God' we understand omnipotence and benevolence of infinite extent?"

"Yes, I do my best," said Despair.

"Then follow this," said Glorian confidently. "Positing the existence of evil, either you—God—cannot rid the world of it and are impotent, or you can but won't, and are malevolent. And also, we learn early through experience that a good and moral life is of no practical value in achieving happiness for ourselves or our loved ones."

"I move in mysterious ways," said Despair.

"Don't we all," muttered Dore.

"For often we have seen the wicked rewarded," said Glorian, continuing his sophistry, "while we ourselves seemingly go from punishment to undeserved punishment. So some of us fall from the ways of grace, attempting to avoid or at least nullify the apparently random distribution of reward. Thus we fall into sin. But of course the wages of sin is death. But it is through sin that we recall the sovereignty of God; by transgressing God's laws we acknowledge their existence. And the acknowledgment of God's lordship works to His greater glory. Every act of man, whether the most holy sanctioned rite or the most heinous crime, works to the eventual Good, the universal and willing acceptance of God's yoke of love."

"Your friend is free," said Despair.

There is no evil. We may all breathe a sigh of relief. I admit that for a moment I was unsure about our brother's fate, but faith worked its advertised miracle. In the background now the giant Despair loosens Dore's bonds, shaking his head and pondering Glorian's high sentiments. The giant is subdued. He grasps Dore's hand and begs his forgiveness. Dore smiles in his beautiful way and says nothing. The three friends walk slowly to the mouth of the cave, where the giant rolls back the huge stone. They converse in low tones, curiously reluctant to say their good-bys.

"Come with me," says Sabt, who has returned as promised. It is time for a break, anyway. I bid farewell to my giant.

I take my notebook, in an attempt to crystallize some thoughts concerning Dore's next adventure. I have, as I said, a general idea, but now I need to incorporate it, to swath such flimsy feelings in firm, stabbable flesh. New horizons, new vistas of action and meaning, new people to kill and love. Perhaps now, walking about our charming house, nodding hello to brothers and sisters going by with papers in their hands, standing on ladders with brushes, kneeling in courtyards with trowels, I will get characters, plot, dramatic impetus. I know where Sabt is taking me.

Outside, on the far side of the house from Our Mother's vacated and already crumbling seat, there is a pen, an enclosure very much like the one in which Dore passed his recent restless hours. If you still have a mental image of that compound merely translate its location. Place it in the middle of a lawn of prickly high weeds, perhaps one hundred yards from the house. There is already a well-worn path from a rear entrance of the house, although the pen was not built until after Our Mother's Desumption.

"Where were these, uh, tenants housed prior to the construction of these, uh, quarters?" I ask.

Sabt marches briskly, not even turning his head to answer. He does not want to waste energy, and is trying to urge me to greater speed with his example. We must not be late.

"In the basement, of course," he says. "There are many more of them now, so we thought it best to move them out here. Fresh air. Exercise."

I shudder. "Who are 'we'?" I ask.

Sabt grants me an unpleasant look. "Tere and Ateichál."

I know why there are many more of them.

At one end of the rectangular corral a high platform has been built, with a balcony overlooking the enclosure and its inmates, my brothers and sisters. The stage looks like a boardless diving tower, a small open box for the Pope or visiting royalty to wave from, slowly. I think of the play by Genet. I think about prostitution, about bartering for power, about identities and images changing as fluidly as motivations. I think about lies. I think about the ugliness inherent in all relationships. I think about some people standing on platforms looking down on other people. I wonder how I might feel to be on that balcony.

"Let's go up," says Sabt. "The lesson'll start soon."

We take our seats. I have time to look down into the pen, against my better judgment. I see horrors; balls and cylinders and pools of animal flesh that used to be human. Several of these unfortunates (oh, Father, what a damned euphemism!) were born that way. 5396 was the next male to be born after me. 9704535 and 40313642 were twins, females originally destined for marriage with princes of high-ranking foreign families. 2940, 7188, and 9305 were all normal males in their youth, until puberty began some strange endocrine-linked transformations in their somatic selves. They were all good friends. Haven't spoken to them in years, though.

But the others . . .

"Isn't that Mylvelane?" I ask in horror.

"You can still recognize her? Yes, she's 49127046 now. A dangerous heretic who couldn't be saved. Oh, Ateichál tried. They spent many nights together. I could hear the loud cries from my room down the hall. But she was hopeless. She is better off here, and so are we."

I can say nothing. Dozens of brothers and sisters were tried, found guilty, and . . . sentenced. And still Ateichál wants to save their souls. She climbs the stairs and takes her place at the front of the balcony. She is entirely naked, unadorned in the service of Dore, her spiritual lover. She wears only a small gilded chain around her thick neck. I don't understand the significance, and I am reluctant to ask Sabt. She has her light blonde hair in tight curls, like a helmet for her pious battle. She carries some flowers wrapped in waxed paper; after a short introductory prayer to Our Father and Mother asking for Dore's safe return she throws the flowers down to the numbered audience. None of those in the pen make any move toward the offering. Ateichál's heavy, unclothed body does not excite me.

"Let us speak today of goodness," she says in her gospel voice. "Does anyone still believe in it?" Naked, large-boned Ateichál lets the silence sweep in, and only Sabt's rustling program disturbs the effect. "Can anyone cite me an example of goodness, now that Our heavenly Father and Our earthly Mother have left us, now that Dore, our priceless Link, has followed?" Once again she permits a peaceless quiet to form around us.

"God has given over the rule of the world to his subordinate angels, and they have proven to be traitors. The very seat of goodness has been overthrown. We must make the best of what we have. Order has gone. Morality is irrelevant. All that is left is *us*. Our Father cleared a home of calmness and justice in the midst of this chaos. Our Mother programed us with the precepts necessary for a good life. We may spend our allotted seventy years in whatever mode we most desire; but it was for Dore, and Dore alone, to be called to his Parents' side, to discover the answer to the question we may know only as 'Why.' We are as machinery, to facilitate Dore's quest. He is doing it not for us, but instead we are sacrificing ourselves for him. It is to be a seventy-year sacrifice for each of us, and for our children, and for each generation to come. It is necessary. Why? I do not know. You must have faith."

I begin to think about Ateichál's words, about the blackness of her universe, and I glance down into the pit, into the pen, the corral that imprisons my heretic brothers and sisters. Ateichál's words are very . . . interesting. They are very . . . interesting.

"There is *only* teleology. The purpose of the world, of the Creation of everything, is to get Dore along on his journey. For us, now that we have played our expediting role, there is only life. Life without further goals beyond selfish pleasures. We have seventy years to kill. All that we do, all work, all play, all cultural, organizational, intellectual, bestial activity represents nothing more than an effort to rid ourselves temporarily of that oppressive fact. Seventy years, with nothing to come after. Such a gross waste of energy, were it not for Dore! Let us be thankful to him for that, at least! Let us be thankful that we have had him, as so many billions have not. Let us be thankful that he may still serve, in prayer, as intermittent diversion. Seventy years, my brothers and sisters! Such a long time to pass. The hours move so slowly.

"Without Dore, what do we have? Hope. And hope is an illusion, a romance. The universe is emptier than we are, my friends. There is no universal Good waiting for you to pass your scabby human trials. There is no Good at all." Ateichál drops her clenched fists to her sides. She begins to weep, and Sabt hurries to her with a dark-blue cloak. Before the departure of Dore, Ateichál was a student of the bones of Home, delighting in the dark and stuffy shafts beneath the ground, and in the mineral treasures to be found there. The brooch that closes her cloak is made of lead, shaped to resemble a fleshless human jaw of teeth.

Tere takes Ateichál's place on the balcony, moving with great dramatic sweeps of cloak and waving of arms. "Come, my children," he shouts through his impervious smile, "sing with me. Move your arms, my dears," he says, his eyes wide, his voice cracking. "Move your feet, move your necks for Dore!"

"Thank you," said Dore.

"Eh?" said Despair, covering his crusted eyes suddenly with his huge, filthy hands.

"For setting me free," said Dore. Glorian had disappeared.

"No, wait," said the giant, stumbling back against his boulder door. "Nothing, there is nothing, don't you see. No goodness left at all. They're right, loo. There is nothing to hope for, loo, nothing to live for." The giant made several strange choking sounds behind his hands, and Dore watched anxiously, worried for Despair, his new friend. The giant straightened at last, and breathed heavily. He recaptured Dore with one quick movement.

"There is no evil, and there is no good," said Dore. "There is some truth in both sentiments, I think, but perhaps a compromise is closer—"

"No, loo, no, loo," said the giant, carrying Dore back through the tunnels, not even stopping to light a torch.

I hear that gentle knock. Dore is back in the cattle fold now; he was nearly free, but now he's back in his foulsmelling prison. The knock on the door means that Dyweyne would like to speak with me. Her brother and lover has just been plucked from the eager arms of freedom, and yet she calls on me. I welcome her. Her face is creased and wet: what distasteful feelings does she read in me? My sister, as much as Mr. Oscar Wilde's wellknown fictional portrait, shows to me my real self, and I choose not to look too closely.

"Why?" she says, weeping. "That is not Dore. You do not describe the brother you knew. What are you doing to him?"

No one else in our family can make me feel—guilty.

"Is it because his quest is so pointless?" she asks. "Why do you not give him a real task? He *was* heroic and noble, but how can he be in your silly situations? You have taken Dore and yes, even Our Father and Mother, and changed them to fit your strange narrative. Why, Seyt?"

Well, I explain, no, I haven't, really. I can't expect her to understand about my allegory or the complex framework I am building. She is too simple, too generous to accept such sophisticated technique. I say nothing more. Dyweyne realizes that she is powerless to make me understand her: My artistic integrity is stronger than her sentimentality, which is as it should be. Romanticism is for adolescents, and stark realism is for the mindless. I demand effort on the part of the reader.

If I *have* distorted my characters, I'm sure Tere and Ateichál would let me know.

Glorian and Dore stood against the wooden railing of the empty pen. Glorian was trying desperately to revive Dore's foundering morale. If only Dore knew how we were all behind him one hundred percent, how we all wished him success, how we all worried about him and even, secretly, tossed unimportant books into the River for his well-being, I'm sure he would have been heartened.

"Did you sleep well last night?" asked Glorian.

"Yes, I suppose," said Dore, "although I was troubled by a strange dream."

"Oh? Perhaps it was some sort of omen. Tell me of it."

"Certainly," said Dore. "I dreamed of a domino."

"Just one?"

"Yes, just the one. All night. No people or sounds in the dream, just the domino. The five-three."

"Wonderful!" cried Glorian. "The five-three is a lucky little devil. It presages victory after hardships. It confirms your inner ambition, but counsels you to avoid extremes, to temper pleasure with practicality. Advances in music, art, and drama are indicated. Rely on good manners and good taste. The five-three is a domino of hope and good news."

"Are you making that up?" said Dore suspiciously.

I am reminded of the many stories, perhaps apocryphal, of Our Father and his fantastic ability with dominoes.

"See what I made you, Seyt?" Lalichë explodes into my closet of a room, carrying a large, colored construction paper gift. On one side is a golden snake with the head of a lion, apparently floating above an altar. Around it is written in Lalichë's childish hand, "I, even I, am the Good Angel or perhaps Spirit." On the back is pasted a triangle of letters:

A
EE
HHH
I I I I
OOOOO
Y Y Y Y Y Y
WWWWWWW

and beneath that is written, "Please keep the contents of Seyt's chest in working order."

"What is it for?" I ask my little sister.

"It's a Gnostic amulet," she says solemnly. "That's Knubis, the Sun of the Universe."

"I know," I say, "but those W's are supposed to be omegas. And why did you give it to me?"

"You have stirred the wrath of Tere and Ateichál," says Lalichë, kissing me suddenly on my cheek and running from the room. At the door she stops and says, "I've never heard of any stories of Our Father being skillful with dominoes."

"You're too young," I say, my mind considering her warning.

"No," said Glorian. "But let us consider your plight. Captured by a Giant Despair, like Christian and Hopeful in Bunyan's ever-popular *Pilgrim's Progress*."

"I could never get through that," said Dore.

"Never mind. Perhaps we could take a lesson from them."

"How did they escape?"

"They were put in a 'dungeon, nasty and stinking.'"

"Uh huh."

"They had neither food nor water from Wednesday morning until Saturday night. Every day the giant beat them unmercifully."

"Say," said Dore, "how do you know all these things?"

"That's what I was put here for," said Glorian, giving me a secret smile. "Anyway, the giant counseled suicide, rather than their continuing a life of pain in his dungeon. Fortunately, Christian had a key called promise that could open every lock in the giant's castle."

"That *was* fortunate. What do *I* do?"

"You consider some more. Spenser. *The Faerie Queene*. Despair's not a legitimate giant, but he's big and he lives in a cave. His charmed speeches persuade everyone who listens to kill himself."

"Apparently despair leads to suicide."

"Yes," said Glorian, as pleased as any tutor with Dore's understanding. "Despair is the greatest of evils, because it limits and denies God's infinite love and mercy. One is saying that one's sins are so great that even God couldn't forgive them. A perverse sort of pride. Do you want to kill yourself?"

"No," said Dore seriously, "things haven't gotten that bad."

"Fine, my lad."

"How does Spenser's hero kill Despair?"

"He doesn't," said Glorian sadly. "His girl friend saves him."

"Oh," said Dore. "Are we done considering?"

"Not just yet. Before Spenser's Despair episode, a real giant is killed. Orgoglio, Carnal Pride. When he's stabbed he deflates like a blown-up balloon."

"That's dumb."

"Well, they used to think the erection of the penis was caused by air. Giants are phallic symbols."

"I've heard that somewhere else lately," said Dore disgustedly.

No, that was Lalichë telling *me* that.

Dore was silent for several seconds. "You want me to stab him in the chest?"

"I guess so," said Glorian.

"With what?" There was no answer. Dore thought of the other giants he had heard about. Glorian was silent, and for a while Dore thought that the mystic ally might have abandoned him again.

"How about pulling an Odysseus?" said Dore to himself.

"Congratulations!" said Glorian. "I was just waiting to

see how long it would take you. Come, let us sharpen the stake. The giant will be back to lead out the goats very soon."

"Let's skip the stake, all right?" asked Dore. "That's too gratuitous. Besides, do you really think he'd lead the goats out blind?"

"I don't know," said Glorian doubtfully. "You'll be easy to spot."

"I will not blind that stupid monster," said Dore. "He's in bad enough shape already. Let's go find the goat pen."

In the terrible darkness the two men stumbled and bruised themselves repeatedly, before the impatient noises of the goats directed them to their goal. Dore was frantic for a while, trying to find something to use to fasten himself to the underside of a large goat. Quite by accident he discovered two large buckets suspended from a pole by long ropes, evidently used by the giant to transport milk. In a few minutes Glorian had tied Dore to the breast of the animal. There was nothing left now but suspense.

Dore's face was pressed against the goat's stinking chest, and thus he did not see the approaching light of the giant's torch. But he could hear the familiar looing, and Dore grew more anxious as he waited to be discovered. But after the she-goats had been milked Dore knew by the motion of his own that the flock was being led outside. Fortunately, Dore's animal neither led the way nor straggled conspicuously, and after a nervous journey Dore was finally outside. He had no idea how long it had been since he had seen the sun, and even now all he could see were gray, curly goat hairs.

He heard Glorian whisper, "Here, you evil-smelling beast!" and then Dore felt a sharp bump, as though Glorian had kicked the goat. The animal began to run, and Dore hoped it would not attract the attention of the giant. At the bottom of Despair's hill he tried to call out; but his voice was muffled by the closeness of the goat. "Tell your next victim my name is Dore," he cried.

"What?" said the giant, looking around for his captive.

"My name is Dore!" shouted our brother, his words still garbled.

"Eh?" said the giant.

"Never mind," said Dore.

"Eh? What?"

And so Dore devised and executed his own escape from

the prison of the giant Despair, bound to the bottom of a raw-boned goat. And, also, he *conquers* Despair, the chiefest of heresies. Tere? Ateichál? All right?

And you, Dyweyne: How's that?

CHAPTER SEVEN

Goats That Pass in the Night

Where is Dore now? Tied upside-down to the bottom of a goat, yes, of course; but where? I had him wandering away from the River, through a forest to the giant's mountain. Now he's gone back down the hill. I don't suppose the goat would pick his way through that dense thicket, so for now Dore's going even further from the River. Slowly we are learning that the River runs as a great life-giving and sanity-maintaining force through our world. The farther one travels from its blessed banks the more irrational become the local inhabitants, and even the environment itself. And now, helpless, Dore is carried deeper into that enveloping chaos. We must fear for his safety.

The goat stopped to eat some grass. "Glorian?" said Dore. "Let me down, Glorian, I'm getting tired." There was, *natürlich*, no answer. "I'm getting very hungry, you know that, Glorian?" Silence, broken only by peaceful, innocent bird songs. A warm sun in a white sky, the heartening sounds of insects at work and play, the friendly welcome of growing things: None of this relieved Dore's aching neck and back, his leaden arms and legs, his parched throat and empty stomach.

Where the goat skips, there skips he. As the goat stood idly munching the early-afternoon grass, Dore began to be aware of noises around him that didn't conform to the vicinage: metal clinking on metal, moanings, sounds of feet tramping across the meadow. The people had to approach very closely before Dore could actually see them. Indeed, a man spoke up before Dore was aware of his presence.

"Hello, I've found some sort of beast," shouted the man.

"A horse, perhaps?" said one of the others.

"No," said the first, "it seems to have horns. It's not large enough for a horse, either. It may be a goat."

"Yes," said Dore, "it's a goat."

116

"It talks!" said the first man fearfully, moving away. Dore could see that he was dressed in a very ragged military uniform. He carried an absurdly ancient rifle over his shoulder, in such disrepair that Dore did not believe it could be fired. The man's trousers were tattered and patched, and his feet were bound up in filthy rags.

"No," said Dore, "it's just me. I'd be grateful if you'd get me down."

"Is it a demon?" asked one of the other men, who had gathered around the goat at a respectful distance.

"No," said the first man, "it didn't seem to burn when I touched it. I think it is merely a talking goat."

"Can't you see me?" said Dore in exasperation.

"No," said one, "of course not. We're blind."

"Blind? An army, blind?"

"We're retreating, aren't we?" said the first man.

"How did it happen? What strange weapon or terror blinded you all, to a man?" asked Dore with his noted compassion recognizable in his voice.

"Oh, we were blind when we set out," said one of the shabby warriors.

"Ah!" said Dore in anguish. "What people could send out such a handicapped and futile force to defend them?"

"It's not as bad as all that," said the first man, as the others began to take up again their stumbling, painful march homeward. "We are from the village of Newburg, and we have constant border disputes with another village, Springfield. But years ago our rulers agreed on this method of keeping the carnage to a minimum. Both villages gather together their sightless citizens of all ages, men and women. We are armed and led on our way out of town. If and when by chance we should meet the blind army of Springfield, we engage them as best we can. This way there is no one to witness the horrors of war, and no one is left with crippling visual memories of the butchery. Indeed, few are ever hurt, and never by design but only through chance and the holy will of God. After a time we regroup, and the army of Springfield marshals itself, and the two forces return to their homes. The sight of our poor band, limping, bleeding more from low-hanging branches than bullets, torn and dirty and tired and completely vincible, is enough to frighten our fellow citizens back into their safe parlors. We look so utterly defeated that everyone expects momentarily the Springfield army of occupation. They wait breathlessly for the new masters, for the life of slavery and hopelessness. Of course, the townsfolk of Springfield are thinking the same thing. And everyone is content to live for a while without interference, happy to be left alone, grateful for the negligence of the conquerors."

"That's horrible," said Dore. "It's absurd to think it could work more than once."

"Oh, I don't know," said the man. "We're but simple country folk. God be with you, goat."

"Stop," said Dore pleadingly, "you have to help me."

"Nay. You cannot aid us, and we have nothing for you. Our task is finished." And the man went along across the meadow after his companions, and Dore was once more left alone. Later, as the twilight deepened, our brother thought he saw another goat, standing motionless on the horizon. His own goat showed no sign of recognition, and so Dore kept his peace.

Today is a special day. The River rose during the night, grumbling and straining its back higher and higher until this morning we saw it from the fields. The sunlight reflected from the boiling surface and shone, sparklike, through the flat gray leaves of the low dey trees along the bank. Peytheida touched me on the arm during breakfast. "Do you think you can leave your history this morning?" she asked. "Long enough to come with us, I mean. You haven't done the book thing in quite a while."

I nodded. I wasn't aware that I have been that lax in my observances. Things pile up. I'm losing points with Tere, Ateichál, Dyweyne, Joilliena, and the family, not to mention Our Father and Mother, and even the River. How difficult it is to be a functioning artist in a demanding society. Such never-to-be-forgotten masters as Wagner and Kafka could afford to thumb their noses at convention and the myth of sociability. But we lesser luminaries must make efforts to conform, at least until our output has purchased for us a modicum of accepted eccentricity.

Peytheida carried a worn blue edition of *Up From Slavery* by Booker T. Washington. Elliavia brought a copy of Branch Cabell's *Ladies and Gentlemen,* complete with dust jacket. I found a volume of Bury's *History of Greece.* My sisters were very beautiful. I was haggard, bleary-eyed from working late and rising early. My clothing was rumpled; I tend to neglect my appearance when I am composing. The younger children giggle at me behind their hands in the hallways. The older brothers and sisters glance at me at meals and turn away to speak in whispers, with creased brows and much nodding. But this morning I made a discovery of myself. I tried to reach my new and changing personality; but it is still, for the most part, secret. A few hints, and some new peace.

The River changed from flat gray to flat green, dark flat blue to a black almost as deep as the moonless night. We stood for a few minutes on the bank, silently, within our individual and unjoined thoughts. Then Peytheida tossed her book into the water. The River changed immediately, keeping its same ominous hues but falling back to its accustomed depth, leaving us higher and farther from the current. Elliavia had to throw her book quite a distance then, over an expanse of mud and shore that was already drying and verdant with new, River-sired sedge. Immediately the Cabell touched the water the River lightened in color. I did not wait, but threw my book into the flood. There were no visible effects, but we all felt them in our souls. The whole world enjoyed the repose of the heart.

I thanked my sisters for asking me to join them. Where before I felt the torture of inconstant emotions, I feel now the joy of unified energies. I am able to verbalize my feeling better—and am now for the first time aware of a sudden love for Dyweyne, and a gratitude for the cherished love of Joilliena. I understand responsibility, chiefly my lapses concerning the proper respect due my house and our River. Tere and Ateichál are justified in their displeasure. I hope that my observances today in some small part rectify my ill-considered neglect.

I receive a note from Tere. He and his sister-in-faith would be pleased if I were to make amends. Terms to be arranged. Peace. Harmony. Good fellowship.

I. I cannot write, not about Dore. I will sleep.

I awoke to find Joilliena kneeling by the side of my bed, praying. I raised my head a little, but she did not notice, so I let it fall back to the pillow. I closed my eyes and pretended to be still asleep. The silence was awful, because the situation was so strange. Perhaps I had been asleep for days or weeks, unconscious and on death's wait-

ing list, and only now had made a miraculous recovery.
My tongue felt all right and the inside of my mouth was
free of unusual symptoms. My limbs could be moved without discomfort. I did not feel the presence of swellings
under my arms or ears. My head and throat were without
pain, and I was neither fevered nor chilled. Physically I
felt fine.

But mentally, no. Where was the well-being that soothed
me to sleep? I could *almost* recall that sense of oneness of
purpose, of solidarity with my family and my world that
destroyed the doubts of the last few weeks. It may be that
I have sunk to deeper depression now, having known and
misplaced a rare religious event. When at last I sat up and
interrupted Joilliena's worship, she merely smiled shyly,
stood, and left without a word. I read over my words of
last evening and experienced only a sense of profound
loss, that the moment of pure devotion had to be so
fragile and short-lived. Later I found beneath my bed a
scrap of parchment with a crudely drawn duck and the
words "O River, forgive him, he doesn't know what he's
talking about" inscribed on the back.

"There is only work. Do it." I will lose myself again and
forever in my history. All else is fantasy. People are
dreams and hopes are less.

The goat; Dore. The countryside flattened as they wandered farther from the safety of the River. From Dore's
upside-down vantage the features of the landscape seemed
to shrink: Tall losperns gave way to stubby, barren fruit
trees, then to shag-barked pollits, to thorny bushes, low
shrubs, clumpy weeds. The tall grass disappeared and was
replaced by the prickly short stuff that we find in hard,
stony soil. Dore was desperately thirsty, but never did he
find help in being loosed from his creature prison. He
traveled bound to the beast for several days. At last he
spied a solitary micha tree in the midst of the plain. The
goat, also, was intrigued by the anomaly, and as Dore
came closer to the tree he discovered that a man was tied
to it, as helpless as our brother.

The tree grew straight and branchless for ten or twelve
feet, and there the trunk was marked by two limbs growing out parallel to the ground, looking like two supplicat-
ing arms. The poor man had his own arms thrown back
over the branches and bound, and his body was thrust
forward painfully by the curvature of the trunk. His head

hung forward as though he were asleep, comatose, or dead.

"Hello," called Dore. The convict jerked his head up in surprise.

"Hello," he said. "Get me down."

"You can see how I am as resourceless as you, roped as I am to this goat. Do you know how I might be released?"

"If you don't get me down, I don't care," said the man.

You can begin to see what the journey and the difficulties have done to Dore. Even Tere and Ateichál in their sanctified rigidity must admit that the things he has seen and the people he has had to deal with must have caused him to change. Surely one can't behave the same, rely on old standard patterns of response in every situation. So of course, Dyweyne, of course it isn't the same Dore we knew. It isn't the same world, either.

But such things as common courtesy go beyond local custom. Situation ethics do not excuse insolence, vulgarity, and discourtesy. How often Our Mother used to say that very thing! Early in the morning, on the way to the chata fields, I used to hear her mumbling away about politeness. She didn't mind bad news, she always claimed, as long as the messenger was polite. We read often in the Greeks, particularly *Oedipus the King* and one of the Oresteia, I believe, of the frightened bearer of bad tidings worrying about his own punishment. Politeness is the key. If we remember the three magic words we can open any door. Soon Lalichë will tell me that she thought Promise was the key. That was *last* chapter.

So Dore had to explain patiently and carefully to the man in custody of the micha tree. He did so to no avail. The man grew angrier, cursing Dore for lacking the compassion to set him free. Evidently the man was of a weak mind in the past, for he seemingly could not comprehend that Dore, too, was as imprisoned as he.

"Are you some sort of mythological hybrid?" asked the man in the tree.

"No," said Dore.

"I mean like a centaur or something. You look like part man, part goat. If you have strange and inhuman faculties, you could easily get me down."

"I'm sorry," said Dore, "but I'm just a man like you,

tied to a goat. Like I said, I can't use my hands to free either of us."

"I can pay you."

"It's not that."

"Look," said the man in a surly voice, "why don't we do this: I'll ask you a riddle. If you guess it, you may pass by unharmed. If not, you have to cut me down. Ready? What is it that dreams at noon and toils at midnight, yet never sleeps or works?"

"It doesn't concern me now," said Dore.

The man was quiet for a few seconds. "It doesn't matter. You aren't real, anyway."

"What *is* reality?" asked Dore.

"Is that your riddle?" said the man sarcastically. "Did you make that up by yourself?"

"Well, what *is* reality?"

"All right," said the man, "I'll tell you." And the man told Dore what reality really is. "Reality is neatly summed up in this poem:

> What is there but to run, and
> having run, rave, and
> having raved,
> ruin?
> What more?"

"Where did you learn that?" asked Dore without interest.

"I always knew it. I'm the corporal manifestation of the spirit of the River."

Now this, we the readers know, is a patent lie. The corporal manifestation of the River is Glorian. But Dore hasn't thought of that yet. Nevertheless, he didn't accept the stranger's word on the matter.

Dore, as a paid-up member of our happy clan, had much experience with manifestations and aspects. They are quite a source of amusement among the younger children. Of course, having divine parents leaves one with the constant uncertainty that the doglike animal or friendly shade tree one is observing may well be Father or Mother off on a spree. We frequently tell the toddlers to be good, or Our Father will get them, usually in the form of a streptococcus or a letmoth. If they are frightened and ask to have the night light left on, we turn the screw and tell them that even the light may be an offended Parent, just waiting for the youngster to fall asleep. . . . That always gets them.

Our Father was compelled to come to Our Mother in various guises, for well-known reasons. The shower of gold was a favorite for a while, until the thrill began to fade. Our Father employed on special occasions the form of the fructifying rainstorm, a very Chaucerian touch that I've always applauded. It took Our whining Mother a while to figure out what to *do* with a rainstorm. And, too, certain errors and miscalculations were bound to result. We like to repeat the jocular tale of the day Our Father came in from his work with the chairs to find Our Mother in bed with a strange swan.

"Isn't this—?" said Our Mother, confusion claiming her expression.

"No," said Our Father, kicking the fowl out of his marriage bed and going out to find a bite to eat. These incidents happened fairly frequently, and Our Mother always had the perfect excuse that she could never be sure that it *wasn't* her husband, who thus was cuckolded by animals, vegetables, and inanimate objects. But nowadays we wonder.

I hear shouts of outrage from downstairs, from outside, from next door and up in the towers: "No, *we* don't wonder. *You* wonder."

Not a note, but Tere himself stands at my barrierless door. He is angry, and even his perpetual, oiled smile cannot hide his outrage. I invite him in, offer him a chair, a handful of gebbins. He does not move. He glares, and after a suitable time, smiling, he speaks.

"We are having a meeting, brother Seyt," he says. "A representative group of us have gathered to discuss your work so far. It would be well for you to attend. The discussion will be salient, instructive, and mandatory. In ten minutes. In my suite."

His *suite*. That tells you something, doesn't it? Let me finish with Dore.

The man chained in the micha tree cursed our brother soundly, promising to bring down all sorts of plagues for Dore's failure to observe the laws of hospitality. Dore couldn't waste any more time with him, so he apologized for his haste and took his departure. After some struggling and painful jabs of numbed feet and hands, the goat

moved on. Dore thought he saw another goat, just like his,
walking slowly across the plain, a man tied beneath it
just like our brother. This time Dore called out, but there
was no answer. Perhaps he was hallucinating.

Tere's rooms were filled with my brothers and sisters. In
the large central chamber was a lovely michawood table,
which I remembered used to be in the state dining room
in the South Wing. Around it were seated Tere, Ateichál,
Sabt, Shesarine, Joilliena, Vaelluin, Blin, Dyweyne, Elliavia, Peytheida, Loml, and several others whom I haven't
spoken to in many months. Chairs and stools were scattered about and filled the room with staring, uncompro-
mising faces: my brothers and sisters, my family, my critics,
my jury. Tere's other four rooms were also crowded and,
while these kinspeople could not see me, word of my
appearance was passed by messenger from group to group.
Nesp, ninth-oldest male (and thus the functioning male
member of our family next oldest to me), stood and faced
me as I hesitated on the threshold.

"Ah, Seyt," he said without enthusiasm, "won't you
come in?" I glanced at Tere. He said nothing, but
smiled dreadfully. I wanted to tell Nesp that I didn't think
I would come in, just to see the reaction.

"Thank you," I said. A seat had apparently been left for
me at the table, between Dyweyne and Joilliena, and I sat
uncomfortably.

"We wanted to discuss with you your journal of Dore's
pilgrimage," said Nesp. It took me a few moments to
remember where I had met him before, but after listening to him for a while I recalled that he was Vice-
president in Charge of Permeation for the Ploutos Corporation. I never liked him.

"Certainly," I said.

"Now, of course, you have been handed a difficult assignment. And, right off the bat here, at the outset, we'd
like to say that we appreciate the diligent way you've
handled the hot potato we passed to you. As far as
quantity goes, you're doing fine." Nesp paused, and I
looked around. No one had changed expression, but Sabt
nodded thoughtfully. "But you have a problem," said
Nesp. "We realize how formidable a task it must be to
chronicle the progress of a near-god—"

"A god," said Ateichál in her lowest voice.

"Yes, quite," said Nesp, looking a bit shaken. Could that

slip have been enough of a sin to warrant turning in his name and several pounds of flesh, for four digits and a place in the sun? We don't know. That's what I'm supposed to be doing, if they'd only let me alone. I'm codifying the faith.

"In any event," said Nesp nervously, "we have Our Father and Mother above, with light, rain, and grace. Dore for a time, as we all know, dwelt among us without any outward sign of his special calling. But is apparent, through the troubled days we have had since his departure, that it was through him that the spirit of Our Parents made itself manifest in our midst. Perhaps we have the divine motivation to unite with God, Our Parents, the River; but without Dore that hope is meaningless."

"Nicely put, brother Nesp," said Ateichál with an edge of impatience to her voice. "But I think what Seyt would like to hear is criticism more to the point. Style. Technique. Point of view."

"Yes," said Nesp, nearly sliding beneath the table in his fear, "yes, quite so. If we may direct our attention to those matters now, then. We, as your patrons and your audience, feel that if and when you stray from your precise assignment it is our duty to instruct you. We do not intend to interfere with your material as such. Please don't interpret this as an attempt to censor you or to discourage you in any way. But we are concerned with the matter of correct thought. Orthodoxy. A minimal adherence to the facts as we understand them. And here is our . . . complaint." Nesp smiled at me. I chewed my fingernail and nodded. "You tend to misrepresent both Our Parents and Dore. You allude to incidents in the past which are not official doctrine. Further, lately you have begun to invent what may be interpreted as myths impugning the well-known and documented moral character of our beloved pantheon."

There was a terrible silence. I was expected to defend myself.

"Thank you," I said. "I appreciate your interest. All I can say is that, of course, the work is yet incomplete, and perhaps you are developing an incorrect impression seeing it bit by bit. I think that it may be best for you to wait until I have finished, when you can see the grand play of narrative, action, suspense, humor, and other tricks. I have spent a great amount of time inventing an overlaying system of color, size, animal, plant, and number symbolism, of which you seem to be unaware, unfortunately. I am using inspirations at such a prodigious rate that my subconscious seems to have formed a protective callus. If I have wandered from my appointed path, forgive me and allow me to try to find it anew."

They all seemed very satisfied. Nesp rose and came over to me while the younger brothers and sisters were serving cider and donuts. He shook my hand and told me that he had enjoyed my giant. I thanked him. He told me to come down and visit him at the Corporation. I thanked him, looking over his shoulder at Tere and Ateichál, those rival pietists. Neither had moved from his seat, neither had spoken. They both were staring back at me, but I couldn't read the meaning of their looks.

I am severely chastised. Could this have happened if Dore had been here? An unfair question, a moot point. This started out to be so much fun. It seems sometimes that objects are designed to defeat their apparent purpose. Pens are made to enable one to write words that mask one's meaning. Frustration is the chief weapon of chaos. We don't have forever, and that saddens me.

A definitely anti-Ateichálian sentiment. All right, fellows. Starting tomorrow I will be better.

CHAPTER EIGHT

Free at Last

It's very quiet today.

There are no unsettling comings and goings of younger family members, asking me if they can be in my book. None of the older brothers and sisters have come in to stand, coughing, by the side of my desk until I acknowledge them. Everyone is leaving me alone today, alone to write my own impeachment, if I will. I feel as if I am auditioning for old age. With what morbid interest are they gathered, to watch me hastening to the thumbscrew and bastinado of Ateichál's sacred mission? Who cheers me on? Is there a section of the grandstand set aside for *my* fans?

Life along the River is exciting, healthful, never exhausting. But I can't claim that we live here without threats to our safety. Besides the somewhat shaky relations with our neighbors, whom we choose to ignore, there are strange beasts and vegetable menaces. Standing on the hill with the banner was not a simple task. I am rather glad that this history excused me from the job, which has been passed on to the eleventh-oldest male, a young man named Thib. We regret that Thib is not as suited, preferring to spend his spare time in dark and damp cellars. I told him that if he wished he could come to me for some pointers, but he never did. I fulfilled my obligation to him.

Happiness has always played a great part in the governing of our family. We were always happy, except for those times when devotional matters by their nature compelled us to grieve. But in the day-to-day maintenance of affairs we were quite contented. Each of us had his own particular area of interest, but each member of the family was concerned for everyone else's business as well. For an instance, I was always messing around in the meadows. Flowers, most frequently the yellow ones, were my sidekicks, though there was a limited amount of experiences which we could share. Nevertheless, I gained through Relp's association with lily pads, for example, or Vaelluin's water birds. She was so lost when they followed Dore down the River.

I don't know if I can convey to you, my now-and-then readers, the pervasive, nearly threatening quality of that *happiness*. We were reminded of it constantly. Our Mother told us often enough that she wept only that we might not have to. But that weeping, bless her soul if it needs it, was the only signal we had that our *happiness* was to some extent illusory. It kept us awake nights. Even today leaves will not grow on the lower branches of the micha tree under which she sat.

Our *happiness* was founded on beauty, pleasure, and fertility. Everyone is beautiful. Everyone has access to everything he desires. And Our Mother was fertile. She was a true mine of information and children. We, for some reason, are not. Our Mother always felt that her greatest sadness since the vanishing of her husband was in never seeing a grandchild. The dew of the subconscious, trampled upon by the cloddish feet of sensual, conscious life, lies all around us on the lawn of existence. The tributary streams of thought, arising from the collected dews and passing from our minds in the form of action, make us what we are. And our dews are beautiful dews. We think joy and sky and silver chalices. We have *happiness*. We dance to express ourselves, oftentimes stopping in the middle of some essential labor to hop up and down with strange, ecstatic expressions on our faces. Others in the chamber or hallway or field will clap their hands. It's a shame that Dore has to miss all this.

And now, sincerely, I want to thank Tere and Ateichál for their custodianship of our *happiness*. Without them we would have been lost in the bogs of individual interpretation. We would have wasted our energies in many fruitless directions, but they have sacrificed their own pleasures to the task of uniting us. We are a great team, moving forward into enlightenment together, watchful for those twin deceitful lords, Rumor and Heresy. Like Hermes, messenger of the gods, the bringer of the Word and the guide of the dead, Tere and Ateichál join the best of both worlds, the male and female principles combined without taint of carnality to the betterment of all concerned. And if Tere's masculinity is less apparent than it might be, and if Tere and Ateichál tend to differ over fine points of doctrine, well, it is only Our Father's way of reminding us that they —and us—are only mortal.

But not for long. I have a plan.

In a perfect democracy such as ours, where each member of the family has precisely the same opportunity to demonstrate merit, those who possess that merit cannot fail to be recognized. Inner worth makes itself known although, due to the total environment of equality, there is little personal gratification. Naturally, those with the most goodness are those least interested in reward, but it is a well-known fact that the existence and impartial availability of reward can act as a motivating factor for those unfortunates born with fewer of God's beneficences. If one can point to another, better person and try to emulate him, for whatever reasons, the results can only work for the general good.

Thus, I herewith introduce a system for canonization, contingent only on the acceptance of the sectarian leaders. My inspiration is obvious, and I beg the pardon of Tere and Ateichál for my lack of imagination, but I hasten to say that I see no reason why the scheme may not be as serviceable now as it has proved to be in the past.

St. Lucy, my researches indicate, was a virgin martyr of quite some time ago. She was an allround fine person and had several miraculous or horrible things happen to her. In art of the church she was pictured with two eyeballs on a dish. Every time you saw a holy lady with two eyes on a dish, it was St. Lucy, because of the similarity between her name and the Latin for "light." Now, if my plan were adopted, Ateichál could be *St. Ateichál*, not necessarily a virgin or martyr but possessed of enough mystic substance to easily defeat all competition. Future graphic representations of her could contain some symbol of her personality or her achievements. I don't know what.

Even Tere. *St. Tere*. Of course, like all new ideas it takes a bit of getting used to. But even the true saints were sometimes a mite ludicrous in the stories and myths that came to be collected. We read of St. Agatha, another in a long series of virgin martyrs. She had her breasts cut off for her faith, and is of course shown in paintings and mosaics as carrying them on a dish. Because of the shape of breasts on a dish she is the patron saint of bell founders. Who knows what Tere might end up to be? St. Apollonia had several teeth put out by an angry mob and became the divine one invoked against toothache. In time we might with a little effort build up an entire *Ars Medica* of helpful souls.

Say it with me now: St. Ateichál. St. Tere. A small beginning, but a sure and practical foundation for a great edifice of faith. Let us prepare now for the eventual passing of these two most generous of disciples. Let us build gorgeous things to house chips of their bone. Let us touch St. Tere and St. Ateichál whenever we can, and tell them of the cures they have achieved. Let us smile quietly at them when they pass. And let us not forget to be on the lookout for others who might, through demonstrations of virtue, be elevated to their lonely rank. Whoever proves that he lives "along Dore's way" may be eligible, and not just those who work miracles or talk to fish. Even a poor hagiographer.

Who will be the first to have a vision and build a shrine? Who will be the first to be eaten in Dore's name? Who will be the first to hold back the River's angry torrent with his simple faith? I tingle with anticipation. It is possible that this work may be equivalent to Moses' well-received Pentateuch, that I institute here the beginnings of something that will endure for all time, even as my avid-for-wealth Ploutonic brethren have indicated?

How quickly the dream ends. Two notes—

From Tere: "No. I will not accept *sainthood*."

From Ateichál, ironic in tone: "We lack virgins."

The rain begins. It is evening. The quiet is still undisturbed, and somehow the daily shower spatting on the narrow slit of a window makes the house even more soundless. I wish I could judge whether I am thought a fool, a dangerous enemy of the faith, or a pious workman who happened to miss his mark. I wish there were external guidelines; I wish my personal doubts didn't so mask the reality of my work. What I write is governed by what I feel, and (St.) Tere and (St.) Ateichál will not give me the time or the liberty to know what that is.

I would like to go for a walk with Dyweyne. I would like to walk beside her through the paneled, tiled, tapestry-hung halls of this house and talk, in low, loving, sentence-less tones. So much could be understood. Perhaps when I became afraid we would stop and I would touch her arm and she would lower her eyes and smile. People going by would pretend not to notice. Then we'd walk some more until I uncovered a new fear. Soon they'd all be gone. Dyweyne, why don't you come? Is it because you do not believe that I have anything to offer you?

Many material benefits can accrue from our association. Gain through inventiveness: In my function here as documenter of the faith I am in a position to make or break you, not that you have to worry about the latter. But I can set you up in a comfortable circumstance. I'm sure you appreciate that. As the companion of the official historian and biographer of our esteemed brother, you will receive extra attention. All eyes will be on you when we enter the cafeteria. Our sisters will copy your dress, your hair styles, your mannerisms. Stories will be written comparing me to Dore, telling of the pain of his memory and linking your name with others in clandestine attempts to ease your anguish.

I'll go out now, I think. I haven't taken a good ramble in months. How grow the hedges beyond the yard? Do the doglike animals still run wild, waiting to nip your ankles when you cross the property line? I think I will take a summer promenade, along the same rude highway that Dore followed, so many dreadful weeks ago. I will take my notebook and search for clues. And perhaps I will meet someone; perhaps Dyweyne will feel like leaving her humid cell for a while.

The house looks as if it has aged a century in the last few months. The paint on the outer walls and palisades and gabled towers is flaking off, as though our very residence weeps for Dore's return. The driveway is a long, gently curving path filled with white cinders. The crunching sound they make beneath my shoes always made me feel curiously *at home*, but today they are reminding me that as I walk down the hill I am going away from our country. I pass the various introductory monuments just within the huge, arching granite gates. Here is Loml's moss-covered obelisk, the oldest of them. It makes me seek out my own shattered pediment, which I began at the age of eight and destroyed at an early stage when I discovered that no one was watching. It is hidden by weeds. Here is Niln's red column, inscribed with meaningless pictographs. There is a new, sad equestrian statue of Dore,

built by Talavesía, Dúnilaea and Lalichë. A bronze tablet
with Yord's name engraved on it; a marble column; several simple pillars; a boulder with strange figures carved
on it which Aniatrese tells me are copied from Sir Arthur
Conan Doyle's "Adventure of the Dancing Men," a Sher-
lock Holmes rouser. I pass by these and other remarks,
under the permanently open stone portals, and out into
the wide world of mystery and disease.

About a quarter mile down the road I came to the
home of the Fourth family, residence of the lovely
Melithiel who is famed in song and legend. As no one
seemed to be out and about, I saluted as I passed. I went
on, and I saw the forest track where Dore turned away
from the road. I didn't.

Continuing down the road, I saw a weather-worn road-
side stand, where the way is met by the drive of the Fifth
family. It was constructed of warped boards and sections
of cardboard, badly fitted together and threatening to surrender entirely at any time. A wooden sign stood in the
uncut grass, with letters of chalk dispersed and emaciated
by the evening's rain. The sign was unreadable, but I saw
pints of strawberries for sale, and apples, corn, raw gebbins, beans, tomatoes, and flowers. The whole thing glad-
dened me; I think that it's because I was gratified to see
someone still working for himself, still providing, still contending successfully, with enough left over to offer in
trade. Our poor attempt at growing chata embarrassed
me, because I know that the Fifths here must resent us
more for it. I went up to the stand and said hello.

"Howdy," said a young boy, perhaps six or seven years
old. He was shy and after his first volley retired behind
his grandfather's chair. The old man, I recalled, was Donald Five, an honest patriarchal sort. He touched the child's
head affectionately. His son and daughter-in-law, An-
drew and Bonny Five, ran the farm now. I supposed Mr.
Donald had been put to pasture here at the stand. Is it
worse than a stone-damp throne?

"Onions and carrots are cheap today," said Donald
Five. I felt my throat choke with emotion; which one?

"Fine," I said. "And let me have a box of the berries,
okay?"

"Anything else?"

"No, that's all for today."

"That's, um, three-six, and one," said the old man, putting my purchases in a stained paper bag.

"Do you have to have cash?" I asked in humiliation. "You see, I'm a First, and I don't usually carry money."

"You're a First, are you?" said the old man suspiciously. "I beg your pardon, but I'm afraid I didn't recognize you." I could see that he didn't believe me. I got out my card, and he examined it for a moment. "I'm sorry, sir, that I caused you this trouble," he said politely, but, I could sense, bitterly. "Take these with our compliments." I took the package and hurried down the road, still away from our house. I had wanted to talk to those people, to let them know of my sudden and dilettante affection, and I only succeeded in playing the lord.

I saw no one for several hundred yards and my thoughts and unpracticed guilts tortured me. I saw Les and Larry Eleven, with whom I played when I was much younger and less discriminating. They were standing on a hill in their yard, looking out over the River with their older sister, Maureen. I yelled to them, and they turned and waved. I went up their driveway and climbed the hill to join them.

"Hi," I said, nervously.

"Hi," said Les. "Haven't seen you for a long time."

"Been busy," I said.

Larry touched Maureen's shoulder and I heard him say, *"For eight years!"*

Maureen smiled at me. "You're a First, aren't you?" she said. I nodded, pretending to be interested in anything else. "You're the one who's writing the story of that other one, the one who went down there, aren't you?" She pointed her bare arm down the River. I nodded again.

"How did you know that?" I asked, kicking a stone down the hill toward the water.

"She gets around," said Larry, grinning.

Maureen stood by my side and pressed herself against me. "I get around," she said. "I come and go."

"She means she comes and she goes *down*," said Les.

"I'm sorry," I said, frightened of their cupidity, "I'm not carrying any cash."

The three were silent, shocked. Maureen stared at me with her head slightly turned, her forehead furrowed. Larry took her arm. "Come on," he said. "Let's go back to the house." His brother knelt and picked up some small stones.

I was afraid that he was going to throw them at me, but he turned his back and ignored me completely, and threw them out into the River. I might have been horrified by his sacrilege, as would about half the other members of our family.

I stayed on the road, coming at last to a small side street which I followed to the estate of the Twentyseventh family. This clan lived in many individual, identically constructed houses; they were painted white or yellow or pale green with a flagstone walk and a picture window, much the same as their ancestors had for centuries on our forsaken shelter, Earth. I took a deep breath and marched up the path to one of the houses.

I rang the doorbell and was answered by a large woman, strong and red and parturient. "These are for you," I said, pressing the bag of vegetables into her hands.

"For me? Thanks," she said, closing the door. I caught it before it shut.

"Wait," I said, "I'd like to ask you a few questions."

"I don't know. We don't want to buy nothing."

"I assure you I'm not selling anything," I said. "Did you ever know Dore First?"

"He one of them that live in that crazy big house up to the end of the road?" she asked.

"Yes, ma'am."

"They're crazy. Don't know the one you mean, he never been by here, ain't likely any of 'em ever will. They're all crazy. Is that all right?"

"Yes, ma'am, thank you," I said and headed home. The road was filled with holes, and I stumbled over large rocks a few times. All the way I felt very vulnerable. It was a new feeling, and I welcomed it. I tried to think of a way of avoiding the Fifth's fruit stand; when I passed it, it had been shut up for the evening.

My room is dark, and it suits me now. I believe that this afternoon I went by a milestone in my development. From struggling artist I have graduated to suffering poet. It is not a happy milestone, and I will endeavor to get through this stage as quickly as possible. What's next? Angry young man? Bored celebrity?

My room is dark; there are two narrow windows set in the heavy stones of the outer wall, and they let in little light. For illumination I depend on tallow candles with which Joilliena supplies me, scorning the overhead fluorescents. The windows are rectangular, standing tall on scanty bases. They are divided into dozens of small regular parallelograms by lines of gray lead. On one of the windows two of the parallelograms are colored; a transparent red and a yellow pane have been inserted by a whimsical glazier. On the other window there is a green and an orange pane, as well as an uncolored pane with a very detailed tempera painting of a scholar in a wheelbarrow.

My room is rectangular, just wide enough for my bed along one short wall. The long walls run parallel to the major axis of the house itself, and thus the two windows look out, theoretically, on the yard of chairs and the vacant throne of Our Mother. But an addition was built jutting out obliquely from the house. On the ground floor the addition makes with the house a sort of open courtyard or bay, and there is a charming cloistered walk in the new wing. On the grass we have placed a table with a large umbrella and four white aluminum chairs. The new wing has a tower which obstructs my view. In the tower is a single small window, about twelve inches long and six inches high.

Dore loved our house. No, I don't mean just the family and Our Parents and the fallow ambience; he loved the house, its inanimate construction, the insane angles and explosions of rooms. Dore was basically a homebody. He never went out to eat. I don't recall his ever once taking someone dancing or getting up a softball game. This may be the reason Ateichál has avoided the rigors of a missionary tactic: We are the Chosen, of course, but we were Chosen for something that had previously occurred. There is little use in going out to convince others that the greatest spiritual guide has already been here, had nothing to say, and left without promise. Ours is a strange faith.

Dore was enthusiastic on the job. He made friends quickly and used materials wisely. He *fit in*. All nature rejoiced to his presence. When he walked across the lawn the grass in his footsteps stretched out toward him, rather than clinging crushed to the ground. From Dore's small, constant smile I gathered that the tiny blades praised him in their grassy tongue, inaudible to us of course, but related closely to the dialects of his woody friends. It was from his trees that we first got a hint of his pervasive influence: One day, as we labored early in the bean fields, we were astounded to hear the branches of the trees groaning and rustling in perfect four-part harmony, with elegant counterpoints, themes, restatements, all a verdant orchestration of a Scottish pibroch or dirge, according to Cillenavei. We had never heard anything like it, and we knew that no one of us had the skill to teach the trees that music. The trees missed him, more, I'm sure, than my meadows would miss me. Soon we became blasé to swarms of bees humming descants to his absence, or River-bank pebbles spontaneously forming intricate mandalas with his portrait in the center.

Dore's established leadership enables us to bear our guilt as well as we do. We console ourselves with trifles. If one of us looks sad, as though he is considering his part in the sacrifice of our brother, someone will say, "What more did he have to look forward to? His hopes were realized. As it was, he had but forty more years of the same. Now he's with Our Parents, doing whatever they do in the great beyond." It's not much, but it's all we have.

Success and personal satisfaction are rarely achieved on one's own. As is usually the case, Dore's happiness was the result of an amicable partnership. This brings me back to my discussion of my courtship of Dyweyne, Dore's amica-ble partner. It has been some time since I have spoken with her. She avoids me. Yes, but why? It may be because I hide something foul among my motives, to which I my-self am yet blind. Or, I choose to believe, because she fears the tempest of feeling that I stir in her. She is too aware of the role she plays, that of grieving mistress; we must assure her that for her, also, life goes on. And here life means . . . me.

We are separated by a distinction of concepts. She clung closely to home, and, meaningfully, to the house itself; her interest was her gardening. She cared most deeply for her small plots of cultivated soil, blooming near her win-dow and cultured by her conscious volition. I, on the other hand, though as charmed by nature and yellow blossoms as she, prefer the wilder sort, untamed and raw. Therein lies the flaw of difference. My mind is creative and free, able to value beauty wherever I find it; and Dyweyne must rule it, bring it forth exactly as she fancies, in a structured, homelike context. But I still love her. She has withdrawn since Dore's journey, but if only she would trust me I know that I could open her up.

It is still so quiet. I expect Dyweyne, Joilliena, even Tere.

If only life mirrored the theater the way theater mirrors life. Then I might have more hope. To a great extent, certainly, my frustration is engendered by the environment: the order and lawfulness of the "city." Here, in this thoroughly governed house, Dyweyne has the resources of custom and system on which to rely. If only I could transport her "to another part of the forest," if, like the abandonment of the town in *Love's L. Lost*, or *Midsummer N.'s Dream*, or *As Y. L. It*, we could bid goodby to this locked-in house and speak with lovers' eyes in the faerie green world, then she'd have difficulty dismissing me.

Seasons change, feelings change. Thomas Nashe, in his unduly ignored *Summer's Last Will and Testament*, can afford from his patronized distance to mock the fool. But he himself says, "Give a scholar wine, going to his book, or being about to invent, it sets a new point on his wit, it glazeth it, it scours it, it gives him *acumen*. . . ." Who will deny that love is my wine? Later Nashe quotes Aristotle: "There is no excellent knowledge without mixture of madness." My madness is Dyweyne; hers is, sadly, Dore. I add the "sadly" for the cause is so futile. Dyweyne, let me make you happy again. Come back, my sister, come back to me and to all of us.

I heard the tiniest rustle of paper. A note has been slipped beneath my door. Is it from her? No. It is FROM THE DESK OF . . . *Loml*. It is in Tere's lovely, flowing script. It says, "You cannot avoid the assignment with fancy footwork. Do you not recall that Dore is still on his goat? Get him off at once. All best, Tere."

Fortunately, Dore came at last to the simple hut of a poor peat-cutter. The honest serf cut Dore loose and carried him into the decrepit shack, where he and his wife nursed our brother back to health. Dore, in his gratitude, gave the goat to the good peasant.

Part THREE

What Fairer Soul E'er Dwelt This Mortal Cell

CHAPTER NINE

A Moral Dilemma

Do you know why this is ridiculous? Because we don't know that any of this ever happened. It's silly to write it down. Someday these words are going to be quoted as gospel; the very topographical discrepancies will be passed off as "miracles." We ought at least to send somebody out to see that Dore isn't lying in a ditch just a little way from here. I mentioned this to Tere this morning and he said, "Wonderful! What a great idea. We should send someone to find Dore, even as he was sent to find Our Father. We could have his words firsthand and end this disruptive squabbling. But whom could we send?"

Who, indeed, *eldest son.*

The squabbling to which Tere refers is the first symptom of a genuine religious war. I had not given my brother and his sparring partner, Ateichál, credit enough for their zeal. I had assumed that the matter of their differing attitudes toward Dore was the equivalent of cocktail party chatter. I apologize. Their respective creeds are shaping up nicely now, and are demanding much too much of our time. Petitions are being circulated, loyalty oaths are being signed, processions of masked monks block the hallways, and my little history is due to become a major battleground. Tere made a few statements in the *Times-Register*, and when Ateichál asked for equal space for

rebuttal she was denied. I suppose that Yord was still
miffed at what our undefiled sister did with Mylvelane, his
best drama and book reviewer. Now Yord is "not available," and Ateichál has requested my aid.

Their strategy is simply this: Any thought which is
printed, either here or in the paper, without subsequent
attack is generally believed to be true. This is not so much
a logical condition as it is a fault of human nature. A long-
standing or constant idea is often equated with a true one.
So Tere and Ateichál want to get out as many tracts as
they can, hoping that the other will overlook some important point, which will then be incorporated in the growing Mystery of Dore.

Tere made some preliminary remarks concerning the
platform of his new party, the Fraternal. He said that
while Ateichál was correct in deifying Dore, a step which
ought to have been taken long ago, she was wrong in
denying that his mission to learn the secrets of the River
was equal to his search for Our Father. Such a denial was
an implied limitation on Dore's goodness and ability.

Ateichál answered this by saying that Tere's insistence
on Dore's contract with us mortals is impious. Tere assumes that we here in the house are worthy of such salvation, an assumption never enunciated or even hinted by
Our Parents or Dore. Ateichál admits that such an eventual reconciliation among all the members of our family
could occur; she is not willing to promise it with assurance.

The Humanist Party, the liberal wing, temporarily leaderless with the removal to the backyard pen of its last four
chairmen, still firmly denies the divinity of Dore.

And everyone is aware of the power I wield. I am in-
fluencing public opinion with each chapter I write. Does
Dore seem to be seeking Our Father? Does he seem to be
gathering facts about the River and our world? The question of the merits of beliefs, Tere's, Ateichál's, *anyone's*,
is to a great extent political. During other periods of time
the war against heresy was a war for the *status quo*, more
than a passionate defense of doctrine. But here the situation is reversed; everyone has left the *status quo*, for it
was so obviously stagnant and sterile. What we have now
is a venomous battle to establish Something, and I feel it is
my part to stay neutral, giving the facts as I see them. I've
gotten myself into enough trouble.

I, uh, think that both Tere and Ateichál's viewpoints have a lot to commend themselves. I question, however, the tendency to put Our Parents in the background, obscured for the moment by Dore's brilliant ascendancy.

Lalichë laughs. "That's it, Seyt," she says. "You tell them."

Dore and his friend Glorian walked on freshly, enjoying the beauty of the forest and the meadows. So far from our house, Dore had difficulty understanding the harsh accents of his green-growing intimates, but he laughed often and passed on the choicest witticisms to Glorian. Glorian said little, and when Dore inquired what was troubling him, Glorian replied, "Our time is coming. I must prepare myself." This was all the information that Dore could get, and it left him puzzled and frightened.

One day, about a month after Dore outwitted the giant Despair, Glorian turned to our brother. "Do you recall the lady Narlinia von Glech?" he asked.

"Von Glech?" said Dore, pretending that he could not place the name of that deceitful woman. "Was she not the sister of Snolli von Glech, who so basely stole my small treasure?"

"That's her," said Glorian grimly. "The castle of old Baron von Glech is not far from here. I trust you'll want to drop in."

Dore was astonished. "Why, yes. I'd feel more secure with Battlefriend at my side."

"And perhaps you'd care to call on Narlinia, too?" Dore did not reply; Glorian chuckled. "But you must know that the way will be no less filled with dangers than it has been in the past."

"That's a shame," said Dore. "I'd like a long, soaky bath and a warm meal."

"I know of a small kingdom ahead where you might be able to achieve those ends, and a clean bed thrown into the bargain. King Herodes is an old-time acquaintance of mine."

"Like Dr. Dread?" said Dore sarcastically.

"I'm sorry," said Glorian, "but you're well aware that everything that's happened has strengthened your moral fiber. That's what I'm for."

"How far to the king's house?"

Glorian just smiled again and pointed. They traveled until late in the afternoon. From the top of a hill Dore looked down into a large valley, bounded on the farther side by rolling green hills and, beyond, a distant, rugged range of mountains. "The River runs just on the other side of those peaks," said Glorian, and Dore spent some time gazing at them with interest.

In the middle of the valley was a small walled town. Dore could see what appeared to be the palace in the center of the village, with towers roofed with bright gold. The two men descended into the valley and reached the entrance to the town just before the rains began, as the guards were locking the gates.

"Who seeks entrance to Monthurst, capital of his majesty, King Herodes?" challenged a mailed soldier.

"It is I, Glorian of the Knowledge, and I bring Dore, a worthy pilgrim."

"How are you, Glorian?" called the soldier.

"Fine. What's new in Monthurst?" said the strange companion, now tall and strong, with long arms and a broad, sturdy back. His hair was brown and fell to his shoulders. He wore a long velvet robe, gathered at the waist by a rope woven of golden threads. On his head was a silver crown with five points, each topped with a polished onyx.

"Nothing, really. Go on in, the king'll be glad to see you."

Glorian turned to Dore and said, "See, they know me here. Relax." Dore grimaced and followed his friend into the town. They went straight to the king's palace, which was built of large stone blocks set together without mortar. Around the building were many gardens and fountains, and the townsfolk seemed happy and prosperous. The guards at the palace door recognized Glorian immediately, and he and Dore were let in.

"Ah, Glorian!" said King Herodes with delight. "It's been a long time. You should come more often; you're always welcome."

"Thank you, King," said Glorian. "I'd like to introduce my friend, Dore First, who has traveled a great distance and is weary. Dore, meet King Herodes of Monthurst."

"A friend of Glorian's . . ." said the king, smiling.

"I'm honored," said Dore with a small, tactful bow.

"Has he met the Queen?" the king asked Glorian.

"Not yet, I believe," said Glorian. "I'm sure he would appreciate a good meal, though, before the rigors of courtly life."

"Of course." The king clapped his hands, and attendants hurried off to prepare the banquet. The king put his arm around Dore and escorted him from the hall. "Wait until you meet my wife. Queen Corylis is the most beautiful woman in the world. Glorian will tell you that I wouldn't settle for second best. Wait until you see her. Better yet, you'll just have to sleep with her tonight."

Dore was horrified. Hospitality was one thing, but Dore couldn't accept the responsibility. There is good promiscuity and bad promiscuity, and another man's wife is an example of the latter. Our Mother drummed this into our heads every four days. We had to have *some* standards.

"I appreciate the offer, King Herodes," said Dore slowly, "but I don't think I could allow myself the liberty. I'm a pilgrim, you see, and we have a sort of code."

The king looked angry. "You'll sleep with Corylis and like it, or I'll be deeply insulted. And your friend here will no doubt instruct you that it is never good policy to offend a powerful monarch within his own palace. Until dinner, then." And the king went away.

Dyweyne will be pleased, I think. I choose to believe that the political frenzy in the house has driven her even deeper into her widow's seclusion, but I will admit that I have added to her agitation. Dyweyne, come out and let the grateful sun kiss your shining eyes. Can you not see the way Dore has grown on these pages? He was intelligent, and that means that he was adaptable: able to mature and change his outlook, blessed though provincial, and learn to live a life of honor and innocence among the screaming ills of the world. I have done well by your lover, and I want to do well by you. You can't cling to the past forever, you know. Come out; it'll do you good.

I think that in the midst of the tempestuous political situation in the house at the moment, the development of jealousies and amative excesses can only work to our disadvantage. A certain unity is required, for it seems that for the most part it has been the solitary, unskillful, visionary thinkers who have been put to the Question. We all heard Nieb ask jokingly if Dore had a hairpiece. Two months ago we would have laughed for hours, but today we sat uncomfortably in our seats and waited for the green- or blue-cowled brethren to lead him away. It is all a matter of a strange sort of affection between Tere and

Ateichál; somehow this is the working out of their unreal betrothal.

Joilliena, whom I have not forgotten but merely set aside, must feel a jealousy for Dyweyne, who must know jealousy for the ladies Dore meets in my spurious history. I am ashamed to admit my jealousy for Dore and for the blinding light of his love which dims my own poor flame. None of this is healthy or safe. United in mutual esteem we could act sensibly in each other's defense. Jealousy stirs the mind to restlessness. One falls victim to an unjust way of thinking; one misrepresents the words of others, hunting within each sentence for fuel to feed that hideous passion. Does this not sound like the symptoms afflicting our virginal sister and our flouncing brother?

A brief bulletin has arrived from the latter, during my preceding meander of ideas. Lalichë will read it, as I am much too concerned with Dore's coming epiphany to care.

" 'A high-level official of the newly formed Fraternal Party,' " says my little sister, innocent of factional ties, " 'defined Ateichál's error as one of observation and interpretation, and absolved her from what he termed "willful impiety, maliciously or otherwise designed to undermine the faith of our family." Dore, the statement continued, obviously had two missions, each precisely as important as the other. Ateichál has not seen the necessity for each, and is thus unable to accept their duality. We pray for her enlightenment.' "

Lalichë and I wait for our sister's reply. It is not long in coming:

" 'From her small, austere chamber in the North Tower, Ateichál issued the following statement of position: "Any presumption of motive is blasphemy; any limitation of action is heresy. I will not dictate Our holy Brother's inspirations, and I will not demand redemption at his hands." I thank Tere for his meaningless absolution, and deeply regret that, until such time as he assumes responsibility for his faulty belief, I cannot extend the same to him.' "

I certainly wish they'd get together and talk things over. I don't understand the difficulty: They make an ideal couple. Tere's inclinations in no way endanger Ateichál's purity. Besides, I've seen the plans for the new and larger heretic compound.

Such are the knotty trials of love. All the half-learned,

misunderstood concepts of honor and respect get mixed up
with personal pride to make a classic approach-avoidance
situation. Dore would not have minded a free amatory
encounter, but his instincts and his training denied him
access to another man's chosen partner.

"King Herodes is a nice enough fellow," said Dore,
"but he won't understand that I can't make love to his
wife. In the first place, where's *he* going to sleep? What's
he going to do while I'm with his queen, read a good
book?"

Glorian was inspecting the vast collection of armor and
weapons in the palace's trophy room. He put down an
impressive double-edged sword and sighed. "Dore, there
are different customs in different places. You're not still
back in that insane house of yours. You ought to be glad.
You ought to open yourself to new ideas."

Dore paced impatiently. "And you're the one who's
always lecturing me on ethics and wholesome thoughts."

"But you're under compulsion. The situation doesn't
present you with a choice."

"What if I make one anyway?" asked Dore solemnly.

"You mean refuse the king?"

"Yes."

Glorian turned and faced Dore. "If you accept, Herodes' expert ministers will disguise you so that the queen
herself won't recognize you. I've been here often, and I've
seen many a duplicate Herodes in these halls. In the
morning no one will say a word, but the king will beam
at you as if you were a long-lost son. You'll be expected
to thank him and tell him how good it was. That will make
him happy. If you refuse, he will be humiliated before his
subjects, even though they will never learn of the thing.
But *he* will know. And the only way he can save his
honor is to kill you."

"Have you ever been up there?" asked Dore with a wry
expression. Glorian did not answer. "Well," said Dore,
"let's go."

"To find the king?"

"No. Back to the forest."

Glorian put his hand roughly on Dore's shoulder. "No,"
he said, "this time you're going to stay and see this
through. Do not think that your path here is predestined,
and that you cannot follow a worthy course. You have
not even thought on the matter, and already you wish to

flee to the unthreatening woods. You have passed beyond them, although you refuse to admit it. Your initial tests were physical, of danger to life and limb. You had no problem with monsters, human and otherwise. Then you contended with intellectual hazards. Now, finally, you are fronted with questions of virtue, to prove your spiritual mettle. If you run to your forests you forfeit all you've gained, and no second chance. Sun and rain and greenery are wonderful, but a man's life is sadly none of these things. There are more strains of courage than merely facing a sword."

Dore was confused for a moment and made no reply. At last he said, "And if I don't accept? If the king's subtle ministers prepare another in my place?"

"Excellent!" said Glorian, slapping Dore's mighty back. "And I know the very man. A member of the king's Praetorian, Belodicos by name."

"Is this man trustworthy?"

"Eminently," said Glorian. "I saved his life once."

"How fortunate," said Dore. "Let us send for him at once." In a short time Belodicos the guard appeared before Dore, and the situation was explained to him. He, too, was hesitant to accept the duty, but his debt to Glorian persuaded him. He would visit the offices of Treneos and Meronidas after the dinner hour and be transformed into an image of King Herodes. Then, after dark, he would enter the royal bedchamber and join the queen, careful to awaken and depart before the first light of morning. Belodicos agreed doubtfully and left Dore and Glorian alone in the trophy room.

The two men were unaware that their conversation had been overheard by Neliastra, a young servant girl engaged in polishing the armor, who had hidden herself behind an arras when Dore, Glorian, and Herodes had entered the hall. She hurried straight to Queen Corylis and told of the plans of the king, Dore, and Belodicos.

"I admire the virtue of the man Dore," said the queen, "and I sympathize with the plight of the honest Belodicos. But, lo, these many years, how I have grown to hate the stink of spirit gum and grease paint! And simple Herodes believes that he has fooled me every time. How like a courtesan I feel, to be displayed to all who visit, and bestowed as a gift, like some golden cup or matched stainless flatware. I must end this charade."

Neliastra spoke up diffidently. "Great Queen," she said, "I do not wish to advise one exalted above my low degree, but hearken to my scheme. The tool of the strangers' plan, Belodicos of the youthful heart, has been my true beloved, though circumstance has forced our paths asunder. I, a servant to your grace, and he, a stalwart of our lord's defense, now rarely meet to share love's joy. Allow me, your faithful bondmaid, to visit those same councilors and have myself made new in your image. Then myself, a grateful hollow queen, and he, king but of my soul, will meet one night for moments of luxury. All innocent, we; and thou shalt have thy joke."

"Delightful!" said the queen, and ordered preparations to be made.

"Look, Seyt—" says Sabt, Ateichál's press representative. Before he can finish, Lalichë shows him to a chair and gives him a large illustrated book to read while I continue my work. Lalichë is becoming indispensable. If she were only a few years older, I'd ply her with candy. My story is simple enough and moving well toward its foreseeable climax, so I will grant Sabt his audience.

"Audience?" he says with distaste. "You're lucky that Ateichál instructed me to meet with you. She's being very careful to point out your frequent inaccuracies, you know; you should be glad that she worries so over your puny soul." I could ask Sabt what Ateichál considers to be the value of a soul without eternal life or any kind of Deific Judgment. But, no doubt, the system of their dogma provides them with answers.

"What can I do for you, my brother?" I ask politely.

"Ateichál requests that you refrain from repeating the vile heresies of our kin; even for purposes of instruction the mere voicing of these beliefs is injurious to the human and therefore assailable maintenance of truth." Sometimes Sabt sounds like a pamphlet of an uplifting nature.

"Whom do you feel to be the most dangerous enemies of your faith?" I ask craftily.

"There are several whose variant ideas may lead to the corruption of straight thinking. For instance, Chel speaks of the identity of Dore's two missions. The very elevation of Dore's quest for Riverlore to an equality with his reunion with Our Father is bold heresy. But Chel takes the Terian error further. He equates the three offices of the

River—Water, Channel, and ineffable Current—with the three members of our pantheon. Our Father, he claims, is the fleshly manifestation of the River's sacred and life-giving fluid. When it is given direction, as Our Father's essence was through the agency of Our Mother, the result is a Current, a force, in our experience it is Dore, who proceeds from Our Father and is made appreciable to us by Our Mother. While Ateichál applauds the sense of copartnership and is amused by the neatness of the analogy, she has seen fit to induce Chel to retract his speculations. Chel may be consulted on the matter in the backyard pen any day before five."

"That *is* very interesting," I say, "but even I can see the impertinence in his suppositions."

"Really?" says Sabt hopefully. "You're coming along, Seyt. We are also dead set against Dalonelle's argument that in Dore the participation of Our Father's will *replaced* the human element we all share. Dore may be as holy and godlike as Our Parents, but he was also, as you have endeavored to make clear, a functioning and normal man." Sabt allows me a smile, as reward for my spiritual progress.

"I have tried to show that," I say modestly. "What exactly is Tere's position these days?"

Sabt scowls. "Tere is the arch-heresiac. He is beyond redemption and, thus, beyond the power of Ateichál's cleansing service. In demanding the good favor of Dore, he demands that Dore's humanity be dominant over his godhead, a concept unique in its absurdity. He suggests that Dore's identity with Our Parents goes no further than a 'willing accord' with their designs. There is nothing salvageable from his apostasy, and no castigation could be equal to his effrontery."

"Thank you, Sabt," I say, chuckling, "for listing so carefully the solecisms Ateichál wants avoided." Sabt looks horrified, nods, and runs out.

"Perhaps if you get them at each other's throats," says Lalichë, "they'll leave you alone."

Late that night Dore and Glorian conceived a great hunger, and resolved to creep downstairs and find themselves a midnight meal. They followed the tortuous passageways of the palace and at last came upon the back stairway, which Glorian knew was situated near the largest of the king's kitchens. In a short while they were in the pantry, and had made for themselves a fine snack of leftover meat pies and warm beer. As they sat eating they heard the sound of footsteps coming down the stairs. The two men hid, for fear they would be discovered and reported by a guardsman, and thus Dore's ruse would be revealed.

"I wonder who left these lights burning," said a voice. "I'll have the heads of those scullery maids yet."

"Quiet," said Glorian softly, "it's King Herodes himself, no doubt tired of his hiding and seeking refreshment."

"It figures," said Dore fearfully.

"Aha!" said the king angrily. "Someone's been stealing himself a meal at my expense. Here are the remains of a hastily enjoyed supper. The thief didn't even have the consideration to clean up after himself. Hmmm, I wonder . . ."

The king pulled back the hanging behind which Dore and Glorian had concealed themselves. "You!" said the king. "Are you not with my queen? Have you then so mischievously rejected my gifts?"

"No, my lord," said the Queen Corylis, stepping out from behind another hanging. "He is not sharing my favors. And, for that reason, I believe he has acted with honor. I fear that is more than you have done. Only out of love and obedience to you have I bedded with your heroes, each of whom I have detested and resented for having stolen my time with you. Perhaps you have acted out of love and husbandly pride, but even a king may act foolishly, though no one may tell him so. Do not tax this man's friendship, for we owe him much."

"You are right, my wife," said Herodes ashamedly. "I will never do it again. I wish to reward the friend of Glorian. What boon is most seemly to you?"

"Perhaps we could endow a seat at the University," said Corylis. "He could lecture to our citizens on morality and the splendid virtues."

"I thank you, your majesties," said Dore humbly, "but I trust you will understand when I say that I am anxious to continue my quest. Indeed, I hope to leave with your blessings in the morning."

The rulers of Monthurst were disappointed, but promised to aid him in whatever way they could. "Materially, you understand, we're a bit strapped," said King Herodes with embarrassment. "But we can provide you with good

advice, warm feelings, and magical contrivances to speed
you on your way."

"Anything you can spare would be welcome," said Dore.

"Well, then, my reluctant lover," said Queen Corylis
with a smile, "you seem to be one who questions his
goals. You have come far and through many strange adventures, and now you begin to wonder if the outcome
will justify it all. Perhaps you think that those who sent
you on this quest were hasty and ill-advised. Perhaps you
think the pot of gold at the end of your trials is nothing
more than a phantasm to lure you to your doom. But
look at it this way: You've come all this distance; it
would be a shame to turn back now."

"My wife is right. Go on and seek your fortune. If
you went home you'd regret it for the rest of your life. Ah,
you young people. I wish I could join you."

The queen clapped her hands, and an attendant appeared and was instructed to fetch a certain parchment.
Dore marveled at the discipline of the servants, as it was
well after midnight. After a brief pause the attendant returned with the ancient manuscript.

"Carry this with you at all times," said Corylis. "It will
guard you against night blindness, injuries of the arches
and feet, ecstasies connected with bad food, and perhaps
against discomforts due to the common cold." Dore bowed
and tucked the amulet inside his girdle. "I understand you
seek the domain of Baron von Glech," said the queen.
"Glorian knows the way, I'm sure, but still I feel it my
duty to warn you of the cave of Love. There are many
dangers there, some so voluptuous as to make the teeth
rot in your mouth just thinking of them. But other evils
there are which are fatal in hidden ways. It is best to give
that treacherous place your back and pass well away from
its sensuous invitations."

"I'll bet Dore doesn't," says Lalichë.

"There is only one matter that I don't comprehend,"
said King Herodes. "Who is it that entered the queen's
chamber this evening?"

"So you *do* spy!" said Corylis with amusement. "Your
actions have not been so charitable after all. *The Voyeur
King*, what a surpassingly fine title for an operetta."

"We shall discuss that later," said Herodes angrily. "I
desire to have my question answered." The four people
climbed the stairs to the royal boudoir, and on the way

Glorian and Corylis explained their schemes. Everyone had a good laugh at the baroque turn of events. At the door to the chamber the king himself dismissed the confused guards, who of course believed their liege to be inside, sound asleep. Glorian, Dore, Herodes, and Corylis peeked into the bedroom and saw Belodicos, disguised as the king, and Neliastra, playing the queen, asleep in each other's arms. "Oh!" whispered the four fondly as they quietly shut the door again.

"My man Belodicos will have a strange awakening in the morning," said Herodes, shaking his head.

"Oh, I don't know," said Corylis. "I'm sure he's recognized his sweetheart by now. We ought to do something for them, too. They've been star-crossed enough."

"Shall I give them half my kingdom?" asked Herodes generously.

"No, I think not, my lord," said the queen. "We'll talk about it another time." And the two rulers and Glorian and Dore sought their beds for a shortened night's rest. In the morning everyone waved goodby, and our brother and his companion set out once more for whatever reasons Dore had.

" 'Whatever reasons.' A clever evasion," says Lalichë. "Without a weathercock army in this house it's difficult to decide if Tere or Ateichál deserves the commitment. Do you think they really love each other?"

"It's not the tides," I say distractedly, as I notice that Tere has been reading over my shoulder for some time.

"Hello, Seyt," he says, smiling, holding out his political hand. Despite all the handshaking he's been doing it's still fat and it's still wet.

"Hello, Tere. How's it going?"

"We have them on the run now. Orthodoxy versus orthopraxy. We have right on our side; Ateichál ought to realize that even in a trivial way our case is the stronger: We have twice the god to rely on that she has. And her point is that she *can't* rely on him. Small comfort for the simple man, eh? Like you and me. Our sister is growing too big for her alb. I take it from your writings that you don't approve of her methods. Her inquisition lacks restraint and taste. Would you care to see a list of her intended defendants?"

I admit that I would. Tere insists that I not reveal the source of his information. I promise. The list reads:

"Loml, Sabt (?), Joilliena, Nesp, Aniatrese, Talavesía, Jelt, Thib, Lalichë (?), Seyt (!)."

"She doesn't plan to rule a large congregation, does she? There won't be many left when she's through," I say, my eye continuously straying to the *(!)* after my name. Lalichë has run out of the room, crying.

"Don't worry, Seyt," says Tere, pressing my thigh so that I will be reassured. "We, the Fraternal Party, were formed for the express purpose of stopping this nonsense. Help us, Seyt. I don't mean by joining the party and raising funds. But a lot of the younger brothers and sisters still follow this fairy tale of yours. You and they can aid us. And perhaps those on this list won't have to turn in their names for numbers, after all. Why don't you think it over, Seyt? Come see me in the morning and we'll talk about it." Tere grins and leaves. The floppy silk crown that he wears makes me sick.

CHAPTER TEN

The Final Struggle

On the way back from breakfast this morning I saw a large gathering of people by the bulletin board. Usually the notices on the board are trivial and totally unexciting: bookcases for sale; invitations to join the River's Ally, a service organization that picks up papers around the yard; sometimes a lost and found notice. No one ever reads the bulletins except the people who put them up. We have a lot of Harvest Moon Balls and Ring Dances that go totally unattended. But today there were *two* announcements worth reading.

The first statement was written with a felt-tip pen on a large rectangle of purple construction paper. It seemed to me to be Ateichál's acknowledgment of the waning of her influence, demonstrating to us all the indomitable nature of (our) human spirit, in the face of her terrorist tactics. The notice said, "Our brother Tere has made certain accusations concerning my investigation into corrupt devotional practices. These accusations were made with the intent to discredit me and my associates, and to support his own malicious doctrine. It is well-known that Tere was in full accord with the measures which I felt necessary; after his desertion of the Benevolent Party he adopted those same measures for his own uses. A list of potential violators of orthodox thought has been circulated, purporting to belong to me. I deny this vile calumny, and further declare my belief that the list of future martyrs was drawn up by the Fraternal Party, possibly by Tere himself. Yours in Dore, Ateichál."

When I finished reading the notice I shook my head. Shesarine turned to me and laughed. "Intrigue," she said. "Busy little wheels."

"See that you don't get caught up in them," I said, and we both laughed again.

Our brother Stug, a classicist and a recluse, quoted

us a line: " 'One man has one sort of ill, someone else has another, and surely no one under the Sun is happy in the truest meaning of the word.' Theognis. It will be most difficult to avoid those wheels, Seyt. Have you read the other yet? We enter a new era, and trade Scylla for Charybdis."

Shesarine and I turned back to the bulletin board and read the other announcement. This one was elegantly done in a flowing hand on a white card. It said simply, "Tere, the chairman of the Fraternal Party, Guardian of the Faith and Scourer of Heretics, proclaims through his seigniory as Eldest Son his accession to the office of first Kalp of Home. All are requested to acknowledge the authority of the Kalp in matters domestic and foreign, spiritual and temporal. Long live Kalp Tere, successor to Dore." Beneath this was added in pencil, "Reception at eleven, in the Map Room. Refreshments and prizes."

"What's a Kalp?" asked Shesarine.

"I'm not sure," I said. "Let's go to the Map Room now and see if anyone else is there."

The Map Room is at the end of the main corridor in the North Wing. It is a very comfortable room with thick carpeting and richly stained panels, designed to produce a mood of confidence and ease. Tere had chosen well. The tables had been pushed against the walls and folding chairs had been set up. One large table had been placed at one end of the room, and Tere sat there when we came in. Many of the chairs were already occupied; when Tere saw me he came over to speak with us.

"Ah, Seyt!" he said, beaming. "You've seen the proclamation, eh? What do you think, lad? You'll be glad to shake this moist old hand now, eh?"

"Congratulations, Tere," I said slowly. "Is your coup legal?"

"Why not? I just thought of it first, and I *am* eldest son."

"*Acting* eldest son," I reminded him.

Tere frowned. "Do you not believe that Dore has been accepted into the bosom of Our Parents?"

"Of course I believe it," I said nervously, "but I think you should have acted more democratically."

"What's undemocratic about it?" Tere asked, beginning

to grow dangerously irritable. "You can't elect an eldest son."

I decided to change the subject. "What about Ateichál? She made some fierce indictments."

"The last gasps of a drowning woman," Tere said happily. "The familiar *tu quoque* fallacy. She can't excuse herself by making her own denunciations." I didn't think it necessary to ask Tere if Ateichál's accusations were true.

"What does your title mean?" asked Shesarine.

"Oh," said Tere with his famous smile, "you like it? It's a neat combination of things. Mostly 'caliph,' because my power is basically the same. The caliphs were supposed to be the successors to Mohammed, who, like Dore, left no son."

"Dore left no power, either," said Shesarine unwisely. Tere lifted his eyebrows, but made no reply. He continued:

"The caliphs, and the Kalp, serve as custodians of the true belief and protector of the faithful. I want you to come to me as you would to Dore; feel free to bring me your problems and questions. My door will be open twenty-four hours a day. Also 'Kalp' brings in associations of other kinds. *Kalpa,* for instance, is the Hindu term for one cycle in the recurring pattern of creation and dissolution. A kalpa is one day of Brahma, equal to four billion three hundred and twenty million years. I think that adds a sense of continuity and promise. *Calpe* is also the old name for the Rock of Gibraltar, a tie with Our Parents' pleasingly odd and tainted world."

"That's real fine," I said, and came back to my room, forfeiting the free cupcakes and lemonade.

Dore and Glorian walked toward the hills with the early sun rising behind them, among the invariably white clouds of day. With the village of Monthurst at their backs, the men looked forward to a lonely march over the heights to the sacred River. It had been months since Dore had been in the healing presence of the mystic waterway, and he was thin and pale.

"You have made great progress in your spiritual development," said Glorian. "To tell the truth, I didn't think you'd make it this far. You're really very noble."

"Thank you," said Dore. "But whatever gain I've made has cost me in anguish and pains of the soul. I see more clearly now, but what I see strikes to my very heart. I see the pettiness of people, their inability to solve their minuscule problems, their needless languishing over trivia when the great and universal ills go neglected. I am oppressed by the meanness of people; I cannot enjoy my expanded humanity as long as I must suffer the ignoble and niggardly strivings of others."

"Don't be condescending. You're not finished yet."

"Well, Glorian my friend," said Dore cheerfully, "I want to thank you for helping me along my way. I never would have made it if it hadn't been for you."

"Don't exaggerate my role. You had it inside you all the time. I just forced you to bring it out."

"No, really; I really mean it. Thanks a lot."

"That's all right," said Glorian generously. "Tell me, if you had to summarize all that you've been through, what do you consider to be the main points?"

"Well now, that's a tough question." Dore paused for a moment, staring ahead at the misty gray peaks. "I think the important thing is dedication and hard work. A lot of people have an idea, but aren't willing to do the actual sweat to achieve success. If I had to advise a youngster, I'd say, 'Work hard, get plenty of rest, eat well, and never forget that there are plenty of people trying to take your place.' It's all a matter of having a clean follow-through. I like to see youngsters starting at an early age, in an organized situation, and going right on through to their adult lives. Of course, we have to remember that children shouldn't be expected to be as proficient as adults; that would be unfair to them, because those years should be a time of fun and learning. But I believe that any boy or girl who sets his goals high and never loses sight of them, who practices constantly and lives clean, can, with a few breaks, make a big name for himself."

"That's very interesting, Dore. What do you think have been the greatest hazards for you in your own amazing career?" Glorian smiled to himself, for his plan was succeeding. If he could get Dore talking, our brother might not notice the cave of Love. Glorian gives me a warning look and motions me to be quiet.

"I think the prime danger is overconfidence," said Dore. "A lot of times I go out there after a big victory, and I feel like nothing can stop me. There's a very real thing in emotional preparation. For instance, if I, say, have just beaten a powerful sorcerer or notorious villain, I come off a strong win with an edge of self-confidence. Now if I meet something less threatening, like a grass dragon or a robber, I'm in for a battle. Supposing I run across a letmoth. Well, two or three of those things can bleed a grown man dry before he can yell for help. But if I'm feeling overconfident I won't think twice about challenging it. Now the letmoth is going to be tough, because by itself it's not so much of a match for me; it's what we call 'up' for the bout, while I'm not going to be as motivated. I believe that's important for a youngster; it's difficult, I know, but they should try to put out one hundred percent. If it's worth doing, you might as well do it to the best of your ability."

"Thank you very much, Dore, for sharing your thoughts with me. But I'm afraid we can't continue this, as much as I would like to. We're just about out of time; these cliffs have grown steep, and they'll take all of our attention for a while."

"You're lucky," says Thib, just in from Tere's reception, "Tere and Ateichál are so busy now they won't notice what you're doing. Or me. Or the rest of us. Unless they need an example, like what you just had Dore say."

"What do you mean?" I ask equitably.

"Dore said any boy or girl can make a name for himself, with the right breaks. He suggests that he'd be happy to help us, too. Ateichál might jump on that if she needs something."

"I guess the Kalp would aid me," I say, with an ironic expression. Thib doesn't notice. He's a very simple and musty lad.

"Tere's too busy signing autographs," says Thib. "He's going to dress up in a clown suit and visit the nursery later."

The hills had, indeed, grown more rugged. The day was drawing to its close; already the sun had dipped below the ice-clad western peaks and the air in the heights was putting on its evening chill. "We'd better start looking for shelter," said Dore. "A cold rain and a bitter night won't do my aging bones any good." Glorian made no reply, but followed Dore's way up the stony path with his fingers crossed.

"Ah!" said our brother with relief, "there's a cave

ahead, and enough daylight left to gather what meager
fuel the mountain sprites provide."

"Beware that cave, my friend. It is the very cave of
Love against which Queen Corylis wisely warned you."

"Well, I'm not falling into any pits, Glorian. We can
just sit under a ledge or something. Just for the night."

"I've accompanied many a young man who spent one
night for the rest of his life. Come away, now. We may
find less ill-famed lodgings higher up."

"No," said Dore stubbornly. "I'm not looking for
trouble there. But I'm tired and hungry, and I see no good
reason to go further tonight. It's about time that I add
initiative to my new-found virtues. I have followed you
for months. This one time we'll do it my way."

"As you will, my friend," said Glorian sadly. "But if you
must stop there, you shall do it without my assistance. I
will await you on the other side of these mountains; below
the point where an underground rivulet emerges and tum-
bles over a precipice, you will see a castle on an island.
This is the stronghold of Baron von Glech. In seven days
I will give you up and return whence I came. Good luck,
Dore, and be prudent. From the Baron's gate it is not far
to the River and your goal. I hope to see you on the
other side. Goodby." Before Dore could answer, Glorian
had disappeared. Our brother shook his head in bewilder-
ment, and continued the climb to the cave of Love.

I suppose the fatal festivals of love are usually celebrated by poets and dramatists. Love is one of those topics
we can't discuss rationally. If someone has something negative to say about romance, he's branded as a laughable
misogynist or a pervert. But there are times when the
course of true love is not only not smooth, it's absolutely
vicious. That is what Glorian meant by warning Dore to
avoid the cave, and I can interpret the episode as my
subconscious trying to warn me to dim my own pilot
light of love.

I have been receiving notes written in a handwriting that
is pitiably easy to identify: Joilliena's. They have all been
variations on a single theme, that my love for Dyweyne
is injurious to all three of us. Love sits on my shoulder
like an impatient carrion-eater, waiting for me to stumble.
I balance my affections and my duty, so that Ateichál,
grown vindictive, or the Kalp may find nothing disrespect-
ful enough to demand immediate correction. But those

tender feelings creep in; Dyweyne was Dore's chief confidante, the one person in the house who *knows* what he thought. Why haven't I interviewed her? Why hasn't Tere or Ateichál brought her into the poisonous center of their struggle? Dyweyne has given up her garden flowers to languish in a twilit corner; perhaps she has turned our minds to forget her, and damns her own intervention with guilt.

Dyweyne is the gentlest, most honest person I've ever known. I risk here some nameless form of heresy in attributing the hyperboles to someone not of the Holy Three. But my experience informs me. Some of us think she has special knowledge, and that she awaits the return of Dore and her own elevation to godhood. Ateichál, with her cold, sexless devotion to Dore, rages whenever she hears it. Not only does a return of Dore negate her beliefs, but her jealousy has grown to unreasonable proportions. The Kalp might welcome our brother's homecoming on theological grounds, but I'm certain that demotion to second-eldest male would upset him. Others of us do not believe that Dyweyne has any secret information, but is merely playing the part of the bereaved wife, a new Our Mother in tasteful style. Would Ateichál be willing to accept a reincarnation of Our Mother in Dyweyne, as she plays with the idea of Our Father's spirit possessing Dore?

Ateichál has fallen on hard times. She has grown desperate in the need to prove her eminence, and the more she struggles the more we shake our heads and feel sorry for her. Brothers and sisters are turning up numbered in the backyard pen with increasing frequency, as Ateichál strives to impress us with her diligence. But it is to no avail. For all Tere's unwholesome character, his claim to authority beats out anything Ateichál has to offer. But still she shrieks her complaints. We see very little of her these days. She hides her icy Brunhildic charms within her tower and plots her futile strategies. No one takes her very seriously, and so she behaves like a frustrated child, intent merely on injury. We are getting together a list of names subscribing to a request that Tere do something about her. She's keeping us awake nights with her rantings, as they echo through the moonlit corridors.

Her efforts are producing strange results. Besides encouraging Tere in his puerile bid for control, Ateichál is throwing the radical members of our family together.

Previously the irregular minds canceled each other out; their various strangenesses were easy to ignore, and they refused to compromise with any party or any person. Now, in self-defense, the curious prodigies are banding together and hammering out a weird, disreputable creed. Their first step was to throw into the River the amber pendant each of us wears. Our Mother firmly believed in the efficacy of amber in preventing fits in children and in guarding their devotion. Their chief idea is that the River is nothing but a *river* and, similarly, that neither Dore nor yet Our Parents were in any way remarkable. The radicals, calling themselves the Mudsitters, can be easily identified as they flaunt their pendantless chests in open society.

Turmoil and revolution in their best guises serve to tear down ancient and meaningless customs, in favor of practical social reform. Ateichál may indeed be driving us further from her own brand of religion, but her admonitions of doom blast like lightning bolts the moldy foundations of our world. And, as Plutarch would have us believe, lightning is the fertilizer of the waters. Ateichál may make no progress with the sense of her bellows, but their very iconoclastic force may do us all some good. I will pause for a moment in anticipation of some inspiration, some sudden insight now that I have discovered her true rewarding purpose.

Proper knowledge defeats the shouting minions of emotion. Will that do? I wonder if I can frame that sensibly.

Proper knowledge. That of course means *correct* knowledge, free from heresy. That is what we're all seeking, some more assiduously than others. By emotion my Muse probably means the angry deeds of Ateichál. Our one defense, then, is to finally locate *Truth* and hide behind it. The whole framework of science and service which we have built since Dore's departure is based on false premises and superficial reasoning. This structure must be destroyed in order to make room for *Truth*.

A hastily scribbled note from Ateichál: "That's what I'm trying to do! Best, A."

A card from the Kalp, himself: "That's what I'm trying to do! Your friend, brother, and ruler, Kalp Tere I." (I wonder where the Tere II, by implication, is going to come from.)

We reap what we have sown, and what we reap is

confusion. I could dream that Our Father visited me and advised me that irritability opens one to the corrosion of error, and the dream would have relevance. We should save our energy, which we are dissipating in numerous projects, and direct our wills toward building a better world for all of us. My flash of perception has faded.

Sabt, Ateichál's uneasy nuncio, has brought a formal statement which our sister of chastity desires read here, rather than merely posted on the board. I am secretly pleased at this acknowledgment of my universal acclaim and, of course, I allow Sabt to proceed. He refuses to let me copy his notes, but forces me to transcribe his oral proclamation. There is a conservative clinging to old forms at work here that I dislike; it contradicts the clear thinking which I have just outlined, and is a definite symptom of Ateichál's inability to grasp our needs.

In any event, her declaration: "To the brothers and sisters, made sacred by Dore's transient blessing, greetings. I feel it is my duty to my faithful adherents to reply in some way to Tere's scandalous actions of this morning. It is clear to everyone that the assumption of any sort of authority in this family is not only immoral but illegal. If Tere can force submission with his upstart party of rascals, he has not become our leader; he is, in effect, no more than the boss of a military takeover of the shakiest sort. I call for unity, forgiveness for past differences, and firmness of purpose in removing the scoundrel from his invented office. Tere deserves no more than the back of our hand, most certainly not our bowed knee. I for one will never recognize his supremacy, and I will have nothing but the wrath I feel for Tere for anyone who will. Yours in Dore, only in Dore and Our Parents, Ateichál."

"She's softening a bit, isn't she?" I ask Sabt, who is already starting for the door.

"What? Huh? What soft?" he says, fidgeting to be away.

"The way she signs the thing. She's adding Our Parents now."

"Oh, yes, she feels that will make her case a bit more palatable. She's getting ready a new platform. She wants to incorporate a couple of novel extrapolations that we suggested."

"Is it too early to tell me?" I ask, knowing that in his insecure job Sabt would desire to please anyone.

"No, I suppose not. Ateichál is going to believe that

perhaps Dore's education concerning the River *is* of importance, but only insofar as it is absorbed in his search for Our Father. The search and the education are equal, because they follow as cause and effect. There is still but one aspect to be worshiped, but the one aspect has two sides. The key point is going to be the mitigating influence of Our Mother. If Dore were human, her mission for him would have been unjust and cruel. If Dore were divine, her years of shaping him for the ordeal would have been pointless. So Dore must be a mixture, and his burden must be a 'hypostasis' or conglomerate of the two, indivisible motives. I believe that Ateichál has been misrepresented as steadfastly claiming that his relationship to us is of no future importance. But Tere's insistence on separating Dore's will into unrelated parts is offensive to intelligent minds."

Perhaps Sabt realizes that he is giving Ateichál's opponents time to build their refutations. He puts his hand to his mouth and opens his eyes wide; then he turns and runs from the room.

Dore climbed the path to the cave of Love, and found to his delight that the closer he approached the easier the way became. There was a small quantity of dry brush around the mouth of the cave, and Dore gathered it and built himself a fire to warm the provisions with which King Herodes had supplied him. He dared not enter the cave too deeply for fear of the infamous dangers, but he sat just within the protective overhang and watched the rain. After a time he stretched out upon the stony floor and fell asleep.

In the morning he discovered that he was not at the mouth of the cave. With a sudden surge of fear he saw that he was in a large cavern, evidently deep within the mountain. But unlike Despair's noxious lair, the cavern was well-lit by an unknown source, and the air was perfumed and pleasant. Still, Dore was anxious to be on his way across the mountains.

"You need not hurry," said a lilting voice behind him. Dore turned to demand his release, but he was stricken speechless; he saw a lovely person of indeterminate sex and surpassing physical beauty. Dore searched the flowing gown for signs of identifying bulges, but could make no evaluation. The face and form, and the infinite grace of the person fascinated Dore. "I am Love," said the person, "and I welcome you to my temple. Many people seek me out, and many find me by chance. It is no matter how you came here. You may enjoy my hospitality as long as you like, though I require your devotion. But mine is an easy worship." Love smiled and pointed to a smooth walk bounded by Love's sacred roses. "This way, my friend. Your way through here is shorter than across the mountains, and you will find that your body's restless hungers will trouble you only when you will them. Stay as long as you like, and if you want anything, just ask." Before Dore could reply, Love vanished.

Dore followed the path for a few minutes, on his guard lest the honeyed words of Love prove treacherous, and the way be strewn with monsters and pitfalls. But he found none, and soon entered another large underground vault. The room was filled on all sides with great chests of polished micha and bronze. Some of the chests were forced open, and by each of these knelt a man. Dore left the path and joined one of them. The man was filthy and unkempt; his hair and beard had grown to a prodigious length as if he had been locked in a foul dungeon for many years. He sat by his chest and sorted an unbelievable treasure: gold plate and jewelry, precious gems cut and uncut, silver in unrefined chunks and stamped into coins. When the man saw Dore he jumped up and began striking our brother. The blows were weak, and soon the man tired and fell to the floor.

"It's mine," whispered the man. "Gold, coins, buy them all. I'll show them."

"Let me help you," said Dore, aware that the love of treasure had held the wretch captive for many years. "You have been on your journey far too long. Your friends must think you dead."

"I have been gone four days," said the man. "Do not trick me. This is mine; find your own." Dore shrugged and left the man to his avarice. Other men in similar condition looked up as he passed, but Dore saw that there was an unlimited supply of unopened chests. He shuddered and continued on his way. He was unaware that the day had passed as he stared at the old man's riches.

The way opened into a third cavern. This one was arranged into compartments furnished with handsome couches and tables, all of different design and construction. The separate rooms were divided by heavy drapes of various pleasing colors and materials. Dore looked into one apartment and saw a woman seated at a round table of polished obsidian. The woman was grossly fat, so large that Dore doubted that she could ever walk away from her feast. Periodically a young man or woman entered and set a new course before her.

The woman waved to Dore. "Come, sit beside me and eat. I'll never be able to finish this myself." Dore had not eaten well in some time, even at the palace of Herodes, and he thanked the woman and joined her. Fantastically elegant dishes appeared and disappeared on the table as the young waiters came in their endless train. Dore enjoyed each course more than the last, as the food grew more and more exotic and sensuous. The woman talked not at all; to Dore she seemed an indefatigable engine of consumption, eating her way through each delicacy only until something else was brought. Soon Dore's desire waned as he watched the woman's relentless progress. He stood regretfully, wishing he could take something with him, but he knew that he could easily fall into bondage to his palate as had the obese woman. She didn't even notice when Dore left. Our brother did not know that he had spent the entire night at her table.

The fourth cavern was dimly lit, with luxurious silks and laces hanging from poles and carelessly draped over cushions on the floor. A soft music was issuing from an indefinable location, and the atmosphere was warm and sultry. One of Love's young pages met Dore on the path.

"Have you come from the salon of viands?" asked the youth.

"Of course," said Dore impatiently. "Is this the way out?"

"Yes, you are making surprisingly good progress. You have time to rest after your meal." Dore looked about him and saw many other travelers taking their ease among the comforts of the room. He decided that a short nap might be refreshing. He followed the page to a fairly unoccupied area. He was soon asleep, but awoke to the strident pleading of another man.

"Won't you *please* fix this pillow for me?" asked the man, his voice urgent but slow.

"Fix your pillow? You can do it yourself and let me sleep," said Dore irritably.

"Ah, but I would so like it if you would do me this

favor. Relaxing here is so . . . relaxing. I could stay here forever."

"Yes, I suppose, but I for one have an errand."

"So do I. So have we all. But the point is, not now. In a while I'll be up and away. Until then will you fix my pillow?"

"All right," said Dore, hoping to quiet the man's demands. As he stood he threw off the soporific influence of the chamber. He plumped the pillow to the other's pleasure and picked his way through the dormant figures to the path. He had slept away the entire second day.

"Seyt," calls Peytheida from the corridor, interrupting my excellent allegory. "Come on, it's important." I tell her that I can't leave my tale.

The fifth cave was the cave of pride, where a bespectacled clerk seated at a large desk skillfully aroused that feeling within our brother's breast, and antagonized Dore into a defensive and vain attitude before allowing him to enter. The cave was filled with others who had received the same treatment, and they contended amongst themselves with boasting and swaggering heroics. Our brother competed mindlessly for some time until one of the others in the noisy chamber mentioned his murder of his parents and usurpation of his father's throne. The very words "father" and "mother" brought Dore back to himself, and he cursed his foolishness. He departed that senseless place as quickly as he could, but he had spent the night of the second day unknowingly.

"Are you going to go through all seven, Seyt?" asks Peytheida. "You'll miss your chance if you don't hurry." In a minute.

Along the path Dore found a couch set out for travelers. Sitting on it was a handsome young man. Dore greeted the man, who invited Dore to rest for a moment and talk. Dore was still angry with himself for falling into the trap of pride, and he thought it best to regain his head before he contended with any more of Love's trials. The man spoke to him pleasantly for a time, asking questions about Dore, our house, and his goals. Soon the questions probed deeper, and Dore began to reveal his most buried desires and frustrations.

"I know exactly what you mean," said the young man at one point. "I always wanted a loving wife and children. Fortunately, I met the most beautiful girl and we're blessed with three wonderful children. I can't wait to get home to see them. I've got pictures. . . ." The man went on, touching on each of Dore's secret wants. Our brother liked the man, but soon his envy colored his thoughts, and he grew dissatisfied and angry. He considered abandoning his quest, which surely could never produce the ends he now knew he craved more than anything. The man talked on, and Dore grew more envious until he was nearly at the point of physical violence.

"Stop!" cried Dore, shaken and despairing.

A note from Tere: "You were doing okay, but Dore's divine, remember? Human temptations are meaningless. It's unrealistic to show him subject to such trivialities as envy. Just a caution, nothing serious. Best, the Kalp."

Of course, I wasn't finished. Dore's inner resources rescued him just in time, and he shook off the mesmeric bonds of the youth's conversation. He wished the young man the best of luck and continued on his way. While he languished in the coils of covetousness, the third day passed.

"We're going without you," says Peytheida. I shake my head in impatience and put down my pen.

What a strange time it was, too. Apparently one of my reckless remarks caused a bit of comment. Aniatrese and Peytheida decided that it *had* been a long time since they had talked with Dyweyne. Now, although Dyweyne has been shy of us since Dore's departure, we still all think of her with affection. It isn't just I who realized her special virtues. Indeed, even Tere has been moved to send her a valentine, different and more sentimental than those he sends the customers of his Ploutos Corporation. I do not doubt that the intent was political, but it demonstrates Dyweyne's distinction.

Several of us spent this afternoon standing outside her door, singing River carols. We hoped she would enjoy them as she pined in her bare cell. We had brought cookies and milk with us, and had prepared a sort of party. Auel and Lalichë had made paper planes and houses to put on her walls, and Peytheida had written a meandering ode. But we sang four long carols and received no reaction. We knocked on her door but she didn't answer. Finally we went down to the rec room and ate the cookies.

"Maybe you scared her with what you said before," said Lalichë.

"What do you mean?" I asked. I rarely pay attention to what I write.

"About Dyweyne's becoming a new reality of Our Mother. That's certainly a thankless task. I know I wouldn't want to," said my little sister with a shudder.

"I didn't really mean it that way," I said evasively.

"Tell us, Seyt," said Aniatrese, our Beauty Queen, "how *did* you mean it?"

I thought for a second or two. "I might have meant that the greater part of a parent's identity is the reflected honor of the children. Certainly the number of children in our family allowed Our Mother a certain bargaining pressure with the lesser families. In our case, of course, that honor means Dore. Perhaps our respect for Our Mother would be less if it were not for him." The subject quickly grew tiresome, and I excused myself and returned to my room. But I continued to think.

On certain dirt days Tere would set up a blackboard near Our Mother's throne. She would ramble in her moist way, and Tere would seize on some of her more intelligible remarks. Afterward there would be a list of key words on the board: *harvest, prosperity, peace, plenty, harmony, sharing, refuge.* None of us could recall what connection they had with what Our Mother said; but thinking back, it seems certain that she was looking forward with optimism. It would be rank heresy now to contradict that hopefulness; Our Father and Dore's evaporations are shrouded in mystery, but Our Mother's was accessible to us all. It must be through her, then, that any future occult manifestations be channeled. And who is the most likely medium? Dyweyne. Perhaps that is what I meant.

This train of reasoning opens the door to whole new vistas of theological error. Neither Ateichál nor Tere have been too receptive in the past to an allegorical interpretation of the record of our family. Our Parents' life on Earth, their voyage and trials here, and the subsequent founding of our family must be dealt with literally. This is what I've done in this history. But I have felt free to coat Dore's adventures, with which no one else can disagree as they are my own private figments, with a subtle flavoring of metaphor. This is for the instruction of the younger children, who will not swallow straight moral tales unless they appear as parables.

I suppose that Tere and Ateichál are not wholly happy with what I've done, but they both seem content to let me finish and allow the work to be judged on its merits. This is eminently fair, and I'm grateful. And, I guess, they are correct in worrying about misinterpretations of my symbology by less astute critics. Nevertheless, the simple instance of allegory ought not to be dismissed as criminal. And my doctrinal speculations I defend by claiming the immunity of the social commentator in a free culture. I do not wish to drive Dyweyne cringing into her corner, waiting for the soggy spirit of Our Mother to possess her, and I do not wish to provoke our spiritual leaders by making the suggestion. Part of my duty as I see it is to guard against an onset of inflexibility. It is good for us to flex.

The sixth cavern that Dore came to was similar to the den of sloth. The air was warm and spiced with unusual incenses, and the room was provided with many sorts of pleasurable furnishings, most decorated after an erotic theme. Dore was wise enough to understand the purpose and danger of this place, particularly when his suspicions were confirmed by the sight of scores of couples coupling. He intended to pass by without pausing, but he was called by a beautiful young woman, apparently a fellow traveler caught by the ambush of desire. She looked so desperate that Dore decided to help her.

"Come and love me," she said, in a low moaning voice that Dore found peculiarly exciting.

"I'm afraid I can't," said Dore apologetically. "I have to meet someone."

The woman smiled sensuously, and trailed her fingertips up Dore's arm and down across his chest. "Surely it won't take you *that* long," she said.

Dore was embarrassed, but also strangely aroused. The woman was almost supernaturally beautiful, and her perfect body was not at all concealed by the filmy stuff she wore. Her half-closed eyes, her writhings, and her black lingerie inflamed our brother, but he remembered the trouble he'd had with strange women before. He told the lovely creature that he was sorry, but that he had to go. "If you like, I think it would be best if you left with me," he said.

The woman licked her lips. "If you want me, take me," she said.

"That's not what I mean. If you just give in to your carnal desires, you'll be here forever. You'll never reach your destination."

The young woman looked at Dore curiously. "I *work* here," she said.

"Oh," said Dore, embarrassed once more. He was not aware of the passage of time, but he spent the third night staring at her. He gathered his thoughts with an effort of will and found the path again.

The last cavern was a sudden change from the lasciviousness of the previous ones. Here the walls of the stone hall were lined with cases of weapons and armor. The floor of the great chamber was crowded with fighting men. Dore tried to pass through unnoticed, but he was accosted by a large bearded man with a short Roman sword. The man spoke in a rough and unpleasant dialect, and Dore understood little. But he did make out that he was being challenged. Our brother tried to ignore it. The man continued, refusing to let Dore pass, and his insults grew fouler. Finally he combined his abuse with a physical attack, and Dore was compelled to defend himself.

Strangely, the bearded man allowed Dore time to find a sword. When Dore had armed himself, his attacker smiled and renewed his assault. Dore was too involved in protecting himself to worry about Glorian, and the fourth day passed as he struggled with the belligerent savage. Dore's arm did not weaken and he fought without tiring, but neither he nor his opponent could win an advantage. At last Dore penetrated the barbarian's guard and cut almost completely through the man's neck. The bearded head teetered for a moment, then settled back in place. The barbarian grunted and felt his neck, showed his rotting teeth in a hostile grin, and began the battle anew.

Dore was disgusted. He threw his sword at the other's feet and turned away. Behind him the man cursed and threatened, but our brother never replied. He located the path and left the last of Love's caverns. As soon as he passed through, the light from behind was extinguished, and Dore was on a rough and dangerous trail. Having abandoned the mystic benefits of Love, his body suddenly informed him that it was weary and hungry after four days abstinence. Dore laid himself on the ground and slept. When he awoke he ate the last of his provisions and stumbled through the darkness of the cave until he reached the exit. He spent most of the fifth day finding his way out, but when darkness came he had emerged on a high, windy cliff. He slept on a narrow ledge that night.

It took Dore all of the sixth day to pick his way down the side of the mountain. In the late afternoon he spied the underground stream that Glorian had described, as it splashed out of the rock like blood from a wound. It fell a great distance, finally forming a large pool at the base of the cliff. A thick cloud of mist hid most of the ground, but Dore could see the island in the middle of the pool, and the castle of Baron Glaub von Glech. Our brother was heartened at sight of his goal, and after the rains he finished his descent by moons' light. He stopped that night in a small grove on the verge of the pool, and the restful forest noises soothed him to sleep.

Dore was awakened by a firm hand on his shoulder. "Come on," said a merry voice, "wake up. I'd nearly given up on you."

"Is that you, Glorian?" asked Dore groggily.

"Yes, and your ultimate test is scheduled for this afternoon. Get up and find your scattered wits. We have plans to make."

Dore opened his eyes regretfully. Glorian stood beside him, smiling broadly. Our brother rose and winced at the pain of his sore muscles. "It was a rough trip," said Dore.

"But you made it. I'm proud of you, though I knew you could do it."

"I suppose you intended for me to go through there all along."

Glorian laughed. "You're like a good sword now, hardened by fire and water. You've mastered the theory; now comes the real thing."

Dore made a wry face, wondering if Glorian really believed that all the past perils were just overture. "What happens now?" he asked.

"Let us find the ferry," said Glorian, "and I will explain the situation." The two men walked slowly, leaving the copse of losperns and following the edge of the water. Glorian said that the crown and jeweled scabbard had been sold and were irretrievable, but that Battlefriend was locked in the Baron's private vault. Dore's sword was necessary symbolically and actually for our brother's success. He couldn't hope to locate Our Father without it, for Our Father had forged it himself from two broken pieces of something.

"Don't forget that Dore's trying to learn about the River, too," says Lalichë. She's right. I was just going to mention that.

The process of initiation is a theme that pleads for development. Every person experiences a time of *becoming*, not only the heroes who must be properly trained and indoctrinated. The grand unfolding of Dore's initiation into the mysteries can be read as the maturing and assumption of adult life by each of his brothers and sisters. Perhaps that is the universal motive that makes the quest so fascinating; every person leaves the shell of childhood behind, and to do so means accepting and contending with the horrors of maturity. The unknown terrors of self-reliance, the necessity to acknowledge the rights of others, the agonies of sexual awareness are the trials and mission of the general. The Master Bard of Bedford, that anonymous dramatist of superfluous wit, author of *A Faust Comedy* and the lost *Tesselatia*, deals with the dichotomy of internal and external pursuits in the *Tragedy of Godric of Essex*. He is unfortunately unable to make any meaningful statement about their relative importance. He is a frustrating playwright to read, and his is one of the first books I consigned to the River's care.

Oftentimes we may notice that a hero's external problems are in reality projections of the internal distress of a moral nature which he is currently enduring. This way the reader is treated to a superficial struggle in physical terms, and a more satisfying though hidden victory on an implicit level. I have discovered that in the best literature everything means something else. Speaking from my own experience, I can say that this gets to be a great drain on the author. I would have been content to confront Dore with a succession of giant lampreys, Danton's toads, or woodcats. There is little skill in doing that, unless the reader can be duped into believing that one dragon represents the evils of Intolerance, a second identical monster Science, and a third the Papacy. But I have taken the difficult route.

"We have a difficult road still ahead of us," said Glorian. "We must plan surely, for the stronghold of the Von Glechs is a tough nut to crack. Getting there will be simple enough; but recovering your needful sword and escaping, and following the stream to the River, will be a harrowing experience. Are you up to it, my lad?"

"No," said Dore sarcastically. "I think I'll go home now."

"You're a real puzzle sometimes," said Glorian. "Now listen carefully. We must assume that the Von Glechs are expecting you. If you go in there with me, they'll be put on the defensive and be more likely to treat you roughly. They know me well and have no great liking for me. But I will change my appearance to an identity with which they are unfamiliar, and I will enter the castle separately. You must find your sword and obtain it on your own. In that I can be of no help, as I have my own work to do; but I do not doubt that the woman Narlinia may give you aid. After you have achieved your ends, whatever they may be, you are to meet me at the front gate at midnight. The gate will be locked, and the guards will allow no one in or out until morning. But if you have your Battlefriend I shall be able to pass you through."

"I don't know," said Dore worriedly. "Couldn't I just forget it? I've come this far without the sword."

"And you'll go no farther without it. Don't be afraid. The matter is not so doubtful as it sounds."

"What if I don't—" Dore was interrupted by a sneeze on the other side of a low hedge along the path. He stopped short, an alarmed look on his face. Glorian reached over the hedge and pulled up a small boy.

"Who are you?" asked Dore sternly.

"If it please your lordship," said the boy fearfully, "my name is Regelard, son of Norble, porter in service to the Baron. I could not help overhearing your conversation, through no mischief of my own."

"You could not help skulking behind that hedge, eh?" said Dore.

"No, sir. You are Dore, of the First family?" asked the boy with respect.

"Yes," said Dore with some amusement. "Am I famous even here?"

"No, sir, but the Lady Narlinia told some funny tales of you. I recognized you by her description and by your speeches."

"What shall we do with him?" asked Glorian.

"I can be of great help to you," said the boy.

"Perhaps so," said Dore thoughtfully. "We must either trust him or dispose of him, which I cannot bear considering. All right, Regelard, now you are one of us. Do our plans sound faulty in any way?"

"No, sir," said the boy with a grin, "they're just fine. And, if it please your lordship, my friends call me 'Bucky.' 'Regelard' stinks."

"All right, Bucky," said Dore, clapping his new friend on the back and smiling. The three companions soon reached the small pier where they waited for the ferry to the island of the Baron von Glech.

"Seyt?" asks Lalichë, who interrupts me less frequently since she began writing her memoirs. "Ateichál is here." I am surprised. Our unspoiled sister has not visited me in many weeks.

"Good day, Ateichál," I say. "How goes your reformation?"

"Better than you report," she says bitterly. "I am not the powerless fool you picture me to be. I wish to make a revelation."

I am enthusiastic, always happy to be the forum for interesting events.

"No one but myself has ever seen this," says Ateichál, handing me a square of heavy paper. On the manuscript is drawn an intricate diagram in washable blue ink. Within and around the lines of the strange sketch are many mystic symbols: crescents, torches, bulls, eagles, pointing hands, eyes closed and open, serpents, stars of varying number of points, lions, pyramids, crosses, suns, and virgins. In the very center an agate has been glued to protect the recipient against large spiders. Hebraic letters are scribbled about the middle, and beneath the whole chart, in a box, is written: "I invoke the fiery force of love by the power of Varuna, in thee, for thee. Irresistible desire, as the gods made in the waters, this I invoked to secure thy love for me. Thou wilt love me with consuming desire. As ever, Dore."

"What is this?" I ask, confused.

"This was Dore's attempt to win me from my devotion.

When he sought himself a mistress he came first to me, and I explained that his special qualities and my religious zeal made our union impossible. He was heartbroken, and tried everything to win my love and my body. But I would not yield, though my secret heart of hearts desired it. He sent me flowers that were picked for him by Dyweyne. He wrote me silly, romantic poems. Finally I told him that I could not receive any more from him, and he went to Dyweyne, his second choice. It is I, not she, that should benefit from the glory of his attentions."

"This is truly remarkable, Ateichál," I say, genuinely puzzled.

"Yes," she says, rising. She smiles minimally at me, gives Lalichë a stern glance, and returns to her tower.

"What do you make of this?" I say, handing the witchery to Lalichë.

"Oh, *this!*" she says, laughing. "I made this for Jelt, but it didn't work. Ateichál must have found it and put Dore's name on it."

"It was a nice try," I say.

"You mean for Jelt? He was too simple to understand it. I'm going to be more direct from now on."

"No. I meant for Ateichál. She's a very sad person."

Dore, Glorian, and Bucky rode the ferry across the clear water of the pool to Von Glech's island fortress. Glorian was careful to keep himself aloof, even though later he would be in a different guise. It was important to their hasty plans that Dore be thought alone. Bucky chatted with the ferryman, and the ride passed without incident.

"Well, we're safely on the island," said Dore musingly. "I hope getting off will prove as simple a task. What now?"

"Now we follow this street through those shacks to the gate of the castle," said Glorian. "Walk ahead of me. Old Von Glech knows you're coming, and I wouldn't doubt but that so do all these townsfolk. There's probably a price on your head."

"What have I done?" asked Dore. He received no reply.

"I have to leave you here," said Bucky when they passed a filthy hut put together from scrap steel plates and rotten planks. "This is the simple home of my father, and

I'll be whipped if I'm late. I wish you gentlemen good luck on your venture."

"He said he'd be of use to us," said Dore, disappointed at losing the boy's aid. "But we can't prevent him from going home."

"He will be of service," said Glorian. "Tonight, after you've secured your sword and I have gotten you through the gates safely, come here. My own mysterious business cannot reach an end before dawn. In any event, there will be no ferry service until morning. I will meet you here at first light."

"Excellent," said Dore. "Unless I'm recognized and captured, of course."

"Of course," said Glorian absently. The air began to shimmer around his body, and for an instant Dore saw flashes of red sparks. There was a glow which brightened until Dore could no longer see Glorian. The brilliance hurt our brother's eyes, and still the light intensified. Then suddenly it was gone, and Glorian stood in a new identity. He was tall and stout, mostly bald with a few tufts of brown hair. He wore plain blue trousers and an open-necked white shirt, with a turquoise ring on one hand.

"What was that?" shouted a man, evidently Norble the porter, as he ran from Bucky's hut.

"What was what?" asked Glorian innocently.

"That light!" said the porter.

"Oh, nothing," said Dore, and the man shook his head and went back into his house.

"That was close," said Dore, and Glorian agreed. The two men separated, and in a few minutes Dore presented himself nervously to the guards at the gate of Castle Von Glech, seeking entrance.

"Who are you and what is your business?" asked a surly warrior.

"I am a prince from a far-off land," said Dore. "And my business is the wooing of the Lady Narlinia."

"Are you Dore of the First family?" asked the soldier. Dore was chagrined, but admitted his identity. "Go on in," said the guard, "they're all waiting for you."

Inside, in the musty entrance hall, Narlinia von Glech sat in an old, grotesquely carved wooden chair. Dore was sure he had seen its mate in our yard. Narlinia rose when she saw our brother. She came to him smiling.

"Hello, Narlinia," said Dore, his mouth suddenly dry. "We have a chair just like that at home." He felt foolish.

"Come with me," she said softly. "We must talk." She took his hand and led him through the dank corridors of the castle to a small chamber. The room was square, with a low ceiling and only the one entrance. There were no windows and no furnishings. It looked like a mistake of architecture. "We can speak freely here," said the lovely young woman. The two gazed at each other for a moment, and then embraced.

"Narlinia?" said Dore uncomfortably. "Honey? You know I'm glad to see you, but I don't have time. I want to get my sword back."

"I know. I had hoped that you came for another reason. But I will help you get your weapon. My father plans to use it in his campaign against the peaceful farmers next year. He believes the sword has mystic properties. Is that true?"

"Yes," said Dore softly, "but nothing as beguiling as the perfume of your hair."

Narlinia laughed. "Come. The guard of my father's vault is a customer of mine. By the way, is your companion with you? Glorian?"

Dore's eyes narrowed in suspicion. "No. No, he's not. He's visiting a friend."

"What a shame. My father was hoping to see him."

"That *is* a shame," said Dore. He followed Narlinia down a secret staircase to the underground vault of Baron von Glech. An unshaven wretch lay sprawled before the massive iron door. Narlinia smiled at Dore and knelt, trying to rouse the drunken man.

"It's me, Crebbit. Narlinia. I've come."

The poor man looked up blearily; he grinned weakly and spoke in a thick voice. "Go on," he said. "Just take it. It's in the back by the secret cheese formula."

Narlinia swung open the iron door and disappeared into the vault. In a few moments she returned with Battlefriend. The sword had grown slightly tarnished and was covered with dust, but Dore was happy to see it. As soon as he touched it the light in the keep brightened considerably. "That was quick. How did he know what you wanted?" asked Dore.

"We're old friends," said the Lady Narlinia.

"I didn't think we'd get it so fast. I have a lot of time to kill now."

"Before what?" asked the Baron's daughter innocently.

"Oh, nothing," said Dore.

"Then let us creep upstairs unnoticed, and pass the time in whatever way seems best," said Narlinia with a bit of a leer. Dore punched her shoulder affectionately, and could see no fault with her program.

All too soon it was time for Dore to leave. He regretted having to abandon the young woman once more, but our brother removed her clinging arms and gave her a last kiss. "I must be off," he said. "But I'll come back again someday."

"Dore, I love you," she whispered. "Where are you going? It's nearly midnight."

"I have an appointment," he said, pulling on his clothes. The two said their fond goodbys, and Dore slipped away into the night's concealment.

Glorian was already waiting for him by the gate. "Do you have—"

"Right here," said Dore happily, slapping his enchanted blade.

"Fine. That's real fine," said Glorian. "Now stand back. I'm going to open a way for you through the wall. Get through as quickly as you can. Go straight to young Bucky's home and await me there. Talk to no one and try not to be spotted. Good luck." Glorian waved his arms, and a tiny crack appeared in the high wall of the fortress. Dore squeezed through with some effort and much cursing, and did as he was bidden. In a matter of minutes he was standing before the door of Norble the porter.

Jelt comes in to disturb the flow of my adventure. "I'm glad he got his sword back," he says. He sees Lalichë sitting in a corner of my room, too engrossed in her own literary venture to follow mine any longer. But at Jelt's words she looks up with a beautiful and predatory smile. She takes his hand and they go off to share their lovers' lies. I shake my head patronizingly. Ah, to be young again.

Even as I am preparing Dore for his one, final, moral dilemma, I am being tortured by ethical considerations of my own. There is the problem of Dyweyne. My infatuation for her knows no bounds, but my affection for Joilliena is in no way affected. Joilliena can't understand this, claiming that I'm trying to make a fool out of her. This is surpassingly untrue; I am well content with what I have, but I worship Dyweyne in a special way. The traditions of Courtly Love demand that you weaken at the knees for only the wife of another man. Indeed, Courtly Love forbids a man from treating his own wife that way. There is an organization to the feeling, so that the stricken man is at once the suitor and vassal of his maid. Only the Courtly, i.e., the well-bred, can Love, because only the courtly understand the vicissitudes of Service. It is this that I feel for Dyweyne: a sort of hopeless longing to be her feudal bondsman and, with fortune, her lover.

When expressed in these terms my love is less like heresy, if Dyweyne has been elevated to a position of official adoration. I do not recall where the matter stands. I think Tere overlooks it entirely, but Ateichál is ready to grant Dyweyne some status. Ateichál will do anything, right at the moment. The struggle has been too much for her.

Other matters try to entice me from my righteous posture, also. Although the interest of my brothers and sisters has waned, and I get no more reviews now that Yord and Mylvelane have been processed, the Ploutos Corporation has not forgotten me. On my desk are ten or twelve different proposals for exploiting my history, just waiting for my signature. Even though none of them offer me a fair deal for my rights, they are a potent temptation. I have the means to set myself up as a great and powerful authority. With shrewd management I could cut for myself a reasonable chunk of political power. Fortunately, I am immune to such threats to my peace and indolence.

Dore has yet to learn the depths of his inner resources. He settled himself in a clear space among the piles of trash in the yard and fell asleep. The rising sun broke through his dreams, and it took him a few seconds to recall where he was. He stood and made a careful survey of the house, but no one was awake. He wondered where Glorian was. The inscrutable companion was always so puritanical about such matters as punctuality and caution. But Dore didn't worry, knowing that Glorian had more ways of getting out of trouble than most people had for finding it.

But after the sun had climbed steadily for an hour and Glorian had not appeared, Dore began to fret. The longer their departure was delayed the more chance there was that they'd be discovered in their theft. Dore was uncertain about the best thing to do. He hated to abandon the meeting place, in case Glorian might arrive in Dore's absence and leave our brother on his own.

"Are you waiting for Glorian, Master Dore?" asked Bucky, startling Dore from his deep thoughts.

"Yes, my lad. I was to meet him here."

"I know. The Lady Narlinia has betrayed you to her father. Glorian is held captive within a glass bottle. He's powerless inside blue glass, you know. The Baron is demanding that you return Battlefriend, or your companion dies."

Dore was horrified. "How do you know all this?" he asked.

The boy grinned sheepishly. "It's the talk of the town," he said. "We've been planning it for weeks. I was supposed to lead you to the castle and lull your suspicions, but you can trust me now."

The boy's speech made our brother furious, but he knew that he was helpless. "Either I can surrender to the Baron, or I can attempt to rescue Glorian," said Dore hopelessly.

"All the Baron's men are armed and waiting," said Bucky. Dore's confused thoughts strayed from his emergency. They flowed backward, over his countless adventures, his victories and defeats. He thought of Narlinia, and then he thought of Dyweyne. He pictured Dyweyne's—

A note from Ateichál: "You need not trouble yourself incessantly about Dyweyne. With one bold stroke I have simplified matters greatly. Our arrogant sister has been 'taken care of.' Yours for a cleaner Home, Ateichál."

A note from Tere: "I am sure that you share my outrage and disgust at Ateichál's most heinous of crimes. Be assured that already we have had our vengeance. Ateichál, that ghoulish apostate, has, in her words, 'been taken care of.' With best regards and deepest sympathy, your brother, Tere (The Kalp)."

"This is it, sir, your moral crisis. You must choose

between the life of a friend and the success of your mission. But you *can't* abandon Glorian, and you just *can't* go in there. You'll be killed." The boy looked up into Dore's eyes with tears in his own.

Dore looked out over the run-down shacks, down to where the pool lay like Our Mother's glassy eyes, reflecting the unstrained pallor of her skin. A small brook ran out of the pool at one end, Dore knew, and the brook ran on through meadows and sweet forests until it merged with the River.

Our brother looked down at Bucky, and then back toward the castle of the faithless Von Glechs. "You're right," said Dore.

CHAPTER ELEVEN

An End—and a Beginning

Dore followed the River, trekking resolutely now as his goal grew nearer. He marched quickly along the side of the rushing water. He stumbled over roots and tangled his feet in clumps of needle grass, but he did not notice. He went on for hours, until his breath was coming in short, painful gasps. His throat was dry from both his exertions and his anticipation. At last he was forced to halt by the evening rains. He sat down among the weeds on the bank of the sacred River, huddling shelterless in the cold storm.

He did not sleep that night. As the white sky broke up after the rain, pulling apart like cotton to show the cheerless stars, he got again to his feet. The River ran harder now under the burden of the day's rain, and Dore followed it further. The grassy meadowland soon began to broaden to his left and to his right, across the River. After a short while he noticed that he was crossing a great, wide plain that stretched to the distant horizon, featureless except for the River. Shortly before the next dawn he camped beside the water and slept through the hottest part of the day. He awoke in the late afternoon and continued his journey, hungry and weary.

Soon Dore observed that the River itself was changing. The great River was somewhat narrower now, as streams split from it and went off at nearly perfect right angles. I suppose these streams always cut through the opposite bank, or, if they did intersect Dore's line of march, that he found some way of crossing them without entering the water itself. Then again, it's possible that he felt that as soon as the water left the main channel of the River it lost its holy nature.

In any event, these streams seemed to happen more and more frequently, and as a consequence the River became smaller. When it had shrunk to about the size that it is as it circles past the faraway house of our First family, it poured into a huge, beautiful, elliptical lake. The lake was set into the grassland like a polished stud in a velvet garment. It was perfectly still; no wind rippled its mirror surface. At what appeared to be the foci of the ellipse were two small islands, covered with shrubbery and trees. The tall, slender, white trees were the first that Dore had seen in days. He addressed a tentative prayer to the swollen section of the River, and the implied swelling of its holiness.

At the farther end the shoreline was broken by five small rivulets which ran out of the lake and diverged quickly. Dore studied them for some time and finally decided that they all must be from the original sacred River, and they all must lead where he had to go. Either he chose to follow the largest of the streams or he chose the nearest.

The undergrowth grew denser. The dry needle grass gave way to bushes and tall, delicate ferns, to tough climbing vines and creepers, then to the deciduous growths, the micha and the oaks, and finally to Dore's beloved dense, dark woods. The stream that he followed gurgled pleasantly, without the rushing roar of the River. Dore could see smooth, moss-covered stones through the shallow water. He heard the singing of cicadas and katydids. He felt at home again, but he knew he couldn't go on much longer.

The brook tumbled over logs and squeezed past boulders. Water spiders made their profane, gliding way on its surface. Unless, being born to the water, they were holy in their own right; in that case Dore addressed a line of prayer to them, too. From the right another of the five streams arched through the trees, joining the one Dore followed and making a larger creek. In a short while they split around a jagged chunk of stone and went on separately. Dore made his choice. Further on two streams joined his, splitting later into two parts. Dore chose again. The streams wound through the forest, meeting and dividing in confusing combinations. Dore became increasingly convinced that it was unnecessary to differentiate among them; he followed the branch that looked nicest at the time. The rivulets continued on, making their roughly parallel courses through the woods.

Toward evening Dore stopped at the edge of a precipice.

The stream leaped over the edge, splashing holiness on Dore and on the dead leaves of the forest floor. He could see that there were four other streams that spilled together: As they fell they mixed again to form the River, reborn in its virgin purity. Dore climbed slowly down the face of the cliff, stepping carefully on the wet, slick rocks. It was dusky and difficult for him to see below. The roar of the waterfall grew louder, echoing from the walls of the canyon into which he was climbing, making him slightly dizzy.

He clung for a moment on a narrow ledge. He paused, gasping for breath and feeling the weakness in his arms and legs. His head was pressed close to the mossy wall. He felt something touch his foot: rodent? reptile? He glanced down.

A hand was grasping his ankle.

Dore's throat felt dry, his head buzzed with fear. He nearly lost his grip on the rocks in his panic.

"Take it easy," a voice said. "There's a wider one just below you. Kneel on the ledge that you're on, grab hold of the edge, and let yourself down. You'll have to swing in pretty far, but I'll steady you. There's plenty of room here for both of us."

Dore did as he was told. He let go and landed on a wide shelf of rock. A young man about his own age was sitting at the far end. The man gestured, smiling, and Dore sat down, too. He looked over the edge: blackness so deep that it stifled even the rumbling of the falling water.

"Make yourself comfortable," said the man. "It's not bad here, better than you might think. I've been here for quite a while, and you're the first person that's happened by; I guess you know how hard the trip is. It'll be nice having someone to talk to."

"Who are you?" asked Dore.

"Well, who are *you?* You're the stranger here, you know."

"My name is Dore, and I am the eldest male of the First family of Home."

"Well, that's very funny. In that case, you're my son. Hello. I haven't seen you since you were that high. How have you been?"

"Are you my Father?"

"Yes. How have you been?"

"I have come to look for you. I never expected to really find you."

"It's fantastic, all right. How are you?"

"Fine," said Dore. "And you?"

"All right, I guess."

"You . . . you are Our Father?"

The man laughed. "I'm *your* father, at least. I think. With that mother of yours I was never certain. By the way, how *is* Sue Ann?"

"Sue Ann?"

"Your mother, boy. How is she? Oh, never mind; I can see that you got her brains."

"You're really Our Father? I mean, I've been searching for you all this time, and you—"

"Yes, you idiot. What's the matter? You want a signed affidavit or something? Who else you know would be sitting on this ledge Ommming out of sheer boredom for the last thirty years?"

"Why are you no older? You look as you must have when you first went down the River."

Dore's father shrugged, then pointed off the ledge into the darkness. "Down there," he said, "the Well."

" 'The Well'?"

"Yes. The Well of Entropy."

The two of them were silent for a while, listening to the murmurings from the darkness, each lost in his own amazed thoughts.

Finally Dore said, "What *about* the Well of Entropy?"

"Down there is the entropic center of Home at least, and possibly the universe. Everything that falls down there becomes more and more dissociated, tending to the primal chaotic state. Matter is destroyed as the electrons constituting that matter slow and stop. When the electrons stop spinning and the atoms fall apart: no more matter, just randomly distributed, wasted energy. Up there, where you came from, is the River, the symbol and essence of divinity on this planet. God is the ultimate Order, the embodiment of organization. The River and the Well are the two poles of existence; I suppose that it is necessary for the River to have its source from the Well to make the cycle complete. Someday someone will explore the River upstream as we have done in this direction."

"But going upstream is sacrilegious."

"Let me decide that. Anyway, this ledge is halfway

between them, tending neither toward destruction or synthesis. Everything here stays exactly the same. We don't need food or water, and time is meaningless. Sit back, pull up a rock. It's kind of boring."

"What?" said Dore. His mind was stunned by the impact of all these new ideas. "How do you know what's down there?"

"I climbed down about a year after I first arrived. I didn't have anything else to do."

"How did you survive? Weren't you subject to the forces of entropy, too?"

"No. I suspected that staying in the curtain of the falling water would protect me. Enough of the water was being annihilated so that I had little trouble climbing down. Besides, I didn't want to go very far. Pretty soon the rocks go, too, and you're left scrambling around on metaphysics."

"What did you see? What *could* there be? Is it Heaven?" asked Dore.

"Caverns, son. Caverns, measureless to man. Mind-bending panoramas of sinuous rills, senses-stunning spots of greenery, and the ultimate in brain-warping romantic chasms."

"Was your brain warped?"

"No," the young man said slowly, "I got the hell out of there." Dore's father stood up and walked to the rim of the shelf. "I want to go up the cliff again. I want you to come with me. We're going to fill that hole with rocks. We can go up there and push down all the rocks and logs we can find. Block it up. Back the River up so there will never be any death for anything. We can do it!"

Dore watched him, frightened by his father's tone. "No, we can't. It's impossible. You can't overload entropy. Besides . . . besides, there are certain forces in this universe that shouldn't be tampered with; I believe that entropy is one of them."

"If you won't help me," the other man said, raging, "I'll do it myself! You can't get back up by yourself; I know, I've tried. You can't climb those rocks against the flow of entropy. Two of us, together, might be able to do it. Those cosmic forces of yours play by different rules here. You can't make it alone; I'll leave you down here. I'll turn time back on for you and you can starve!"

"Look, if I don't help you, you won't get up there,

either. You just said so. And when you turn time back on, if you could, won't you suddenly age all those years that you've lost? You'll be an old man. You'll never make it back to the house."

"What makes you think I'm going back to the house? I wouldn't go back there if . . . That lousy mother of yours. We wouldn't be here in the first place if she hadn't gotten us into debt so far we'd *never* see daylight. Every time I had us settled she'd trot out her charge cards and get us snowed under. We had to keep running until we ran here. The first thing I did was put the old icepick to her frontal lobes. This is *my* Home. I made certain that making your wife into a vegetable was strictly within your rights. Then I stuck her out on her silly throne so I wouldn't have to listen to her valve clatter all night. She had the coldest ass in bed you ever saw. I'm not going back *there*."

Dore was silent once more. Finally he stood up too, and went to the edge. He knelt; he swung his feet over and searched for a secure footing.

"What are you doing?" Our Father screamed.

"I'm going down there. I'm looking for my Father. He wouldn't be just sitting up here raving. Not Our Father. You're an imposter and a liar."

"Get back up here! You can't leave me like this!" The man grabbed Dore's wrists and pulled, scraping Dore's arms raw on the rock wall.

"All right, let go," said Dore. "Let go or I'm coming up and beat you to jelly. You're mad."

"You don't know what you're doing!"

Dore gazed at him through the gloom. Our brother's eyes were steady, as steady as his voice. "I think I do," he said.

The man grappled furiously. Dore jerked both arms in an attempt to pull free. His right foot slipped, and he fell out over the chasm, held only by his Father.

Dore cursed. "Let me go," he said. "Swing me into the wall and I can grab hold. Then let me go or we'll both go over."

"No," the other man said, "I can't. I can't let you fall and I can't let you go down there voluntarily." He had dropped to his knees when Dore slipped, and now he tried to stand again. He rose, bent at the waist, and as he moved closer to the edge to pull Dore up, our brother swung himself into the cliff. The older man was forced down again, but this time he lost his balance. He toppled over the brink, never letting go of Dore's wrists.

"AIIEEEE!" they screamed as they fell to their doom.

Well, it wasn't a grass dragon after all. Plummeting to certain death with Our Father. My brother, the Kalp, has informed me of our family's dissatisfaction with my Procopian account. He has added, moreover, his own personal disapproval. This won't be the official version, I guess. (Tere also told me, smiling that puffy grin of his, he told me that he would be inclined to go easier on me if I were reclined to go easier on him. I told him that I already had a heavy date down the road, which was, of course, a lie.)

Our Mother is gone, he said, and her memory is holy to us (Like hell it's holy to him; he was measuring his hyperbolic bottom on her throne last night. Not Our Father's. *Her's*). The remarks I made about her were profanity of the worst sort. I don't know exactly where I did get them (maybe Our Father *is* around and transmitting?), but at worst they are creative reportage. Anyway, our family doesn't see it that way. I've already finished packing. I'm honored to have the task of going out to find Dore and Our Father and bringing them back. I'm taking Tere's place. The Kalp's been wondering how he was going to work this. But I don't get the wallet of bread and cheese even. Certainly not a sword: I'm not old enough.

I thought they left Earth because of things like censorship. Ah, utopia!

I also go without the blessing and various rites that are exquisitely Melithiel's, the princess from down the road. I'll miss that. My brothers are always standing around and joking about her. She must be really something. I'd probably like our material better, anyway. (That's just sour grapes. How would I know?) Last night Joilliena came to my room. She was one of the few who would talk to me after the meeting. She wanted to come with me, but I said (rather nobly), "No," I said, "stay and finish your education. If you're in school, *stay* in school. If you're out and want to get back in, call your State Office of Education Opportunities. I will send for you when I get settled." Of course she cried. I never know what to do.

This morning my little brother Jelt knocked on the

door. I shouted to him, so that he wouldn't come in and embarrass Joilliena. I said, "What do you want?"

"Beware the plant men and the great white apes at the end of the River," he said. I don't know what he meant; I don't read his books.

Lalichë was with him, of course. When she spoke she sounded as if she were crying. "This is for you, Seyt," she said. "Be careful." She pushed a piece of white paper under my door. I smiled sadly, thinking it was another of her magic charms. It had a red heart drawn in crayon, and shaky letters that said, "We love you, Seyt."

I thanked them and they went away. Then I got up and brushed my teeth. Joilliena was still asleep and I left before she woke. It was so romantic that I nearly wept. I kissed her cheek, and she smiled in her dreams. Her hair spilled over the pillow like a wave of amber. Lovely, lovely.

I won't worry about any plant men. But I *will* watch out for the Ship of Fools. And those Rhinemaidens, guarding their refound horde of magic gold, as delightfully depicted by Richard Wagner in his opera *Götterdämmerung*. What real dangers there will be, I cannot say. I don't know. The River I see over there, and the River I described for Dore probably won't be the same. (If they are, I'm already lost.) But, as Fluellen says to Gower in William Shakespeare's immortal play *Henry V*, "There is a river in Macedon, and there is also moreover a river at Monmouth. . . . But 'tis all one; 'tis alike as my fingers is to my fingers, and there is salmons in both."

That is in the seventh scene of Act Four.

Other SIGNET Science Fiction You Will Enjoy

☐ **THERE WILL BE TIME by Poul Anderson.** Only a natural-born time traveler stood between man and a future which could destroy human civilization.
(#Q5401—95¢)

☐ **THE FALLIBLE FIEND by L. Sprague de Camp.** Could a rational, literal-minded demon survive in an irrational world of men? (#Q5370—95¢)

☐ **THE CITY AND THE STARS by Arthur C. Clarke.** A tense story set millions of years in the future, when one man sets out to unite Earth's sole survivors, two isolated nations ignorant of each other's ways. (#Q5371—95¢)

☐ **THE WEATHERMAKERS by Ben Bova.** Harnessing weather was the goal, and the man who could perform this miracle was Ted Marrett. But the opposition he faced was almost overwhelming and his greatest opponent was the weather itself. (#Q5329—95¢)

☐ **OPERATION: OUTER SPACE by Murray Leinster.** A television producer, his secretary, and a psychiatrist find themselves trapped inside a spacecraft, being hurled far beyond the confines of the Solar System toward a planet inhabited by bizarre creatures—a volcanic world strangely similar to Earth. (#Q5300—95¢)

More SIGNET Science Fiction You Will Enjoy

☐ **LEVEL 7 by Mordecai Roshwald.** A horrifying prophetic document of the future—the diary of a man living 4000 feet underground in a society bent on atomic self-destruction. (#T5011—75¢)

☐ **CLARION: An Anthology of Speculative Fiction and Criticism from the Clarion Writers' Workshop edited by Robin Scott Wilson.** The Clarion Workshop is the only writers' program dealing with speculative fiction. The alumni represent twenty states and from this workshop many fresh and important voices will emerge to set the tone and influence the direction of science fiction in the seventies. Included are **Fritz Leiber** and **Samuel Delaney.** (#Q4664—95¢)

☐ **THE WORLD INSIDE by Robert Silverberg.** An unflinching look into a future as frightening as it is chillingly believable. It is the time of Urbmon, unlimited procreation and group identity. "One of the most fascinating and ingenious science fiction novels to appear in years." **The Science Fiction Book Club** (#Q5176—95¢)

☐ **A CIRCUS OF HELLS by Poul Anderson.** The story of a lost treasure guarded by curious monsters, of captivity in a wilderness, of a journey through reefs and shoals that could wreck a ship, and of the rivalry of empires. (#T4250—75¢)

Still More SIGNET Science Fiction Titles You Will Enjoy

☐ **GREYBEARD by Brian Aldiss.** Science fiction with a difference about an almost desolate future in which mankind and mammals have been rendered sterile by a cosmic "accident." (#Q5141—95¢)

☐ **DOWNWARD TO THE EARTH by Robert Silverberg.** Earthman Edmund Gundersen gambles his body and soul in an alien game where the stakes are immortality. (#T4497—75¢)

☐ **THE DEMOLISHED MAN by Alfred Bester.** A science fiction tale of a ruthless killer who pits his resources against infallible mind-reading detectives. (#T4461—75¢)

☐ **ISLANDS IN THE SKY by Arthur C. Clarke.** An engrossing novel of a future Earth encircled by terrifying dangerous manned satellites. (#Q5521—95¢)

☐ **TOMORROW I A Science Fiction Anthology edited by Robert Hoskins.** Five fascinating speculations on tomorrow featuring **Poul Anderson, John D. MacDonald, James H. Schmitz, Clifford D. Simak** and **William Tenn.** (#T4663—75¢)

SIGNET Science Fiction You'll Want to Read

☐ **ROGUE QUEEN by L. Sprague de Camp.** From out of the sky came the magic. From out of the hive came the queen. (#Q5256—95¢)

☐ **THE HEIRS OF BABYLON by Glen Cook.** After the bombs had stopped, there was still . . . THE WAR! (#Q5299—95¢)

☐ **THE OTHER SIDE OF TIME by Keith Laumer.** When time runs backward, can a world be recaptured? Imperial Intelligence Agent Brion Bayard had to find the answer to this question, for if he failed, the Imperium and all the known universe would vanish. (#Q5255—95¢)

☐ **WHO CAN REPLACE A MAN? (Best Science Fiction Stories of Brian W. Aldiss) by Brian W. Aldiss.** Fourteen of the best stories by one of Britain's top science fiction writers. "A virtuoso performance."—**Saturday Review** (#T5055—75¢)

☐ **ELEMENT 79 by Fred Hoyle.** A noted astronomer and science fiction author leads an excursion into a fantastic—but scientifically possible—future universe in this engaging collection of stories. (#Q5279—95¢)